D0952149

somebody's baby

somebody's baby

LURLENE McDANIEL

DELACORTE PRESS

Text copyright © 2017 by Lurlene McDaniel
Jacket art copyright © Kseniia Perminova/Shutterstock

All rights reserved. Published in the United States by Delacorte Press, an imprint of Random House Children's Books, a division of Penguin Random House LLC, New York.

Delacorte Press is a registered trademark and the colophon is a trademark of Penguin Random House LLC.

Visit us on the Web! randomhouseteens.com

Educators and librarians, for a variety of teaching tools, visit us at RHTeachersLibrarians.com

Library of Congress Cataloging-in-Publication Data
Names: McDaniel, Lurlene, author.
Title: Somebody's baby / Lurlene McDaniel.
Description: New York: Delacorte Press, [2017] | Summary: "A young woman who has skyrocketed to fame is guarded but hopeful when she receives an email from a stranger who claims not only to have information about the father she never knew but also to be her half sister"—Provided by publisher.
Identifiers: LCCN 2016018770 (print) | LCCN 2016037574 (ebook) | ISBN 978-0-385-74423-2 (hardcover) | ISBN 978-0-385-38401-8 (ebk)
Subjects: | CYAC: Fame—Fiction. | Fathers and daughters—Fiction. | Sisters—Fiction.
Classification: LCC PZ7.M4784172 So 2017 (print) | LCC PZ7.M4784172 (ebook) | DDC [Fic]—dc23

The text of this book is set in 11.5-point Goudy Old Style.

Printed in the United States of America
10 9 8 7 6 5 4 3 2 1
First Edition

Random House Children's Books
supports the First Amendment and celebrates the right to read.

To my grandson Josiah McDaniel—
may your music be blessed!

For the Lord sees not as a man sees:
man looks on the outward appearance,
but the Lord looks on the heart.
—1 SAMUEL 16:7 (NKJV)

one

$\sim$

"This was in today's batch of emails. I printed it out for you. Do you think it's legit?"

Sloan scanned the paper, then glanced up at Kiley, Terri Levine's young assistant, who stood anxiously waiting for her reaction.

"I know Terri warned you about people trying to latch on after your big win," Kiley began. "I know you've said you didn't have any family in Tennessee, but this sounds so . . . so genuine. Even desperate. I have two sisters. They mean the world to me. So I started thinking that maybe you should see the message. I mean . . . just in case." Kiley's breathless explanation petered out.

Sloan stared down at the letter in her trembling hands. She'd read through it twice and felt shaken to her core. Of course she remembered Terri Levine's warning! *"People will come out of the woodwork, Sloan. You're a hundred grand richer and a rising music star, so you're going to be swamped with all kinds of offers and 'opportunities.' Everything must come through*

1

my firm, and I mean everything. Building your career isn't a sprint, Sloan. It's a marathon."

Sloan reread the letter in the glaring sunlight.

Dear Sloan Gabriel,

We have never met, and maybe this letter will never reach you, but I had to try. My name is Lindsey Sloan Ridley. Sloan is my maiden name, same as your first name. I live in Windemere, Tennessee, and I'm your sister—well, really your half sister. You might think I'm some crazy person, but please believe me. I can prove to you the things I'm writing.

I never knew you existed until about two years ago because our daddy, Jerry Sloan, kept you a secret from me. A secret he was wrong to keep. I'm seven years older than you, and there is a long story attached to both our pasts, too long and too private for me to write in a note you might never read.

But if you do read this, I'm asking—begging—you to contact me. Please . . . it's a matter of life and death.

My phone number and address are below.

Lindsey

A *sister*? She had a *sister*? Sloan had never known her father, and all her mother, LaDonna, had ever said about him when Sloan was growing up was that he was a dirtbag who'd abandoned them. If the words in the letter were true, LaDonna had given her daughter the dirtbag's name—Sloan. *Perverse*, Sloan now thought. *Spiteful*.

Sloan walked to the bank of spotless windows of Terri

Levine's Public Relation firm's expansive glass-walled twentieth floor. Far below, Los Angeles traffic inched down the boulevard. "Yes . . . I remember what Terri said about complete strangers taking advantage." She'd learned that much from LaDonna. *"People will screw you every chance they get, so don't trust nobody. Ever."* Not trusting LaDonna had been Sloan's first lesson.

In November over a year before, Sloan had fled her former life in Tennessee, determined to leave her past and its heartrending memories behind and follow her dreams. She'd hitched her way across the country and arrived in Los Angeles friendless and broke, armed with nothing but hope and an old guitar to audition for the *American Singer* contest open auditions to be held in the summer. In the meantime she'd taken jobs waiting tables and serving drinks, rented a musty room in a run-down apartment building, taken in a roommate who'd made a pigsty seem inviting, and learned to navigate LA's public transportation system, limited as it was. When *American Singer* had held open auditions she'd stood in long lines of singer wannabes for hours under a hot sun waiting for a chance to go before the judges. She had made the first cut. And the second. And finally landed a spot on the nationally televised program that had aired in January.

Six weeks later, on Valentine's Day, she'd stood onstage between the emcee and one other finalist, her heart crashing inside her chest, her mouth cotton dry, her face aching from smiling. And the crowd in the theater where the show was telecast live across the country had whooped and stomped, and confetti had fallen, and the *American Singer* anthem had played when she, Sloan Quentin Gabriel, had won it all.

Now, only two weeks after the announcement, her life in

LA had done a 180-degree turn, until this email had crashed her party.

"Then it was okay to show you the letter?" Kiley asked. "Sometimes it's hard to decide the best thing to do. I mean, some of the email stories fans send winners can break your heart. Others just want some stardust—that's what Terri calls mail dumps from perfect strangers. It's easy to decide how to handle most of the stuff that comes in. Delete, delete, delete. But sometimes . . ."

Terri Levine, owner of the PR firm, was now Sloan's agent. Overseeing media accounts, Facebook, and fan-driven emails was part of Kiley's job. Sloan didn't want to run afoul of Terri Levine, but she didn't want to ignore this particular email either. The letter certainly should have gone to Terri first, but softhearted Kiley had delivered it to Sloan, a risk that could mean her job.

Sloan turned from the window, saw Kiley toying nervously with her necklace, and offered an encouraging smile. "It's fine, Kiley. Thanks."

Kiley relaxed. "Do you know where this Windemere is?"

"It's a small town not too far from Nashville." Since coming to LA, Sloan had been telling people she was from Nashville, which was partly true—she had left Windemere for the Music City, where she'd honed her solo style of sultry country pop in small bars and restaurants in the Music Row area. Calling Nashville home on the *American Singer* show was far more glamorous than confessing she'd grown up in rural Windemere, in a trailer park, with an alcoholic mother who slept around.

Currently Sloan was in the midst of her wardrobe and image makeover, and of laying down tracks for an EP—an extended play CD that was going to radio stations and into stores to quickly cash in on the instant fame of her winning the contest. The record label that held her new contract was banking on the EP to climb the music charts and also whet the public's appetite for her debut album she had yet to record.

But now, with a star-studded future in front of her, Sloan's past had come calling, and with it, possible answers she had craved to know since childhood. Who was her father? Why had he walked away? Of course, anybody living back in Windemere, where she'd grown up and gone to school, could have written the letter to scam her, but Sloan couldn't confess this to Kiley. Her singing voice had been her escape from the hard life and bad memories of that small town.

"Are you all right?" Kiley asked.

Sloan turned, flashed a bright smile. "Just fine. No need to worry about this, so don't put yourself in the line of fire with the boss, Kiley. I'll handle this with Terri."

"You sure?"

"I'll talk to her tonight," Sloan assured the nervous girl.

Sloan watched Kiley flee the room while she folded the letter and slipped it into the back pocket of her brand-new ridiculously overpriced pair of jeans. She *would* tell Terri about the letter. But not just yet.

⌒

"I'll pick you up at ten in the morning," Sloan's driver said as she exited the car. She watched him drive away from the front of her apartment building in the gated complex. This was one of the perks Terri and the record label had given her—a car and driver to and from her scheduled appointments. She liked not having to drive on LA's overly congested freeways, but she disliked the restrictions placed on her by her "handler." Terri had been firm about Sloan sticking to a list of rules that included, *"If you want to go someplace, call your driver."* A safety measure to keep newly minted and suddenly richer winners in check.

Sloan took an elevator up to her luxury apartment, a spacious corner unit of modern design and designer furniture, none of it belonging to her. She wondered how many other *American Singer* winners had been squirreled away in the place. No matter. She'd one day own a place bigger and grander.

Sloan grabbed a bottle of water from the fridge and looked at her schedule, which was posted so she always knew where to be. Terri was in charge of building Sloan's image, so Sloan's time was well organized. Tomorrow at eleven she worked with the voice coach. Mandatory. Sloan's voice and versatility had won her the contest, but the trainer was helping her with exercises to better control her breathing and song phrasing. Her stage presence was under reconstruction too. She loved performing, but in these big leagues everyone could be made better.

After the voice coach, the recording studio. The song she'd sung to win the contest was already going on the disc, and two others were under consideration. She was eager to get the EP CD into stores and then concentrate on the new album. *Her album.* And the big money advance that had come with it. She fantasized about hit albums, concert tours, and all the joys that came with fame. Then she sobered. Would this Lindsey *Sloan* Ridley pull her back to a place she'd thought she'd left behind forever? But if the woman really *was* her half sister . . . if she truly was a link to long-buried family roots—

Sloan growled and flopped onto a large leather chair, slugged down her water. She pulled her cell phone from the pocket of her jeans. Or rather, her agent's cell phone. *"Keep this on you at all times,"* Terri had said when handing it to Sloan. *"Never know when I might have to make changes in your schedule. This phone is our communications lifeline."* Sloan sighed, realizing it would be a long time before she'd be able to again come and go as she pleased.

She pulled out the folded paper. The phone's time stamp showed one p.m., which meant it was two hours earlier in Windemere. She reread the letter and, with her heart hammering, punched in the digits. To the empty room, and with sarcasm, Sloan said, "Okay, *Sister,* you want me to reach out and hear your story? It's time to tell me what you got."

two

―――

Sloan listened to the sounds of a ringing phone coming from hundreds of miles away, her mind tripping backward to growing up in Windemere, her dark childhood and her school years, the boy who'd loved her, and how she'd walked away. Dragging her mind from the edge of the swell of memories, she hissed, "Answer!" into her cell. She was about to hang up, when a breathless voice said in a hushed whisper, "Hello."

Sloan went momentarily speechless, then cleared her throat and asked, "Is this Lindsey?"

"No, I'm her friend Gloria. Can I help you?"

The thick sludge of the woman's Southern accent reminded Sloan again of her roots. In LA most people's voices were homogenous. She was working to shed her accent, but people still heard it, often asked where she'd come from in the South. "Is Lindsey there? I'd like to speak to her. Please."

"She is here, but she's nappin'. I can't wake her just yet."

Gloria said *cain't,* dragging out the word in a voice that Sloan found irritating. Napping? What grown woman napped in at eleven in the morning? A *drunk,* she quickly realized. Like Sloan's mother.

"Can I take a message for her?" Gloria asked.

Sloan drew a blank, fumbled for an answer. "You have any idea when she'll be awake?"

"She tries to be up when Toby comes home, if she can." Gloria was talking in riddles, throwing out names. She offered information, but Sloan had no context. "If you want, I'll have her call you when she gets up."

"No. I—I'll call back later . . . at a better time. When she's awake."

"That would be nice," Gloria said. "Can I say who's callin'? She likes it when friends call to talk."

"Later. It . . . it isn't important." Sloan disconnected, sat brooding, the honey drip of Gloria's voice still inside her head. Who were these people? Did she even *want* to know them? Her embittered mother had held back information about her father, a man who'd walked away and never *ever* acknowledged Sloan's existence. That pain and, yes, anger too had lain inside her heart for all twenty-three years of her life. No birthday cards. No Christmas gifts. Nothing.

Sloan shoved up from the chair, went to her bedroom and the walk-in closet, and sorted through a pile of clothes on the floor until she found her bikini. She would lay out at the pool, work on her tan. In LA, glamour radiated from the depths of glowing bronze skin. In Windemere most people sported "farmers' tans," necks and forearms browned by the sun, torsos as pale as milk.

In their first meeting following Sloan's win, Terri had insisted, *"No secrets. I can't shape your future if there's something that blindsides me from your past."* Sloan slipped on the bikini, realizing that now she had a dilemma. There were

9

things in her past she didn't want to talk about to anyone. This letter had hit her hard, and she was unsure how to tell Terri, or even *if* she should say anything until she personally checked out the story. And not over the phone but in a face-to-face meeting with this Lindsey person. If the story was bogus, Sloan could deal with Lindsey without involving Terri at all.

Sloan went down to the pool, mulling over a way to slip out of LA without too many questions being asked.

———

"You seem distracted. Any problems?"

Sloan glanced up from her dinner plate at Terri sitting across the table. They were in a restaurant, eating a late supper, Sloan with a platter of fries and a burger, Terri with her small green salad. The woman was in her fifties, waspishly thin, dark haired, and stylishly dressed, always looking polished and pulled together, even after a fourteen-hour day. "No . . . no problems."

"I wouldn't think so. Three of your songs from the show are topping iTunes downloads. All we need is one more song to round out your EP."

They'd spent most of the evening in a recording studio listening to songs and trying to pin one down that was special enough for the extended-play CD, but so far the producer, Tom Jackson, wasn't satisfied. "Tom's being too picky. What's wrong with just grabbing another song from the show?" Sloan dragged a fry through a glob of ketchup.

"We want something extra special, something original, if possible." Terri's phone vibrated. "A text. Excuse me."

Sloan was anxious to get started on her *solo* album, and a

successful album would launch her even higher than the contest. She jiggled her legs, impatient for Terri to finish texting. She also checked out the restaurant, its low lights, the candles on every table, and the pale pink linens, all giving the room an elegant ambience intended to enhance the dining experience. There weren't many diners this late in the evening, but the ones Sloan saw were couples, a reminder that she hadn't had a date in much too long. She shelved such thoughts, reminded herself that relationships were complicated, and breakups painful. She wanted to focus on one thing only—a singing career.

Terri laid down her phone and picked at her salad. "You ever write any songs?"

"I'm better at performing others' music."

"You stated on your *American Singer* audition form that you were once lead singer in a band. Don't you have any music from those days? Most bands write their own stuff."

It had been necessary to put some of her musical experience on her contest form, but her time with Anarchy had ended badly, and she didn't want Terri to dig up her former band days. "That was high school, and we played a different genre of music."

"Doesn't matter. Songs can be rearranged. So you got something lying around?"

Sloan heaved a sigh. "I worked with the lead guitarist on a few numbers." Jarred's image flashed in her mind, and then Dawson's and all that had happened. "The songs aren't very good."

"So you *do* have some recordings of you with the band? An old CD, maybe? I'd like to hear the music." Terri was like a bulldog, and not letting go. "Tom can judge their worth. Where can I get the music?"

Sloan gritted her teeth. "Some stuff is stored on my old cell phone, back at the apartment. Battery's totally dead."

"I'll pick it up when I drop you off tonight. Give it a listen." Terri took a sip of her wine. "Don't be embarrassed. Lots of singers have material they'd like to forget. I'm your agent, Sloan, your promoter. I have one purpose in your life now, and that's to keep your momentum moving forward. This is a tough business, but if you're lucky, very lucky, you'll be able to climb into the stratosphere and become a star. Don't you want to be rich?"

Of course Sloan wanted the money, but fame was even more of a lure. She ignored Terri's question and tossed another ketchup-laden fry into her mouth.

Terri stared longingly at Sloan's diminishing pile of fries and sighed. "You won't be able to eat that way all your life, sugar. Trust me about that."

Sloan spitefully gobbled another fry.

Sloan was lying on a poolside lounger considering how to best smoke out this Lindsey character, when a shadow fell across her. Sloan winked open one eye, saw Terri backlit by the sun. "Let's go up," Terri said. "I've got news."

Once inside the cool air of the apartment, Sloan wrapped herself in a thick terry cloth robe, poured Terri a glass of pinot grigio that she kept on hand for the agent. She grabbed a sparkling water for herself. Handing Terri the glass, she asked, "What's up?"

Terri placed Sloan's old phone on top of a stylish stone coffee table. "Tom and I listened to the songs on your old cell, and you were right. Most of the songs are as you said—not very good."

"Told you so."

Terri handed Sloan the outdated phone. "Except for one."

"Really? Which one?"

"'Somebody's Baby.' Great title. Great song, and your voice is perfection on it."

Sloan felt as if her knees were going out from under her. She dropped to the leather sofa, the room spinning. *Not that one.* She'd totally forgotten about the song she'd written late one night in a spasm of pain and tears. She didn't remember recording it, but apparently she had.

Terri's eyes narrowed. "You don't look as pleased as I thought you would. Maybe *you* should have a glass of wine."

"Why that song?"

"Because it's a great song, Sloan. Tom likes its slower pace, and the lyrics. He thinks it will balance the EP, and he has good instincts. He also likes the way you sing it, your passion, your tenderness." Terri waited a few beats, inviting Sloan to speak. When she didn't, Terri added, "He wants you to hit the same vibe at the studio, with all the bells and whistles of additional musicians and a good sound mixer. This is a huge opportunity."

Sloan said nothing. The song had come from a dark place inside her, from a time of unfathomable sadness. She felt her eyes fill. "I—I don't know if I want—"

Terri stared at her. "Are you *kidding*? Of course you do! And if the label's full support can't persuade you, think about getting double royalties for penning it *and* singing it. More money, long copyright. I don't understand your reluctance."

The plush apartment was flooded with sunlight, but all

Sloan saw was herself alone in a basement bedroom with her old battered guitar, a melody chasing her soul, and words spilling out of a well of personal pain.

Terri eased down beside her, took Sloan's hand. "It's a breakup song, isn't it? About some guy you loved and lost. Like the singer Adele. You know, those amazing songs she sang about her and her boyfriend splitting up. They're classics."

Instantly Sloan saw how Terri had made the assumption. "Somebody's Baby" was indeed filled with the lyrics of goodbye and brokenhearted loss.

Terri's voice soothed, saying, "It's a wonderful song, Sloan, and no matter how personal it was at the time, this is the here and now. We want that song for the EP and your album. Don't bog this down. It's just words and music. And isn't that the business we're in?"

Sloan shut down her feelings, raised her eyes to meet Terri's gaze, and mentally balanced her private inner chaos with recording the song for the world to hear. Wiping her eyes, she said, "You're right. It was a breakup song, but it happened a few years ago, and I'm over it now."

Terri offered a delighted smile. "Excellent. I'll schedule the recording studio. I have a good feeling about this, Sloan. A very good feeling." She stood, picked up her purse, and headed to the door, where she turned. "He must have been a hell of a guy to leave you this shaken up so long after the fact."

Sloan made no comment, heard the soft click of the closing door as Terri left, then whispered, "He was. He truly was."

three

⸺

Dawson Berke realized that moving forward with Alana Kennedy, the girl he loved, wasn't going to be simple. He was, after all, a doctor's son, so he knew about survivor's guilt, post-traumatic stress disorder, depression, and other psychological issues brought on by trauma. Still, he wanted Lani in his life no matter the heartaches of their shared past, and he believed that together they could get beyond what had happened. From his perspective Lani's feelings of guilt were self-imposed and undeserved.

This April marked a year since his return from Chicago to Windemere, and reuniting with Lani. He'd been unsure if she would come to see him when he'd asked, but she had, and over those early euphoric spring months, they'd grown closer. He had assumed they would move forward together, but over time, he had seen that what had happened was keeping her from the life she deserved and the future he wanted with her. Grief had immobilized her.

He had rented an apartment not far from the interstate,

close to his construction worksite, in an area booming with suburban growth. Windemere was expanding, changing, and he had settled miles from the streets of brick and stately trees and renovated Victorians called Old Town, where Lani lived with her sister, Melody, an attorney, in a brick building of refurbished apartments built in the 1940s. Dawson thought Melody, the apartment, and its location added to Lani's inertia and that as long as Lani lived so close to places linked to sad memories, she wouldn't move forward. He wanted Lani to live with him, but Melody vehemently disagreed.

Dawson had argued his case with Melody, meeting inside a small eatery flush with aromas of coffee and fresh pastries. A table had separated them, but it may as well have been an acre of land. He'd said, "I love her. And she loves me. When we're together, she's happier. You've got to see that's real."

"I know what you feel for each other is real, but don't you get it? *You're* part of her problem. That's not your fault, Dawson. It's the circumstances. You're not to blame in any way, but her emotions are wound around you like a coil. Living with me represents a time when she didn't have this weight on her heart, this idea in her head that she's to blame for what happened. She's my little sister, and she needs my support."

He didn't think Melody gave his and Lani's love for each other enough credit. He was with Lani almost every night. The gaps between her dark spells were growing wider. He saw it in unguarded moments when they joked and laughed together, felt it in the way she burrowed into him, holding on in the dark—two souls searching for comfort. "I need her too, Mel. It isn't over for me either, you know. She's the one helping me go on, day in, day out. I want to wake up with her every morning."

"She needs space, Dawson, separation. She needs more than you. She needs a purpose, a direction!"

"I won't walk away from her. End of discussion!" He had scooted his chair from the table. The legs had made a screeching sound that had turned heads in the café.

Melody had reached out and caught his hand. "And don't you walk away from *me*. This might be our only chance to talk in private, while she's out at Bellmeade with her damn horse. Think about it. Lani is a few terms away from her finishing her RN degree, something she's wanted all her life. I've met with her supervisor, and she could have her old job at Windemere General in a heartbeat. And yet she spends her days grooming horses, mucking stalls, and shoveling animal shit at Bellmeade for Ciana Mercer. What a waste of Lani's talent and ambition!"

Melody's tortured expression had given Dawson pause. He'd calmed and said, "That job *is* helping her, Mel. I went through the same thing. I did hard physical work, but . . . *news flash* . . . when your body aches and you're physically wiped out, your mind catches a break. You're too tired to think and rehash a past that can never be changed."

"She can work just as hard in school and at the hospital. Be patient." Melody had waved her hand in dismissal. "Maybe I can find her a good therapist."

Dawson had fisted the table. Why hadn't Melody been able to see that Lani's hard exhausting work at the Bellmeade Stables *was* therapy? "Don't push her. She'll come through this."

Melody's desire to help Lani return to the enthusiastic, gung-ho girl that Melody had watched grow up was also an invisible coil. One night, wrapped in his arms, Lani had said,

"My horse, Oro, is like a good friend. He never ever pushes me. Sometimes I ride Oro bareback and we run against the wind. I feel his mane stinging my face, hear his hooves pounding on the track, dirt flying like stones against my legs, and for a few minutes the pain inside me goes away . . . and I'm free. Oro runs, he carries me, and all I have to do is hold on."

Dawson had pressed his lips against the crown of Lani's head, knowing he was hearing her deeper meaning. Melody's pushing and urging Lani to return to her former self was hurting more than helping. He knew Lani in ways Melody never could, because he and Lani shared a mutual and a brutal wound, in some ways the same wound, but also very different. It had left deep scars on them both. Once she'd fallen asleep that night, he'd whispered, "If you fall, my love, I'll catch you."

That day in the coffee shop, resigned to nothing changing between him and Melody, Dawson had known they were at an impasse, so he'd said, "Enough. We're getting nowhere, and I've got to get back to the job site."

Still gripping his hand, Melody had said, "Please promise me you won't push her, Dawson. You have a power over her I don't. You and I can fight like dogs whenever you want. I don't care what you say to me, or think of me, but don't take her away yet. Right now she's very fragile. I know we can agree on that."

The pleading look in Melody's eyes had dampened his frustration with the woman. Their love for Lani rose from different streams, each just as passionate. And they both knew that he held the winning ace—he held Lani's heart. "I get that we both love her. I won't use my 'power,' Mel. But I won't let go either. Sooner or later, she'll come through the pain.

And when she does, you'll have to step back. No matter what, you are her loving sister. You need your own life too."

Almost imperceptibly Mel had nodded, and Dawson had left the coffee shop knowing he'd told only a half-truth. Darkness and pain lurked inside him, but over time it had grayed, and the sharpness had dulled. Life had resumed, a new rhythm had been discovered, new paths had been followed, memories had gotten shut into boxes and tucked away inside closets. They slipped out occasionally, but more to comfort than to wound. He knew that one day the same would happen for Lani too.

~

Lani understood that her sister and the man she loved were fighting about her. She wished they wouldn't, but she had no inner resources to cope or change things. She loved them both, but she was smart enough to know that release from her internal prison was something she must achieve on her own. Neither Melody nor Dawson could do it for her.

After what had happened, having Dawson in her life felt like an undeserved gift, one she'd wanted for a long time, never dreamed she'd have, and didn't want to lose.

She had helped him search for his apartment, had gone with him to choose furniture—some new, some used—and had arranged places for everything in the single-bedroom unit. She'd suggested colors, chosen small appliances, pillows, pictures, tabletop decorations, bed linen. "White," she had said, standing in front of shelves stacked with bedding in a department store. "And this comforter." She had held up one with multicolored stripes because he'd insisted, "No flowers."

He hadn't cared what she chose, because she had seemed engaged and happy, once more like the Lani he remembered. "Buy anything you like," he'd told her, secretly hoping that if, despite Melody's objections, Lani moved in with him, she'd feel like the apartment was *her* home too.

When the buying fervor had been over, the apartment decorated, the activity completed, Lani had crashed. The world had spun around her. Melody's life was filled with law cases, court filings, late nights at her office, dates with a guy she'd met online and really liked. Dawson's life was busy with juggling his workload at Hastings Construction and classes at Middle Tennessee State University toward a degree in construction management. One day he would design houses. Meanwhile, he learned all he could about the business. And she, Lani? She had fallen into limbo. She couldn't find her way back to wanting her RN degree and a job at the hospital. She wasn't sure she ever would.

When Ciana had asked her to resume her former high school job at Bellmeade Stables, Lani had been grateful to be given a reason to get up every day. No task was too difficult, too dirty, too big, or too small for her to tackle. Exercising and bathing horses housed at the stables, helping Jon work and train quarter horses that were to be sold, spreading fresh straw in stalls, even giving Ciana a helping hand in the fields kept Lani busy and feeling useful. Life had had a rhythm that summer, an easy ebb and flow tied to the rising and setting of the sun, the blooming and fading of seasonal flowers, the solitude of rainy days puttering around the barn and talking with Ciana. Her evenings had had a rhythm of hanging with Dawson, making dinner together, going to movies or for late-night swims in the lighted pool, the water warmed from the heat of the day . . . and of lying in his arms on sheets of white cotton, skin to skin and sleepy-eyed. Sometimes she'd stay the night, but she usually returned to the apartment she shared with her sister. To keep the peace.

The memories that normally haunted her had retreated, but would sneak out to wound when she passed a playground of laughing children. She remembered the time when she and Dawson had been in the mall and had been watching a mother chasing after a squealing exuberant child who'd broken free, and who then careened into Dawson's legs full tilt. "Whoa!" he'd said, catching himself and the little girl before they'd both hit the floor. A grateful mother had retrieved her child, but the wistful look on Dawson's face as the mother and little girl had melded into the crowd had broken Lani's heart.

That first summer had turned into autumn, and as the leaves had turned vibrant colors, Lani had turned a page in her book of life. And when she looked back now, she saw that the pain that shadowed her was becoming paler in the waning light of the past. *"Love changes things,"* Ciana had told her as they'd worked in the barn one rainy day. *"It changed me."* And by the time autumn had come that first year, Lani had known that Ciana's pronouncement was absolutely true. Love, indeed, had changed her.

four

The recording session in March for "Somebody's Baby" went better than Sloan had expected. She was able to hold herself together, to sing multiple versions for mixing, and to ignore the ache inside her about the song's history. When the EP was completed, Tom took Sloan and Terri into the sound booth and played all four songs. "I like it," he said. "We'll press it, send it out to top forty stations. It'll be in stores in no time."

Later in the week, sitting with Terri in the publicist's plush office mapping out a schedule, Sloan ramped up her courage and said, "I want to take some time off."

Terri looked up from the paperwork strewn on the conference table between them. "I'm having lunch brought in, and we'll take a break then."

Sloan took a deep breath and sat on her hands to control their tremble. "I want a real break, Terri . . . days, not hours. I—um—I need some time for myself to decompress." In months ahead lay studio time for the expected album, as well as weeks of touring with more high-profile singers and bands. Summer and fall was life lived on planes and buses and in motel rooms in quickly forgotten cities. A life of burning through arenas and convention halls and stadiums, of rehearsals followed by performances, then packing up and moving to the next place.

"Are you serious? At this stage of career building?" Terri leaned back in her cushy leather chair, studied Sloan's face. "We haven't settled on the songs for your album yet, plus I've a long list of interviews lined up on radio stations. This isn't a good time, Sloan. You're hot, and we want to keep you that way."

For a while Sloan thought about leveling with Terri but decided against it. She told herself it was to protect Kiley, but she knew it was really to cover the things she hadn't aired to Terri months before. She'd grown up tough, turning herself deaf to gossip about her mother, to taunts from kids at school. Who needed them? She'd learned to go her own way in life, ignore what she could, leave behind what she should.

Sloan stood, went to the windows, and stared into sunlight at the ridge of brown hills in the distance. The letter, the lure of a potential sister, was all she thought about these days. "I wouldn't ask if I didn't need a break."

She heard Terri rustle papers behind her. "Where would you go to chill out?"

"Nashville. Just for a few days. I'd like to kick back, reconnect, and celebrate. I do have friends, you know." The white lie was partly true. The Slades at the bar where she'd worked singing and serving food and alcohol liked her, or they *had* until she'd left them without a word of goodbye and without a singer. But of course, it wasn't really Nashville that Sloan wanted to revisit. She turned, leveled Terri a look, willed tears into her eyes. "Please."

Terri steepled her fingers, her expression one of cool composure. If Terri refused, Sloan knew her plan to go look up Lindsey Ridley was sunk. "I'll have Kiley arrange a doctor's appointment for you."

"I'm not sick. I just want a few days—"

"Well, you can't go running off simply because you want to. You're under contract."

After the contest, Sloan had signed many pieces of paper, most she hadn't bothered to read, but at the time it had hardly mattered to her because she'd been capturing her lifelong dream. She knew there were expectations and standards she had to meet, and that in many ways *American Singer* and the record label owned her. So while Terri's proclamation about seeing a doctor seemed senseless, Sloan knew better than to argue. "Why a doctor?"

"Because the honchos in the front office will need a reason why their newest sensation is going on vacation."

A day later Sloan found herself in the office of Dr. Chen, a kindly Asian man who gave her a thorough physical exam. He suggested that while she had no fever, she might have mononucleosis, so he recommended two weeks of bed rest, beamed her a smile, and sent her on her way. Apparently a doctor's excuse was like a hall pass—necessary to skip school.

"You have ten days," Terri said when she handed Sloan her plane ticket. "Get it out of your system, come back, and get to work. Your EP is getting air time, so we need to ride the wave." Terri stood and knuckled the tabletop. "And for the record, don't go nutsy on me in Nashville. The press loves a good 'celeb fail.' Be careful out there."

Sloan understood that the limelight loved to zero in on blemishes. "I won't do anything to hurt myself. I know what's at stake."

Terri offered a terse nod. "Have a good time. Just not too good."

Three days later the car service picked up Sloan and her suitcase and drove her to LAX, where she caught her Nashville flight. She settled into first class wearing a pair of sunglasses, her pulse racing, knowing that the unhappiness and heartache she'd fled in Windemere had not gone away, and now, with the lure of a stranger's letter, she was hurtling toward it like a runaway train.

⁓

A car service met her at the Nashville airport and drove her to a downtown luxury hotel, everything prearranged by Terri's firm. As soon as Sloan checked in, she went to the concierge desk and arranged for a rental car to be delivered. She planned to drive to Windemere and meet this Lindsey face to face without any warning. Sloan wasn't going to be scammed, but she wanted to know the truth, whatever it was.

The next morning she exited the interstate and drove familiar rural back roads, edged by lines of budding trees and open pasture land of freshly plowed red dirt. Wildflowers bloomed in long stretches of yellow, lavender, and white. She'd forgotten how pretty spring could be. In Los Angeles acres of concrete ruled the landscape. Plants were assigned to baskets hanging from lampposts or giant pots lining sidewalks. Fuchsia bougainvillea vines climbed fences and stucco walls to survive, and green grass was confined to patches of manicured lawns and apartment entryways, like the place where she lived. Without rain the LA hills turned brown, looked scruffy. Tennessee's rolling hills were lush with green.

On either side of the rural road taking her to Lindsey's

was open farmland, with an occasional house and a roadside mailbox the only markers differentiating one person's property from the next. Sloan slowed to follow the box numbering until she found the one from the letter. At the end of a long loose rock driveway was a redbrick ranch-style house with hedges of budding azalea bushes across its front. She turned in and parked near the front porch. No one came to the door when she pulled up, and thankfully, neither did a barking dog. She sat for a few minutes listening to birdsong, building courage. Then she went and peeked through a screen door. She rapped on the frame, making it rattle. "Hello. Anyone here?" No answer. "Lindsey? Mrs. Ridley?"

From somewhere in the back of the house, Sloan heard a crash. She jumped back, shivers racing up her spine. "Hello!" she called again. She heard a cry. Was someone hurt? In trouble? She didn't know whether to run away or barge in. "Lindsey?"

Sloan tried the flimsy handle, swung the door open, and stepped into a furniture-cluttered front room. She called again. No response. She carefully wove around two sofas and several chairs, toward a hallway on the left. The narrow hallway was dark, with only one door standing open. The air was laced with a sharp medicinal odor. Sloan stepped cautiously into the room and saw a woman lying on the floor, blood pooling on a rug beneath her body. An IV stand also lay on the floor, tubes pulled from the woman's arm, bags leaking clear liquids. "Oh my God!" Sloan rushed over, crouched next to the woman. "What happened?"

The woman didn't open her eyes, only mumbled, "Help me."

"I'll call 911. Hang on." Sloan fumbled for her phone, couldn't find it, dumped her purse's contents onto the floor, grabbed her cell, hands shaking, heart thudding, thoughts screaming, *Go! Run.* She managed to sputter out the address to the emergency operator, dropped the cell phone, and looked around wildly for something to sop up the blood. So much blood! She saw a towel on the arm of a chair, grabbed it, froze. The blood was coming from the woman's arm and nose. She panicked, unsure of where to start, laid the towel on the woman's arm, watched it stain bright red. All the while Sloan was saying over and over that help was on its way. Where was the ambulance? Why couldn't she hear any sirens? Sloan tasted bile in the back of her throat.

She dabbed dripping blood off the woman's face with a tissue that had lain in the heap from her purse. The woman was unresponsive. Her skin had a yellowish cast and deep dark hollows under lashless eyelids. A bandana wrapped around her head had slipped off, exposing the woman's perfectly smooth hairless scalp. Sloan caught her breath, did a butt scoot to one side, her stomach heaving from the coppery smell of blood and chemicals. She was cupping her hand over her mouth, about to throw up, when from the doorway behind her a deep male voice barked, "Who are you, and what the *hell* have you done to Lindsey?"

five

Sloan screamed, looked up at a man coming straight at her. She scooted until she felt a wall against her back, and her brain rode a flashback. *A man's big hand groping for her, stretching, reaching, his fingers clutching at air just inches from her body. She pressed her back into a wall in the inky darkness. She shivered, terrified, unable to scream, her voice trapped in her throat. Smaller. She had to make herself smaller, thinner. She held her breath. . . .*

For a moment a black haze sucked at Sloan. When it cleared, she was again in the room of a woman unconscious on the floor. Sloan gulped air into her lungs. *Can't pass out,* she thought. *Can't.* The man advancing on her now glared her a warning that said, *Stay put.* She couldn't have moved if she'd wanted to.

He turned, dropped to his knees beside the bleeding woman, and lifted her partway across his lap so that her head and shoulders were higher than her body. He stroked her cheek, "Help's coming, sweetie. On its way. Hang on."

Sloan sat stark still, afraid to move, as frightened of the

man as she was of the woman on the floor. *So much blood!* Sitting ramrod straight, she finally heard the wail of a distant siren. Minutes later, two men and a woman hurried into the bedroom carrying medical bags and a collapsible metal stretcher. EMS.

One of the men gripped the shoulder of the man holding Lindsey. "We've got it from here, Cole."

The man, Cole, handed off his patient, and the team went to work, slapping on a blood pressure cuff and starting an IV. As they worked, Cole rattled off some medical jargon, then added, "I heard the distress call on my scanner. I got here as soon as I could."

The woman on the team asked, "Any idea what's happened?"

"*She* might." Cole gestured to Sloan. "When I got here, she was leaning over Lindsey."

The woman's gaze swept to Sloan. "I—I found her like that! All the blood—" Sloan stammered a recap of what she'd seen and heard after she had knocked on the door.

The team eased their patient onto the wheeled stretcher and began pushing it toward the doorway. One of the EMTs held the IV bag aloft.

"Go on. I'll meet you at the hospital," Cole told the crew. Once they'd left and the siren wail had faded, the room went deathly quiet. He crossed to Sloan, still sitting with her back scrunched to the wall. He crouched in front of her. "You okay?"

She was trembling, unsure she could stand just yet, shocked by what had happened to Lindsey, terrified of the horror she'd felt in an unexpected flash of—of what? What had happened to her in those few dark moments? She forced a nod at Cole.

"Sorry I yelled and scared you, but I didn't know who you were. And when I saw the blood . . ." His voice had gentled. "Lindsey's friend Gloria must have taken Toby to school and gone on to work." He shook his head in disapproval. "Lindsey should never be left alone. I've told Gloria that a hundred times." He held out his hand, but she didn't take it. "I'm Cole Langston, Lindsey's neighbor, next farm over. Also a paramedic with the town's EMT unit but off duty today. When I heard the 911 call come in and realized it was Lindsey, I beat a path here, and now . . . Well . . . again, sorry." He took a deep breath, offered her a contrite smile. "Who are you?"

"I'm Sloan Gabriel."

"This is an awkward way to meet, but I'm really harmless."

She hesitantly took his hand, felt warmth, and realized her hand was icy.

"Want to stand up?"

He helped her to her feet. "You're not a local, are you? I would have remembered you." A look of appreciation as he took in her blond hair, blue eyes, and trim body backed up his words.

She shifted under his scrutiny. She didn't think him a handsome man. She'd seen her share of good-looking men in LA—models and struggling actors, but instead she pegged Cole as "outdoor-rugged." He was muscular, broad across his chest and shoulders, had brown hair and amazing electric-blue eyes. His smile showed straight white teeth, and a deep dimple on the left side of his mouth turned his fierceness into charming.

"I live in Los Angeles. I just stopped by for a visit."

"Look, I'm heading to the hospital. Want to ride with me so we can check on Lindsey together?"

She nodded, bent, grabbed her purse, refilled its contents, and followed him outside, where she saw a gleaming black pickup truck, the driver door flung open, the warning bell about keys left in the ignition still dinging. She glanced back toward Lindsey's house. "Are you going to lock her front door?"

"You're in Windemere, not LA," he said with a disarming grin. "Besides, neighbors look out for each other. They all knew where the ambulance was going when they heard the siren." He helped her into the truck's cab, went around to the driver's side. He started the engine and rolled down the driveway to the road, turned left toward town.

The day had grown brighter, warmer, and the smell of spring air was flowery. "Will she be all right?"

"Yes, this time."

The landscape of small farms streaked past the truck's window. "What's wrong with her?"

Cole, his right wrist draped over the steering wheel, his other hand resting on the armrest, didn't take his eyes off the road. "Cancer. Stage four. She must have fallen and torn out her IVs. Chemo thins the blood. That's why she was bleeding so badly."

"Cancer?"

Cole gave his passenger a quizzical look. "She's very sick. Isn't that why you came all the way from California? To see her?"

Sloan said nothing, simply bit hard on her bottom lip. She'd been blindsided by all that had happened that morning. It had been nothing like the controlled confrontation she'd planned in her head.

Cole turned into the parking lot adjacent to the main

hospital, parked in front of a redbrick building with lots of glass. Inside he said, "Wait here while I check on her in triage." He pushed open doors marked RESTRICTED AREA STAFF ONLY.

Sloan paced the small waiting area like a prisoner, struggled to quell her sad memories of Windemere General Hospital, a place she had never wanted to enter again. However, this building was new, built in the five years that she'd been gone. A brass plaque on one wall read THE ARIE WINSLOW CANCER CENTER.

Cole returned. "She's awake, and getting IV fluids. She'll be moved upstairs into a room soon. She remembers you coming into the house, and she really wants to thank you."

"Yes, I want to see her too."

"We can go up after she's settled." He tipped his head. "Can I buy you a cup of coffee? There's a coffee bar on the second floor that brews good java. I know I sure can use a cup, and I owe you a cup after scaring you half to death."

The coffee bar was located within a spacious cafeteria flooded with sparkling sunlight, and was full of colorful tables with stainless steel trim and brightly painted chairs. Cole walked her to a red-topped table, where they sat and waited for the barista to brew their coffees.

"Place looks new."

"It opened a couple of years ago, the pet project of Ciana Beauchamp Mercer. She owns Bellmeade, a working farm and horse-breeding spread west of town. Seems she had a childhood friend who died of cancer. Ciana gave money and raised more money to get this place built. I hear nobody says no to her." He gave a wry smile. "Everything here is state of the art, and it's a godsend for patients like Lindsey, who used to have to go to Nashville for treatment."

Of course, Sloan knew the Beauchamp name because everyone in Windemere knew it, but she listened attentively, unwilling to confess her connection to the town. "How long have you lived here?"

"About four years. I grew up in northwest Indiana, where I got my EMS and paramedic training. My grandparents lived on that farm next to Lindsey's, but Grandma died and I moved down to help Gramps. He died a year afterward and left me the house and property. I liked it here, the wide-open spaces, the people I met, winters that didn't leave inches of snow and ice on the ground. Plus I had a free place to live, so I went for state certification, and here I'll stay."

Cole's open, easy manner put her at ease. She liked the sound of his voice, the way he freely shared details of his life. Nothing she would do. Sloan had been gone for close to five years—she'd fled Windemere the first time to rejoin Jarred's resurrected band in Nashville with her high school bandmates. The group had spent two summers touring and playing festivals, making a name for themselves, gathering fans . . . and then, as the band's star was ascending, came the disaster that destroyed all their hard work and scattered them.

Sloan had been forced to return to Windemere, where she'd pleaded for help from the one person she'd hurt the most. He had agreed, and those few months had stabilized her life. The time had also allowed her to discover a love she'd never expected. For a short time Sloan had caught a glimpse of what might have been if she'd stuck around the first time. But the door of the past was shut forever, first by another woman, then by a grief unparalleled in all the years of her life. So she had returned to Nashville, where she'd begun a solo singing career, and then gone to LA and the contest. Memories from the past assailed her. She shook them off, glanced at the coffee bar. "Our coffee's ready."

Cole snagged the cups and returned to the table. "So how do you know Lindsey? She's had cancer for years, but you acted surprised when I told you."

"I'm not sure I do know her. I came to check out whether or not I do."

"You came all the way from LA to meet someone you're not sure you *know?*"

"It's a long story, and I want to talk to Lindsey first. It's only fair."

He took a swallow of black coffee, studying her over the rim of his cup.

"Are you and Lindsey"—she fumbled for a word, settled on—"close?"

"We're friends. She's had a rough go of it, and I help out as best I can. She's suffered enough."

Sloan watched his expression turn guarded, his earlier camaraderie gone, and she thought better of prying more information from him. She offered one of her best smiles. "Sounds neighborly of you."

"It's the right thing to do." When they finished their coffee, he stood. "In triage I was told Lindsey would go to room 303. Let's check."

They rode up in silence, and Sloan was fairly certain that if she said or did anything to upset the sick woman, Cole would drag her bodily from Lindsey's room. Sloan would have to be careful.

The elevator opened into a wide hallway where a skylight threw a swath of sunlight onto cream-colored walls and a shiny pale blue floor. The place didn't look like a hospital, but the antiseptic smell couldn't be masked. Sloan knew she was in a hospital, all right. She would never forget that smell. She gave a small shudder, and followed Cole down the corridor.

They found Lindsey lying in a room with walls painted soft pink, on a bed covered with pale blue sheets. The slats of the automatic blinds were turned upward, allowing sunlight to give the room a rosy glow. Monitors with lines running into Lindsey's chest kept tabs on her vital signs. When Cole spoke her name, Lindsey's eyelids fluttered open. "Hey, sweet lady. How you doing?"

His tender side was the polar opposite of the side Sloan had first witnessed.

"Cole . . ." Lindsey's voice sounded drowsy, thick. "I fell."

"We've got you fixed up now." He stroked the back of her hand, purple with bruises. "I heard your call come in and got there as soon as I could. You're safe now."

Her head had been draped with a soft terry cloth turban, but her skin still looked yellowish to Sloan, and paper thin, as though it could tear with any movement. Her facial bones jutted, but even so, Sloan caught a glimpse of what, with health, would have been a pretty woman.

Lindsey's expression clouded. "There was someone . . . a woman. . . . She knocked on the screen door. . . . I thought Gloria was there, but she wasn't. . . . I tried to get up."

Sloan, standing to one side and slightly behind Cole, recoiled. *She* had caused Lindsey to fall?

"I brought her with me." Cole stepped away and urged Sloan closer, planted himself firmly behind her.

"Hi. I'm—I'm—"

She got no further. Lindsey caught her breath, clutched Sloan's wrist. "Oh my gosh! It's you. You came! You believed me, and you came. Cole! This is Sloan Gabriel. This is my *sister.*"

six

"Your sister! You never said you had a sister."

"I didn't know myself until a few years ago. Daddy told me everything before he died." Lindsey cast sad eyes up at Sloan. "I'm sorry you had to hear the news about our daddy like this. I was hoping to tell you in a better way." Her voice had a soft Southern lilt.

The news jolted Sloan. She had expected to face the man who'd abandoned her when she was baby, a man who'd vanished and left Sloan alone with a mother like LaDonna. She had many things she wanted to say to him, many unanswered questions, and now there was no one who could answer. "How did he die?"

"I want to tell you the things I know, Sloan. I have a box at the house where I've saved stuff to show you, old photos, but for now I'm shot full of painkillers and everything's getting fuzzy." Her attempt to squeeze Sloan's wrist was feeble. "So sorry 'bout today. . . . Come over after they send me home . . . please. . . ."

"It's okay. I understand." But Sloan felt frustrated at being so close to learning something—anything—about her family, and being told she had to wait longer.

Lindsey shifted her gaze to Cole. "You'll go to the house? Tell Toby I love him and I'll be home just as soon as I can."

"You know I will."

Her gaze slipped back to Sloan. "Toby's my sweet angel, the light of my life, and he worries 'bout me."

Cole stepped in, lifted Lindsey's hand and tucked it under the covers, bent and kissed her forehead. "Get some rest."

"Sloan's famous, Cole," Lindsey mumbled into his ear. "And real pretty." Her gaze again shifted up to Sloan.

Sloan watched Lindsey drift to sleep. Immobilized and exhausted, Sloan stood staring at the woman claiming to be her half sister. She felt Cole's arm slip around her waist. "Come on. She'll be out for a long time." He led her into the hall, where she slid away his arm and leaned against the wall, profoundly disappointed. Cole braced a shoulder on the wall beside her. "Is Lindsey right about you two having the same father?"

"I don't know. My mother never talked about him unless it was to call him 'the dirtbag who ran out on us' after I was born. I have no warm fuzzy memories of any Daddy." *And fewer good memories of LaDonna.* "Mom never even bothered to fill in the blank for *Father* on my birth certificate, so when Lindsey's email came, I was pretty shocked. And damn curious," Sloan added. "So I hopped a plane to come check it out in person."

"She's never said anything to me, and we've had some long talks."

His comment made Sloan wonder if his claim that he and Lindsey were "only friends" was the truth. "She wrote that his name was Jerry. Did you ever meet him?"

Cole watched a nurse coming down the corridor carrying a meds tray. "Let's get out of the hallway. How'd you like another cup of coffee?"

She felt like having something stronger, but settled for the coffee. They returned to the cafeteria, now peppered with personnel coming on duty for a shift change. He shuttled Sloan to a table shoved into a corner, went to the coffee bar, and returned minutes later. He had remembered what she'd ordered earlier, and set the cup in front of her and took the chair across from hers. She asked her question again. "Did you ever meet Jerry?"

"No. She talked about him, though. She adored him. She was his princess." The words went all over Sloan. She'd never been anybody's princess. "I know she was raised in Memphis, an only child."

Except for driving through the city on her way west, Sloan hadn't been in the city of Memphis. Had LaDonna? Is that where she'd met the man who might have been Sloan's father? "What happened to her parents?"

"A car accident before she moved to Windemere."

"Why did she come here?"

"She bought the house next to mine about two years ago, but you'll need to ask her about her past. . . . It's her story to tell."

He'd cleverly fed her own words back to her, and she didn't like it. She'd been honest with him and didn't like him withholding information she wanted. Lindsey was very sick. Who knew if she'd be well enough to really talk to Sloan over the next few days, which was all the time she had to hang around? Food trays rattled in the background. Someone across the room let loose with a loud horsey laugh.

Studying her, Cole chewed on the wooden stir stick from

his cup. She was one of the prettiest women he'd ever seen, and he couldn't forget Lindsey's whispered words, *"Sloan's famous."* He offered a smile. "Look, I'm not trying to stonewall you, Sloan. As a paramedic, I'm trained to keep confidences. You'd be surprised at what people say when they think they're dying on an ambulance ride. Once Lindsey is able to talk to you, she'll fill you in."

Sloan reminded herself that all of Lindsey's evidence could be of no value if they weren't related. She took a slug of her coffee, burned her tongue. "Can you at least tell me about Gloria and Toby? I'd like *some* answers today. I came halfway across the country to get to the truth. Please help me!"

He rested his forearms on the table. "Gloria Harrold is an LPN and Lindsey's best friend. She came from Memphis with Lindsey and moved in to help care for her and Toby."

"She's a nurse?" Sloan had limited knowledge about nursing, had known only one nurse in her life. Lani's face surfaced, but she shoved it away.

"Gloria's a licensed practical nurse, different from an RN, who has a degree. LPNs do basic medical care and can handle most emergencies. Gloria works in an assisted-living care facility, which means Lindsey's alone more than she needs to be."

"And Toby?"

"Lindsey's six-year-old son. Cute kid, in first grade, and whip smart." The mention of the boy softened Cole's features. "Way more grown-up than he should be, if you know what I mean. He's watched his mama suffer a lot."

The idea twisted her stomach. She'd grown up way too fast too. But Sloan caught on to what wasn't being said, and asked, "In her email she signed her name Lindsey Sloan Ridley. Is she married?"

"Divorced."

Between the question and the answer, Cole's expression had turned ice cold. Another wall Sloan wouldn't be able to breach. "Her story to tell?"

"Exactly." Cole flashed enough of a smile to show his dimple. "I have a few questions for you, if you don't mind. Lindsey told me you were famous. And true confession—you do look familiar." She rolled her eyes. He laughed. "I know, sounds like a lame pickup line, but it's the truth. Will you fill me in?"

She wasn't going to get any more out of him, so she slouched in the chair, considered what to tell him. "I—um—I'm a singer. Country pop. I won a contest—"

"Wait a minute!" Cole slapped his forehead. "Of course! The girl on that talent show. I should have recognized you. . . . Everybody in town was talking about you all during the contest."

"You watched the show?"

He looked sheepish. "Toward the end, when it came down to the finals. The show said you were from Nashville, but people in Windemere said you grew up here."

"I spent a time in Nashville before going to LA to audition for the show."

"Stores around here put VOTE FOR SLOAN signs in their windows. I'm sorry I didn't make the connection before now. . . . I blame it on this crazy day."

"They put up signs for me?" The news was startling. She had no fond memories of Windemere while growing up, and only angry thoughts of mean girls from high school.

"People love stars."

"I'm no star." *Not yet,* she added silently. Plus, she'd jeopardized her ascent by coming here. If Terri discovered she'd lied, or at least held back the whole truth . . . "I didn't come here to be recognized, and honestly, I'd rather no one recognize me. I'm the one who's sorry. For Lindsey. I'm glad you were there this morning to help. I didn't know what to do. . . . All that blood . . ." She shivered with the memory.

"You called 911. That was the best thing to do."

Sloan's purse, sitting on the table, vibrated, startling them both and making them laugh. She reached inside, pulled out her cell phone, and saw she'd missed four text messages from Terri. "I have to return some calls." She glanced around. "But not here."

Cole rose. "Let me see if I can pry some info out of the medical staff about how long Lindsey might be here. Go back down to the ER and wait for me. I'll drive you to Lindsey's."

Where her rental car and the drive to Nashville waited for her, and probably a blowup and lecture from Terri. Sloan had promised to call and check in with her publicist that morning, but hadn't. While she rode the elevator, she read through the messages ranging from chatty to terse, her brain working on plausible excuses, and when the doors slid open, she stepped off the elevator and bumped straight into a man's chest.

He grabbed her upper arms to steady her. "Whoa!"

"Whoops! 'Scuse me!" Sloan peered up, and her heart grabbed. She was looking into the dark brown eyes of Dawson Berke. And for an instant, time stood still.

seven

For a shocked moment they simply stared at each other. Sloan was the last person in the world Dawson had expected to see, yet here she stood in front of him. Behind them the elevator doors quietly slid shut.

Sloan's knees turned rubbery. It had been some time since she'd looked up into those dark brown eyes and told him goodbye. Seeing him now, tall, fit, and browned from the sun, took her breath. And then came the tumble of heartbreaking memories. . . .

He recovered first. "What are you doing in Windemere?"

She fought to control her racing heart, and also to answer him without telling the whole truth. "Just a quick visit. I was in Nashville . . . drove over for the day. How about you? Is someone sick?"

"One of my construction crew got hurt a few days ago. I'm checking on him. But why are you here in the hospital?" He couldn't forget how much she detested this place.

"I came with someone else. He asked me to wait while he

checked on a friend." Vague, a partial truth. She hoped he'd step to the elevator and go his way. He didn't.

"You changed your name, and you won that singing contest."

Her throat swelled shut. He'd hit the one nerve that could unravel her. "Name change meant a fresh start. I was over being Sloan Quentin." She was over being a lot of things, and she didn't want questions about her choice of a new name. She quickly changed the subject. "You watched *American Singer*? Did you vote for me?"

A ghost of a smile turned up Dawson's mouth. So like Sloan to evade what she didn't want to talk about. "Of course I voted for you. It wasn't much of a contest, you know. No one else on the stage had a voice to match yours, or your talent."

He didn't have to say that, but it touched her that he had. Ever since they'd first met, he'd known of her lifelong dream, a small-town girl with a lofty goal, and yet here she was poised on the brink. "I've been told that Windemere put up window signs asking people to vote for me."

"True story."

"I never thought these people—" She nibbled her bottom lip. "Well . . . you know."

"A lot of those kids we went to school with have moved on."

"You mean they up and left this little corner of *paradise*?"

"Yes . . . just like you did."

Her face grew warm with his gentle chastisement. "But you've stayed."

"It's home." He had once thought it never would be, but if it was true what was said about home being where the heart is, then he'd found his. "And for the record, Lani voted for you too."

His message was oblique, but she got it, and it was no surprise that Dawson and Lani had ended up together. "Tell her thank you."

Just then she heard the clearing of a throat, glanced sideways toward the sound, saw Cole. The here and now returned with a jolt. She and Dawson turned in unison, and she offered Cole her best smile. "Cole Langston, I'd like you to meet an old friend from high school."

The two men sized each other up.

Sloan fidgeted. All she wanted to do was walk away, because seeing Dawson so unexpectedly had opened doors that she wanted to remain shut. New her. New life.

"Dawson Berke," he said, shaking Cole's hand.

"I've seen you around," Cole said, loose and friendly, all the while his head spinning over how close Sloan and this Dawson had been standing, and staring into each other's eyes. "You from here?"

"I was a transplant from Maryland. Finished high school here."

Sloan gritted her teeth, hoping Dawson wouldn't divulge more.

Dawson shifted his stance and said, "You look familiar too. Weren't you one of the EMTs who came to the Hastings' construction site two days ago? One of my workers was hurt and I called for an ambulance."

"That guy who fell from the roof of a new build? He had a nasty compound fracture of his right femur, simple fracture of left leg and right arm. Concussion too." Cole offered a sheepish grin. "TMI . . . sorry. I may forget names and faces, but never injuries. How's he doing?"

"I'm on my way to check on him now. You all did good fast work. The guy was in agony."

Cole shrugged and flashed his grin. "Glad we could help him."

Dawson reached behind Sloan, thumbed the elevator button. He said, "Nice seeing you, Sloan. You in town long?" His friendly tone didn't quite match the cautionary look in his eyes.

"No. Just passing through. I live in LA these days. Too much green space in Tennessee for my taste."

"Safe trip," he said, and stepped into the elevator.

Sloan turned her attention to Cole. "Ready to leave?"

Inside the elevator, Dawson didn't immediately send the otherwise empty car upward. Encountering Sloan had been a head trip, and he needed to regroup. The *American Singer* contest was a show Lani loved to watch, and so in January they had cozied up on his sofa to watch the start of its new season together. When the preselected contestants for the show had been announced, he and Lani both had been shocked to see Sloan take the stage. "Should I change the channel?" he'd asked.

"No," Lani had said softly. "I'm okay with watching her. She's always been a terrific singer, and the world should hear her." Lani had squeezed Dawson's hand. "Please believe me. I wish her only happiness."

He had believed her because this was Lani's basic character—sensitive and compassionate, except when it came to herself. Lani had come a long way over the last year but could still be her own harshest critic, fair to all except herself. At the end of last summer, as autumn leaves had begun to turn vibrant colors, through sheer force of will she had made up her mind to begin again. "Because of you," she'd whispered one night in his arms. "And because I can't have you and Mel fighting about me anymore."

She'd hunkered down, kept her horse but quit the Bellmeade job, returned to college, finished her RN degree, and graduated that December. In January she had returned to part-time work at Windemere General. She remained living with her sister and nurtured a sunny disposition, but Dawson could tell when old ghosts wiggled their way out of Lani's subconscious to haunt her, often times showing up in routine and ordinary circumstances. Of course, seeing Sloan on a national television show in a singing competition wasn't ordinary or routine. Watching Sloan in fifty-five-inch living color hadn't been easy for him either.

When Sloan had announced to the camera that she came from Nashville, he had said, "She altered history. What's wrong with being from Windemere?"

"She's moved on, Dawson. A person has to move on . . . ready or not." He thought Lani's words more telling than she might have realized.

On that first night of the show, he'd clicked off the TV, drawn Lani to him, and slowly, leisurely kissed her eyelids, her cheeks, her mouth, the hollow in her throat, until he'd heard her breath catch. "It won't hurt to miss the show tonight, love. We'll catch it next week."

And so week after week they had watched Sloan's heart-shaped face, full lips, sky-blue eyes, and perfect cheekbones illuminate the screen in liquid crystal clarity. She'd wowed the judges, the live audiences, and the millions of viewers who'd voted for her from their phones and computers. She had left the other contestants in the dust.

The ding of the elevator call button snapped Dawson out of his reverie. Seeing Sloan in person had thrown him off balance. He breathed deeply, fought to regain composure and reconnect with his current world. He should tell Lani about running into Sloan. But Sloan had said she wouldn't be in town long. Why needlessly stir up old ghosts? Perhaps it would be best to say nothing. He jammed his finger onto the button for the orthopedic floor and rode up to visit his worker.

～

Cole walked Sloan across the ER lobby and out into the warmth of the afternoon, he feeling as if he'd happened upon a wreck with unseen damages, she pensive and withdrawn. The body language and undercurrent of tension between Sloan and Dawson when he'd walked up unnoticed belied Sloan's claim that Dawson was simply an "old friend from high school." Plus they had spoken in code—recognizable to his trained ears by the cadence of words ripe with hidden meanings.

Once Cole and Sloan reached his truck, he said, "I hope you can hang around for more than a few days. They couldn't tell me upstairs how long Lindsey might be here."

Her mood darkened, but he was pretty sure the change-over was more about running into Dawson than about Lindsey. She said, "I—I want her to get better, but I can't wait around too long. I've a big summer schedule ahead—rehearsals, and an album to record." All she truly wanted was to get information from Lindsey, return to LA, and forget Windemere. "When she's released, will you call me? I'll give you my cell number. In the meantime, I'll be in Nashville."

"Shucks, lady, we have hotels in these parts too." He waggled his eyebrows and grinned, hoping to improve her mood.

"No thanks." He held out his phone, and she tapped in her name and number and handed it back, saying, "For your eyes only."

He opened the passenger door for her, and she offered a perfunctory smile and climbed into the truck, leaving Cole to understand that whatever had happened between Sloan and Dawson, no matter how long ago, wasn't yet over. Not by a long shot.

eight

When Cole pulled up to Lindsey's house, the screen door flew open with a bang, and a small boy streaked outside and down the porch steps. He hopped onto the truck's running board on the driver side before Cole turned off the engine. "Hey, slow down, Little Man."

"Where's my mama? Did something bad happen to her?"

"Hold on, buddy. Let me get out." The boy hopped down, his face a mask of fear. Cole stepped out of his truck, and Sloan followed from the passenger side, coming around the truck's back end to stand near Cole. "Let me introduce some-one to you. This is Sloan Gabriel."

The boy barely glanced at Sloan, frowned, and crossed his arms. "I want my mama."

Cole crouched in front of the boy in order to look him in the eye. "Your mom is doing all right, but she took sick. This lady found her and called 911, and we took her to the hospital."

The boy eyed Sloan with more interest. "Who is she?"

Cole stood. "A friend of your mom's." He took the boy's shoulder and nudged him closer to Sloan. "Where are your manners? Is that how you meet somebody?"

The boy looked pouty but held out his hand. "Nice to meet you, Miss Sloan. I am Tobias Ridley . . . Toby."

"You have nice manners, Toby, and call me Sloan," she said, smiling and shaking his hand. How small it lay in hers. She felt a tug on her heart. "Your mama's all tucked into bed at the hospital and was feeling a whole lot better when we left."

Toby's upturned gaze never left Sloan's. His eyes were large, light brown flecked with green, and his russet-colored hair lay straight and sweat-matted to his forehead. His face held a smattering of freckles, his reed-thin arms were tanned, and both elbows looked freshly scraped. He wore a Titans football team shirt, but it was too small and rode up on his belly. His shorts had a torn side pocket, and he was barefoot.

At that moment the screen door reopened and a heavyset woman stepped out. "Hi, Cole. Didn't hear you drive up. Was back in the kitchen frying up supper."

Sloan thought it amazing that the woman's thick drawl could turn every word she spoke into multiple syllables.

"Hey, Gloria," Cole said as the woman came toward them. "We took Lindsey into the hospital this morning."

"Widow Jenkins come over and told me, so I knew if Lindsey was in the hospital and with you, she was in good hands."

Cole shook his head, looked exasperated. "Why weren't you here with her this morning? She was on IVs and shouldn't have been left alone."

"I had to take Toby to school 'cause he missed the school

bus. But just when I let him off, the nursing home texted saying two people didn't show up for their shifts, and they had an emergency, so . . . well, I just kept going. I'm real sorry, Cole. She was sound asleep, and I left her a note."

Sloan guessed that the note must have gotten lost in the chaos.

"Why didn't you call one of the neighbors or *me*? I was off duty. You could see my truck in the driveway." He gestured to a house a quarter of a mile away. "And I posted a list of our neighbors' phone numbers on the refrigerator. Lindsey *fell*, Gloria . . . if Sloan hadn't happened to stop by . . ." He shook his head.

Gloria blinked back tears. "I called at lunchtime, but her phone went to voice." Gloria's contrite blue eyes sidled over to Sloan. "I had to pick up Toby after school too. I'm real sorry, Cole. You know I love Lindsey and didn't mean her no harm. I cleaned up her room and started supper. I figured you'd be coming back 'cause of the car sitting there."

"My rental," Sloan said.

Cole knew Gloria had the best of intentions. He nodded, and gesturing, said, "Sloan Gabriel, meet Gloria Harrold."

Gloria focused on Sloan and took a step backward, and her expression shifted from remorse to astonishment. "Oh my word! Are you Sloan Gabriel the singer? You're here . . . standing in *our* yard? I recognize you! I do. From the contest. I watched every minute of that contest and voted for you every single time! And here you are standing in our front yard. Please . . . come on inside. I'll fix you some sweet tea. I—I can't tell you how wonderful it is to meet you to your face. You're so pretty." Gloria gushed, her accent thick, words coming fast and accented . . . *cain't* and *purty*.

51

For a moment Sloan thought the woman might throw her arms around her, and she took a step backward.

"My mama watched you on TV too, and when you sang, she cried." This from Toby.

Sloan's gaze swept from Cole, angry at Gloria, to Gloria awash in adoration, down to Toby, who kept staring at her. Surrounded by three people she hardly knew discussing the woman who might be her half sister lying in a hospital bed, Sloan felt dazed and outnumbered. She glanced over her shoulder at her car. "I—I have to go."

"No, no!" Gloria said, rushing at Sloan. "Stay for dinner. We got plenty. I'll tell all my friends you had supper here!"

Cole stuck out his arm, cutting Gloria off. "Let's not knock her down. Sloan will come back when Lindsey comes home, won't you?"

"Yes . . . sure. I will."

Keeping himself between Sloan and an excited Gloria, he gently took her elbow and walked her to the car. "Sorry. Didn't mean for you to get caught in the middle of that. Gloria's a good person, and Lindsey couldn't make it without her, but she should have never left Lindsey alone. So what if Toby's late to school?" Cole raked his hand through his hair, offered Sloan an apologetic smile. "Listen, I promise to keep you updated. Fair enough?"

He opened the car door for her, and she got in, but before she could start the engine, Toby shouted, "Hey, singing lady, Sloan."

Sloan froze, felt color drain from her face. It had been a while since she'd heard someone call her that. . . . Toby's innocent term *singing lady* had shaken her to her core. "Y-yes?"

"Thank you for helping my mama today."

"Yes, thank you," Cole echoed, eyes narrowing as her face turned pale and colorless.

With shaking fingers, Sloan thrust the key into the ignition and started the engine, and once she was on the rural road, she pushed her accelerator to the floor, speeding to the interstate and Nashville. And away from this town with all its memories.

~~~~~~

She talked to Terri, lied about spending a day in the spa and resting, told of plans to go places with her friends. In reality Sloan was as restless as a caged cat, waiting for Cole's call. She spent her days poolside, or shopping but buying little, and spent her evenings on Music Row, Nashville's famous area made up of restaurants and bars, almost all with stages or floor space for live performances by bands and singers. She thought about stopping in at Slade's Saloon, where she'd gotten her start as a soloist, but decided against it because she really didn't want to reconnect with her former life.

To blend in with large groups of tourists on nights out, she dressed simply in T-shirts and capris, wore a ball cap with her ponytail pulled through its back band, and kept makeup to a minimum, half-anxious she'd be recognized, half-disappointed when she wasn't. She moved from place to place, sat alone, nursed a drink, listened to the music, and made notes in her phone about songs she thought she might like to try out for her album. If a guy hit on her, she left the bar and merged with the foot traffic, returned to her room alone, willing her phone to ring. Four days later, Cole called.

"How's tomorrow look for you coming over?" he asked.

"She's home?"

"Yes, and I'm off shift tomorrow too. Not that either of you want me there when you meet, but I wanted to be around if I was needed."

"Is she well?"

"She's stronger." Cole paused. "But she'll never be well."

Sloan drove over the next morning, but this time when she rapped on the screen door, Lindsey opened it dressed in jeans and a T-shirt and wearing a soft terry cloth turban of bright pink. She wore makeup and a smile that crinkled laugh lines around her mouth and eyes. "Please come in! And tell me I look better than the last time you were here."

Lindsey's voice, soft and Southern, was as light as sunshine. Sloan couldn't stop staring at her, searching for some resemblance to herself. "A whole lot better than before."

"Toby's at school, and Gloria's at work, so it's just you and me. I have a tray of pastry and tea for us. We can sit on the sofa."

The room still seemed overstuffed with furniture, but all was tidy, tabletops cleared, décor pillows fluffed. The air smelled faintly of lemon oil and fresh linen, and the medicine smell was gone. Sloan followed Lindsey to the worn sofa, where they sat together in front of a coffee table that held a serving tray. Sloan twitched nervously, feeling conflicted about this woman, only seven years older than her and dying of cancer.

"Hope you don't mind tea instead of coffee. I love coffee, but the medicines I take make the smell of it unpleasant for me."

"Tea's fine."

She watched Lindsey pour steaming liquid from a teapot into matching finely painted flower-splashed porcelain cups.

"This was my grandmother's on Mother's side. We used to have tea parties with it when I was a child."

Sloan was out of small talk. "Tell me—" She stopped, swallowed down her jitters, took the cup and balanced it on one knee. "Please tell me why you think we're related. I—I've never met anyone from my family. Are you my sister or not?"

nine

⸺

Lindsey's gaze roamed Sloan's face. "I see Daddy in your eyes and your chin, in the cleft." She traced her finger down her own chin with a similar cleft but not as deep. "His was shaped just the same." Goose bumps skittered up Sloan's arms. Lindsey bent down, retrieved a large scrapbook from the floor beneath the coffee table, and held it out to Sloan. "Look at this, and I'll let you decide."

Sloan replaced the teacup and saucer on her lap with the heavy oversized book, and flipped open the cover. Fancy cursive letters said *The Rock N Roll Legend of Gerald (Jerry) Sloan and the Pace Setters*. Lindsey said, "You come by your voice honest, you know. Daddy had his own band. He played guitar and he was lead singer. He loved the music of the eighties. In the nineties they played Southern rock."

Sloan turned the pages, saw a faded photo of four guys, one at a piano, a drummer sitting with his drum set, another holding a slide guitar, and in the center, standing in front of a microphone and posing with a guitar, a grinning Jerry. He looked tall and rangy and had blond hair to his shoulders. The image was blurry, but she stared hard at his face, judging, measuring, evaluating.

"Here's a close-up," Lindsey said gently, and turned a page to an eight-by-ten full-on head shot in glossy black and white, a professional publicity photo. Jerry had had high cheek bones, a smooth forehead, blond hair, and a cocky grin. Sloan saw his cleft chin clearly.

"Daddy was very handsome, don't you think?" Lindsey said, smoothing her palm across the photo's surface. "He was twenty-three when this was taken. He was just starting to get a buzz from the music world." Lindsey turned a few more pages to show off playbills, flyers with performance dates, and reviews from newspapers and regional music magazines. "Everything was print in those days. None of these magazines exist anymore, but getting your name in them at the time was important. His band cut two albums in Muscle Shoals, Alabama. Sold quite a few and was getting radio air time too. I have the albums in a file drawer if you want to take them and listen."

"I will." The old vinyl albums would require a phonograph, and Sloan didn't have one, but certainly Kiley could find one for her. Sloan flipped through more pages thick with informal pictures of the band playing inside bars with sawdust floors, or playing in grassy fields, surrounded by clusters of adoring fans, mostly teenage girls. There were fuzzy, muddy-looking photos of hotel room interiors, tabletops littered with bottles of beer and liquor, and photos of pretty half-dressed girls smoking and laughing, lying across the beds with the guys. Sloan honed in on Jerry in each photo, always with a different girl.

"Mom took most of those pictures. She and some of her

friends followed the band and partied after the shows. That's how they met. She was a 'groupie.'" Saying the word made Lindsey smile.

Sloan thought about her days with Jarred's band, the days from high school and also her second time with the group and the tragic and disturbing way it had ended. *No going back.* "The band looks pretty successful. What happened?"

"People's tastes in music changed. Grunge bands and punk rock came along, with Kurt Cobain and Nirvana, and the heyday of Dad's music world went away. Venues dried up. Broke his heart because making music was all he knew and all he wanted." Lindsey flicked her hand. "History now."

Sloan understood. Her own hunger to sing had been all-consuming when she was growing up. Musicians, music genres, bands, and singers came and went like a flavor of the month at an ice cream store. Adaptability was the key to success. Talent was necessary, but so was luck, being in the right place at the right time.

Lindsey pointed to a photo of Jerry with his arm around a petite dark-haired woman. "This is Karen, my mother." In the scrapbook's next pages, the images changed from ones of the band to ones of Karen and Jerry, first in wedding garb, then of Karen pregnant, then of her holding a baby, followed by pages of Lindsey morphing from a newborn into a curly-haired girl in flowery dresses and shorts sets. There were photos of holidays and birthdays, of new toys, a pink bedroom draped with gossamer layers of tulle and lace and pictures of fairies and mermaids. And there were photographs of Jerry kissing Lindsey's chubby cheek and cuddling her on his lap. Sloan's insides twisted. No Daddy Dearest in *her* memory banks.

The final photo was a school picture of Lindsey. "First grade," she said. "It was the last one Mama put in the book, because that's when everything changed." Lindsey took a long sip from her teacup and leaned back into the sofa cushions, her gaze fixed on the ceiling. "That was the year I turned six. The year Daddy left us."

Sloan mentally reviewed the happy photos she'd seen of Jerry with his wife and child. Had the smiles been only for the sake of the camera, moments frozen in time but faked? And yet Lindsey had looked so happy and content nestled in her daddy's arms. Lindsey went silent. Sloan waited for her to continue, grew squirmy, picked at a hangnail on her thumb. A dog's bark came from far away, and an overhead fan squeaked on its looping journey.

"I knew my mother was a hypochondriac. Well, to be fair, she did suffer from migraine headaches, but now that I understand what real suffering is, I can honestly say Mama exaggerated every little twinge with a moan, a groan, an 'oh, baby, your mama's so sick.'" Lindsey quickly looked at Sloan. "I don't mean to speak ill of her. She was a good mom in lots of ways. She loved me. Took care of me . . . but I can hardly recall times when she was healthy and happy."

"My mother drank." Sloan hadn't meant for the words to slip out, but they had, short and to the point.

"*Daddy* drank." Lindsey shifted on the cushion to again look Sloan in the eye. "But his real drug of choice was other women. It took me years to see the ways my parents hurt one another. But when I was six, the only thing I knew was that my daddy moved away and left me and Mama. I cried buckets, prayed every night for God to bring my daddy home. I thought I'd done something wrong to make him leave. Or that I'd said something that had made him not love me anymore. None of that was true, but when you're a child . . ." She shrugged. "Then about a year later, Daddy came home."

"Maybe I should have tried praying," Sloan said, half under her breath, thinking of LaDonna and her own childhood.

"He returned because Mama tried to kill herself. OD'd on sleeping pills one day while I was in school. I found her on her bed, ran to a neighbor's, and she called nine-one-one. The doctors saved Mama's life, but she was committed to a psych ward. That neighbor lady took me in. I overheard her tell her husband, 'Poor little Lindsey. No one to take care of her. She'll have to go into foster care.'"

Sloan swallowed the bad taste in her mouth, recalling the times when she had thought she'd be taken away by social services. Maybe she'd have been better off than she'd been with LaDonna. "Did you have to go?"

Lindsey shook her head. Her turban slipped, and she righted it. "No . . . Daddy came back to take care of me, and when Mama got out of the hospital, along with an infinite Valium prescription, we moved into a new house on the far side of Memphis. I went to school, made friends, graduated high school, and refereed my parents' war games with each other."

Sloan stretched out a cramped leg, rubbed her calf. "I don't see what this has to do with me, Lindsey."

"Sometimes it takes years for a story to come together. This story did when I filed for divorce and moved in with Mom and Daddy. Toby was only three, and I was already fifteen months into cancer treatment. I remember it was in October, a pretty fall night. Toby was tucked in, Mama had gone to bed, and me and Daddy were sitting on the back deck under a harvest moon. Light so bright a person could read under it."

Sloan remembered those kinds of autumn nights. In LA the city lights overtook the moonlight, canceling it out. "Go on."

"Daddy had had a couple of beers, and we'd started talking about all that had gone wrong in both our lives, when suddenly he looked up at the moon and said, 'You have a sister, Lindsey. I haven't seen her since she was a few months old, but her first name is Sloan . . . named after me.'"

Sloan felt as if all the air had been sucked from the room when she heard the words. "Go on."

"He told me that's why he'd left me and Mom. A woman he'd met during his band days, hooked up with him again and was having his baby, and he'd planned to divorce Mama and take me to live with him and her and my baby sister as soon as his and Mother's divorce was final. He said you were the prettiest little thing he'd seen since I was born." She chuckled. "Daddy had a way with words. He told me Mama knew all about the other woman. No surprise. She'd watched him cheat on her for years. But he'd never gotten another woman pregnant. And he and Mama had been unhappy together for years. He told me he saw this new baby as a way to start over."

Sloan again tasted LaDonna's venom. "Every day of her life, my mother hated my father for leaving her. I hated him too."

"Fine line between love and hate, Sloan. Anyway, when Mama heard that you'd been born, and that he wasn't coming back, that's when she took the pills and almost died. It was a risky thing to do, but she wasn't going to let go of him, and he wouldn't let go of me. At least that's the way he explained it to me that October night."

"But now he's dead." Sloan could never meet him, hear his voice, or ask why he'd never contacted her, sent her a birthday card, or come to see her.

"Daddy and Mama died together in a car wreck. Mama was driving the two of them on a back road and hit a tree.

Wrapped the car clean around it. Police said it was the oddest thing, no ice on the road, no skid marks like she'd tried to hit the brakes. Only tree roadside for twenty miles, and she managed to hit it."

Staring into Lindsey's haunted eyes turned Sloan icy. Lindsey's implication all but shouted: *She meant to hit it.*

Sloan blinked, gathered herself, saw that even through her makeup Lindsey was looking pale and drawn, and that she could hardly keep her eyes open. Sloan had a hundred questions, but she realized that Lindsey was spent. "You should lie down."

"I should." Lindsey squinted at a wall clock. "I can tell you the rest of the story later, because there's more."

Sloan helped Lindsey stand, steadied her when she swayed, and walked her to her bedroom, now neat and orderly and scented with lavender air freshener. No IV pole either, just bottles of pills lining the top of a dresser across from a bed with a floral-patterned coverlet. Sloan eased Lindsey into the bed. The pink head covering slid off, exposing Lindsey's smooth scalp. The sight was unsettling. Sloan placed the turban on a bedside table. "Get some rest."

Lindsey's eyes closed. "Thank you . . . my sister. You can go on if you want. You don't have to worry. I'll be just fine after my nap."

Sloan wanted to run as far and as fast as she could. A tiny smile played on Lindsey's mouth, and she added, "Cole's home today. Go see him. . . . I know for a fact he's taken a real shine to you, Sloan Gabriel."

ten

Cole stood on the upper back deck of his house, methodically cleaning the wood with a pressurized stream of water from the wand of a pressure washer. He glanced up to see Sloan walking toward his house from across the field that separated his and Lindsey's homes. Alarmed, he shut off the machine, but her leisurely pace assured him that Lindsey wasn't in trouble. Lindsey had told him that Sloan was meeting with her that morning, but seeing her walking in his direction was an unexpected pleasure. Sunlight struck her hair, making it shimmer like spun gold. *Beautiful.*

He called to her, "Hey . . . Come on up, but watch the puddles."

Sloan stopped shy of a muddy mess at the bottom step, shielded her eyes from the sun's glare to peer up at him. He was soaking wet, barefoot, stripped to the waist, wearing cutoff jeans riding his hips. Broad shoulders, well-muscled arms, and flat well-defined abs. On the back of his left shoulder she saw ink, the black outline of a great white shark with a glowing red eye. Long time since she'd seen a half-naked man so perfectly chiseled. She said, "Everything's fine with Lindsey. She needed a rest, so I thought I'd pop over."

He bounded to the bottom step and offered his hand. She grabbed hold and took a giant step to avoid the mud and join him on the small strip of clean wood. She teetered, caught the railing, as his arm shot around her waist to steady her. Molded against him, his skin felt cool. Their blue eyes met, hers as clear and bright as a summer sky, his the deep blue of sapphires. He wore the scent of fresh water and clean skin, she, the allure of a flower that tantalized but that he couldn't name. Sloan was the first to break the spell. "Are we going up, or just balancing on the edge the rest of the day?"

He caught the double meaning in her question, turned, and, still holding her hand, took her to the top of the partially washed deck. Over his shoulder, still rocked by the physical contact, he asked, "You hungry? I was about to break for lunch."

He'd stirred a primal hunger in her she hadn't wanted to experience, so at the moment, food seemed like a good substitute. "Sure. I ate a light breakfast." Her racing heart slowed, and she followed him inside.

"Make yourself at home while I grab some dry clothes. Back in a jiff."

She eyed his space. Sunlight poured through a bay window and onto a contemporary-style table that offered a commanding view of the deck and a backyard that stretched to a tree line. On the other side of the kitchen, a half wall divided the space from a great room. The kitchen, painted a rich creamy vanilla, with bisque-colored stone countertops, held a stainless steel industrial-looking stove with red knobs centered on a wall lined with simple cherry wood cabinetry. "Nice place," she said when he returned wearing jeans, a body-hugging black tee, and flip-flops.

"Thanks. I've slowly been remodeling the place since my grandfather died. Sit, and let me see what I've got to feed us." He gestured to the table. She settled into a padded chair and watched him rummage through the refrigerator. "I've got leftover chicken cordon bleu, pasta primavera fixin's, old-fashioned meat loaf. . . . I can make a salad to go with anything, if you'd like."

The selection was mouthwatering. "Whatever happened to sandwiches?"

Still leaning over and moving cartons, he chuckled. "I eat enough of that kind of food on the job. When I'm home, I cook."

"I'm impressed."

"It's just a hobby. EMTs are stationed at the firehouse—twenty-four hours on duty, forty-eight off. Three of us are paramedics, but everyone in the firehouse takes a turn cooking and feeding the crew. At home I cook because cooking is a stress release after a long day. So, what sounds good to you?"

"Surprise me."

She watched him work, chopping and dicing with quick, even strokes with a large knife, and in minutes, water boiled, spaghetti was cooked and drained, and the aromas of olive oil, garlic, basil, and fresh tomatoes filled the air. "You teach yourself to cook?"

"Yes. It was a matter of self-preservation," he said with a laugh. "I grew up with three older sisters, and Mom and Dad worked. The girls didn't cook, so I decided to learn, and they got stuck with cleanup. How about you? You like to cook?"

"I was raised on fast food and pizza delivery. My mother wasn't much in the kitchen." *Or anywhere else.*

He set a plate of primavera in front of her and took the chair nearest hers, so that they were sitting almost elbow to elbow. She wondered why he hadn't sat across from her instead of crowding in. His closeness made her skin tingle, every cell on alert.

She spun the spaghetti on her fork, savored each mouthful. "Very yummy."

He dipped his head to acknowledge her appreciation. Having her here in his space only a finger touch away was heady. He'd thought about her for days, not only because she was beautiful and talented, but because of Lindsey and their possible familial connection. Sloan's appearance had sparked an unmistakable glow in Lindsey.

After they finished eating, Cole said, "Come sit in the other room with me."

"I can do cleanup."

"You're a guest today, but next time I'll put you to work." The idea of a "next time" made her pulse tick up, but she shied from the thought. Her life was in LA.

She followed him around the half wall into a space with a cushy sofa and comfy chairs. An enormous television over a fireplace mantel took up the wall facing the seating arrangement. "You think the TV's big enough?"

"I confess to being a sports nut. Nothing like NFL in king-size." She chose one of the chairs and he took the sofa. A square coffee table offered further separation. "How was your talk with Lindsey?"

Her mellow feeling from the meal fled. "She showed me a ton of pictures, told me stories, some pretty sad."

"Jerry's scrapbook. . . . I've seen it. I know some of the stories, but none about you being her sister."

"That's a problem for me."

"You don't believe her?"

"I think *she* believes I am." Sloan understood how protective Cole was of Lindsey, so she chose her words carefully as she repeated Jerry's tale to his daughter from one October night. "It's troubling. . . . He vanishes for a year, and when he comes back, he resumes his family life but never mentions another child, a sister, maybe *me*, until years later. Why?"

"She was just a kid. Her mother was in a psych ward. I wouldn't have told her the truth either."

"I have Jerry's name as my first name, and I'm a singer, but where's the proof? She told me in a letter that she could prove her claim."

"Did she prove it?"

"She was wiped out by then, so I tucked her in for a rest and left. But I plan to ask her."

"How about your mother? Can she confirm the story?"

Sloan startled, then realized he hadn't grown up in Windemere, so he might not have heard local gossip about LaDonna and her. "My mother only spoke about my father in expletives. One Christmas, when I was five, I asked if Daddy would come for a visit, and she slapped me so hard across the mouth, I bit my lip and bled. I didn't ask again. If my father *was* Jerry, he left me with *her*. And unlike with Lindsey, he never came back for me. Never once contacted me. I don't know where my mother, LaDonna, is these days, and I don't care, so if I never see her again, that's just fine with me."

To Cole, who'd grown up in a great loving family, her revelation was heartbreaking. Hard to imagine a mother being so cruel. He wanted to take Sloan's hands in his, but the table took up the space between them, and he guessed that Sloan was not a person who wanted anyone's sympathy, so he veered by asking, "Do you want it to be true? Lindsey's story about you being her half sister?"

Sloan weighed her answer, finally said, "Growing up, there were times when I wished with all my heart for a daddy to come and pick me up for the weekend like girls at school who had divorced parents. I heard them whine and complain about having to live in two places. And about how they hated their dad's new 'girlfriend' or their stepmothers, and sharing spaces with 'sisters' and 'brothers' they loathed. I'd have traded places with them in a snap." Her expression turned defiant. "Instead I learned to play guitar and sing. I always believed my voice was my get-out-of-jail-free card. And now, nothing's more important to me than making it in the music world. Nothing."

The fervor in her voice lit a fire in her eyes. Her hunger for success was palpable.

"And thousands of people felt the same way when they voted for you on *American Singer*."

She became self-conscious, realizing she'd told this man, a near stranger, way more about herself than she ever wanted to say. Not only in words, but in attitude and nuance. "I won't be sidetracked in my career, but I've been lied to all my life about my father. I *do* want to know the truth, Cole."

"I'm sure Lindsey will tell you more when she's able. Chemo takes a lot out of her." Cole sat up straighter, cocked his ear. "I hear the school bus. Toby's coming home."

Sloan strained to locate the sound, but heard only the white noise of the air-conditioning system.

Cole stood, held out his hand. "Let's walk to Lindsey's together. I haven't seen Little Man for a few days, and I'd like to toss the baseball with him." She hesitated. He didn't withdraw his hand. His palm looked strong and steady, never wavering. She stood, took his hand, calloused and rough, and let him walk her to the front door, where he paused. "For the record, Lindsey had a daddy who loved her but a husband who abused her."

"While she had *cancer?*"

"Even then. When I asked her why she stayed, she told me, 'Bo kept saying he was sorry, and I believed him. Besides, I'd watched Daddy stick it out, and figured I should too.' And so she stayed with Bo Ridley, who kept slapping her around. Then one day he started hitting Toby. That's when she took their son and left."

"She said she divorced him. Doesn't that mean she's rid of him?"

"He's Toby's father. He still has rights under the law."

His comment was sobering, and Sloan saw a bigger piece of the picture. Cole had become a self-appointed guardian, a watchman over the makeshift family next door. Sloan had grown up with a revolving door of men who had come and gone through hers and LaDonna's lives. No watchdog to protect little Sloan. She gave an involuntary shiver.

"You cold?"

"I'll warm up on the walk over." And once outside in the dazzling sunlight, she did.

eleven

—

Lindsey and Toby were huddled together on the couch look-ing at a book when Sloan and Cole came inside the house. Seeing Cole, Toby broke into a gap-toothed grin and shot off the cushion.

"Hey, Little Man. How's the book?"

Toby half turned. "Boring. No monsters. No aliens. Bor-ring."

Lindsey laughed. "He's reading real good. I'm so proud of him."

Cole cupped Toby's chin. "You learn to read that one, and we'll go buy you a book you want."

"Any book?"

"That your mama approves."

His enthusiasm waned, so he glanced shyly at Sloan. "Hello, Sloan."

The image of Lindsey and Toby together side by side, cozy and loving, had unexpectedly wrenched Sloan's heart, made her think of another time, another child. She cleared emotion from her throat, said, "Hello to you too."

Cole asked, "Still have that glove and baseball I gave you?"

"Yeah!" Toby darted around the sofa and down the hall before Cole could say another word.

Lindsey and Cole burst out laughing. "You don't mind me stealing him for a little while?" Cole asked, because he knew how precious the boy's time was to his mother.

"Course not. He needs to have fun."

Once Toby and Cole exited to the yard, Sloan felt awkward. Perhaps sensing it, Lindsey patted the sofa cushion. "I know I flaked out on you earlier, and after seeing the scrapbook and hearing about our daddy, you must have questions."

Sloan edged onto the sofa, unsure of where to begin. Certainly not with *Where's your proof?*

"Would you like to see the scrapbook again?"

"That's all right. I—um—I was just wondering how you ended up in Windemere from Memphis."

"That's an odd story too. Mine and Bo's marriage hadn't been good for some time." Lindsey dropped her gaze. "After my diagnosis, things got worse. I couldn't be the wife Bo wanted. I also think when Bo married me, knowing Daddy had been a recognized musician, he thought that I'd have money." She shook her head, forced a sad smile. "I stuck it out for a time, but when Bo started picking on Toby, I left and moved in with my parents. Daddy drove me to and from my chemo treatments, three times a week at first. Toby was barely three, and my treatments could take a while, so Daddy stayed with him in a playroom at the hospital. One night driving home, with Toby asleep in his car seat, Daddy says to me, 'You know, princess, if you decide to get out of this big city and away from Bo, check out Windemere, not too far from Nashville.' I told him I'd never heard of the place, but he said it was a real nice little town, small and friendly, and that it would be a good place to raise Toby."

Sloan's pulse quickened. "Why would he pick Windemere?"

"At that time, I had no idea. But he said it to me more than once. Between chemo and being sick, taking care of Toby and leaving Bo, I was a mess. But after the accident, after his and Mom's funerals—" Her voice caught. Sloan waited patiently. "They left me all their worldly goods, including their house, which I sold. Bo was starting to become a problem too. I had to get a restraining order to keep him away and—well, I remembered what Daddy said about Windemere. I came and bought this house. Got lucky, getting Cole for a neighbor."

"And Gloria?"

"A dear friend who didn't want me moving here by myself. She may be a little rough around the edges, but her heart is pure gold. She takes good care of me and Toby too. Plus . . ." Lindsey paused, toyed with a tissue she held. Sounds from outside, the crack of a bat and Cole yelling, "Run, Toby! Home run!" floated through the screen door. A ceiling fan moved stuffy air above the sofa.

Lindsey said, "Plus I want to give you something, Sloan, because I believe it belongs to you. When I cleaned out the old house before selling it, I found this envelope. It looked like it had been opened many times." Lindsey reached into the pocket of the housedress she wore, withdrew a folded paper envelope worn thin, and yellowed with time, and handed it to Sloan. "Daddy had it hid in a shoebox. As you can see, he wrote the word *Windemere* on it."

Sloan saw the scrawl of the town's name in faded ink. She lifted the flap, pulled out a very blond curl of baby hair tied with a silky pink ribbon. "You—you think this is *my* hair?"

Lindsey closed Sloan's hand around the curl. "It's not mine. I had dark hair like my mother. . . . A piece of it is in my baby book."

Tears filmed Sloan's eyes. LaDonna had never saved anything from her infancy that Sloan knew of.

Lindsey raised her fingers as if to touch her head covering, today a bright cotton scarf of red, yellow, green, and white, but she paused, then lowered her hand. "Sometimes I forget I have no hair." A rueful smile crossed her face. "Wigs are hot."

Sloan opened her hand and stared at the soft tuft of fine baby hair. In her palm the hair lay weightless, the ribbon limp from its long bondage in the envelope.

"Oh, Sloan, when I saw you on that TV show, when I heard you sing, when people started buzzing about Sloan, one of Windemere's own, being a contestant . . . I knew. I just *knew* you were the baby Daddy left behind. I see him in your face. I hear him in your voice. Jerry Sloan is our father."

Sloan felt as if the room were shrinking, the air suffocating. The emotional side of her brain wanted to believe, but her skeptical side pushed back. Everything Lindsey had told her was speculation and circumstantial. There were no photos, no notes between LaDonna and Jerry, no letter to a long-lost baby girl. . . . *Nothing to see here.* With trembling fingers, she tucked the envelope into her nearby purse.

The screen door clattered open, and Gloria hurried inside. "Oh, thank goodness you're still here, Sloan. I rushed home and"—she panted—"and I'm so glad I did."

Sloan was startled, but also grateful for the interruption. Gloria was breathing hard, her face red from exertion.

Lindsey looked alarmed. "Gloria! Sit down, girl, before you have a heart attack! Sloan's not going anywhere yet."

Gloria flopped into a recliner that had seen better days, and fanned herself with her hand. She plunked her purse and a shopping bag on the floor. "Oh . . . I was afraid I'd miss you." Her bright eyes glowed. "The women I work with didn't believe me when I said you were here in town, and that you knew Lindsey and that I'd met you."

Sloan gave Lindsey a sidelong look.

"I've told Gloria that our friendship goes way back."

Sloan appreciated the little white lie. She didn't want rumors all over town about her being Jerry's "love child." She'd endured enough gossip growing up just being LaDonna's daughter.

"Well, I'm just gonna prove to those crows at work that you are real and I wasn't lyin'." Gloria reached down into the shopping bag. "They're gonna be so jealous when I bring in autographed CDs."

She held out two jewel cases, and Sloan saw her own face smiling out from the covers, along with the song titles. The sight jolted because Sloan had left LA before seeing the finished product. She took the cases from Gloria. "Where'd you find these?"

"At Target." Her self-satisfied smile stretched from ear to ear.

"Let me see." Lindsey eased the cases from Sloan's hands, beamed a knowing smile.

"Can you sign inside on your picture?" Gloria asked. She hefted up her purse, fumbled for a pen. "Make sure you say *To Gloria Harrold.* . . . I want to wave it under their snooty noses! That'll teach them to call me a liar."

Lindsey returned the cases, and Sloan opened them. She dutifully wrote per Gloria's wishes, signing her name with a flourish. She was capping the pen when Toby and Cole burst through the old screen door.

"Look, look what I got!" Gloria waved the CDs. "Sloan's music."

Cole took the CD and squatted so that Toby could see also. The two of them smelled like Tennessee red clay dirt, sweat, and the leather of a baseball glove. "That's *you!*" Toby looked astounded.

Cole's gaze found Sloan's, and he winked. "That's her, all right."

Onstage performing, Sloan relished attention, but now in this small setting, she felt unnerved, and the sexy twinkle in Cole's eyes wasn't helping her to settle. The walls seemed to be closing in on her. Sloan stood abruptly. "I should go. I owe my agent a phone call."

"But I was gonna call for pizza!" Disappointment spilled from Gloria's voice. "Pizza Palace has the best in town."

"Please stay," Lindsey said from the couch.

Cole rose, said, "Tell you what. I'll be on duty for the next twenty-four hours, but I'll have a cookout for all of us at my place day after tomorrow. How's that sound?"

"Thanks, but I return to LA day after tomorrow."

Everyone looked disappointed. "Will you come visit again?" Lindsey asked.

Against her better judgment, Sloan said, "Sure."

Cole gestured toward the door. "I'll walk you to your car."

The afternoon sun was low when they went outside, and Sloan felt that the spring air had turned cooler. She crossed her arms against the chill. Cole opened the driver's door, leaned down when she'd settled behind the wheel. "Sooner or later you're going to have to break bread with this crowd. May as well be over my grill. Next visit, okay?"

Sloan steeled herself against his dimpled smile. "There's still no solid proof, Cole, no hard evidence. I . . . I just don't want to get her hopes up if it isn't true."

As he watched her drive away, he said, "Too late for that."

In her hotel room, Sloan took a shower, slipped into the suite's oversized terry cloth robe, and ordered dinner from a room service menu. Her head was spinning with all Lindsey had told her, and all she wanted tonight was to watch a movie on TV and sleep until noon the next day. She had just fluffed king-sized pillows against the bed's generous headboard, when there was a knock on her door. She wondered how room service could have come so quickly. She crossed to the door and opened it, but no waiter greeted her. Instead she looked into the cool gray eyes of Terri Levine.

"May I come in?"

Shocked to see her agent, Sloan stepped aside. "What are you doing here? I—I mean . . . is everything okay?"

Terri stepped into the room, and the door automatically closed behind her. "You tell me, Sloan. What's really going on with you? I want the truth."

twelve

Terri commandeered the suite's brightly patterned love seat, and Sloan eased onto a matching club chair, her heart thumping. Terri had arrived from LA without even a mention to Sloan in a text or voice mail. Sloan was unsure how to interpret the sudden visit. Had Terri come to deliver bad news? "What makes you think something's going on?"

Terri drilled her with a cool-eyed stare. "I have other business in Nashville. You're not my only client, you know."

"I—I told you I needed a break. I'll be home in two days."

"I'm well aware of your schedule. And that you haven't checked in once since you've been gone. Seems odd. Your EP's in stores, and most clients get all excited about that. They usually call to tell me how excited they are."

"I am excited. I saw it in a Target store." It was a half-truth but all she had to offer. She'd been so absorbed in her trip to Windemere and the people there, she'd missed the jump start of the EP, the progress of iTunes downloads, the publicity schedule Terri had arranged. "Sorry."

"Think back to that day in my office when you signed your contracts, and how I told you once your music dropped, we'd have to hit the ground running. Established artists and new artists . . . all scrambling to be heard. And bought by fans. You're up against some big releases by big-name artists, Sloan, and we want to get you seen and heard. Loyal, die-hard fans are your bread and butter. We don't want to give them any time to forget how much they loved you on the TV show. Kiley's been hitting on social media on your behalf. But we need your undivided attention and efforts."

"What can I do to make it up to you?"

Terri steepled her fingers, heaved a sigh, gentled her stern expression. "You can start by telling me why you really came back here on the verge of jump-starting your career. Not to relax, I'm thinking. To reconnect with an old boyfriend? The guy you wrote and sang about in 'Somebody's Baby'? Is he still hanging around and poisoning the well of your attention span?'"

"No, no . . . nothing like that." Sloan closed her eyes, gathering herself while considering the best place to start. She was granted a brief reprieve when room service rapped on her door. It had been a long time since her pasta lunch with Cole, and she was hungry. Or she had been before Terri had appeared. The waiter pushed in a rolling cart draped with white linen. She signed for the meal and he left.

"Please, eat. I've got all night," Terri said. "My room's just down the hall."

Sloan had ordered chicken fingers and fries, but the food went untouched as she weighed the best way to explain things to Terri. "I came to Nashville in order to return to Windemere, about fifty miles away. It's where I grew up."

"I've always known about Windemere, Sloan."

"You have?" A revelation she hadn't expected.

"Background checks are run on all contestants once they make the cut. We have to be careful. One year a guy made it through auditions with an outstanding drug warrant against him. Another had posted some pretty nasty photos on the Internet. So it's policy to do routine checks." Terri massaged her temples with her fingertips.

Sloan went very still. "What did you learn about me?"

"I learned you were raised in Windemere by a single mother, graduated high school under the name Sloan Quentin, and that you never had so much as a parking ticket. We only look for bad stuff, Sloan, criminal actions, inappropriate photos and rants on social media. As I've told you, digital input lives forever. Relax, you passed."

"I changed my name." Sloan's heart was thudding hard, banging inside her chest. She was grateful some things from her past were still guarded.

"Lots of artists do that. Nothing wrong with the name you chose either. It worked for Peter Gabriel." Sloan knitted her forehead, and Terri sighed. "Before your time, but he was big in the eighties. My point is, you won one of the biggest career-launching contests in the country, but for reasons I can't fathom, you wanted to return to Tennessee before your EP launched. You could have relaxed in Los Angeles. Plenty to see and do there. So tell me, what's really going on?"

Sloan nibbled on a limp french fry, wondered if the background check had turned up LaDonna's history of drunk and disorderly arrests. She tossed the half-eaten fry onto the plate. "My single mother never told me who my father was. LaDonna gave me her maiden name when I was born, and I grew up without any family. After my win, I was contacted by a woman in Windemere who claims we're half sisters." Terri rolled her eyes but held her tongue. "I came because"—Sloan stared into her hands, open in supplication on her lap—"because I wanted to know . . . *had* to know if it's true."

"Sloan, didn't I discuss this with you after you won? I told you about scammers—"

"Stop! Please, I'm not stupid. I know about fakers and liars, and dipshits. I've met plenty of them." She felt the sting of hot tears, blinked them away. "Just hear me out." She didn't mention how Lindsey's letter had come to her, only that when Sloan hadn't been able to make phone contact, she'd decided to personally confront Lindsey to catch her in a possible lie. "What I discovered instead was a woman sick with cancer, convinced that we share the same father." Sloan repeated Lindsey's account, offered names and dates, and parallel time lines, pausing only to take tastes of chicken turned soggy. She gave every detail, every assumption and similarity that Lindsey had given to her.

Terri listened, her expression neutral. When Sloan wound down into silence, Terri said, "I remember Jerry Sloan. He was real. What do *you* think about Lindsey's story?"

"I don't know. I understand how she could have made the connections. Windemere's a small town, and Jerry told her to move here more than once."

"Has Lindsey asked you for anything . . . like money?"

Sloan shot out of the chair. "No!"

"Calm down. It's my job to protect you and the label." She also stood up. "You need some rest tonight. But here's the bottom line. I need you back in LA. I've got a lineup of radio station interviews, local TV shows, and two mall appearances booked. We need to promote you . . . keep you out front in the public's faces. And most of all, we need an album from you." Her tone was all business. "I don't want you hanging here another day. There's a noon flight tomorrow, and I've booked us seats. I understand about you wanting to know your roots, but you'll have to sort it out later." Terri walked to the door, where she paused, hand on the handle. "One more thing. If you want positive proof of Lindsey's claim, do genetic testing. A swab from the inside of both of your cheeks takes seconds. Results come in days. It's done in paternity suits all the time. It's the only way to know for sure."

Cole and his crew had been called in as emergency help for a seven-car pileup on the interstate about an hour after Sloan had driven off. Once the accident was cleared, Cole and his crew had their duty roster adjusted, and now they were crowded into a booth in a busy restaurant, downing nachos and beer. He raised his bottle. "Good work, people. Nobody died tonight."

The team clinked bottles with his. After ordering, he checked his phone messages. One from Lindsey saying good night, two from his family in Indy just to say hello, one from a store about the arrival of his special-order hiking boots . . . nothing from Sloan, but even though he hadn't expected a message he was still disappointed.

He liked being around her . . . *wanted* to be around her. He'd downloaded her CD, and through his earbuds had heard the power and complexity of her voice, had felt an intimacy that had sent ripples through him. She was the most interesting woman he'd ever met, not to mention one of the most beautiful and talented. He admitted he was starstruck, but it went deeper than that. She intrigued him. She'd set up walls and barricades around herself. He saw them in her eyes, her posture, the tone of her voice. *Stand back . . . don't come too close.*

While waiting for food, Cole absently glanced at other tables and booths. His gaze halted on a couple sitting near a window, holding hands and deep in conversation. *Well, well.* "I'll be right back," he told his team. He walked to the couple's table, stopped, blasted the couple an affable grin, and said, "Hey. It's Dawson, isn't it?"

Dawson looked up. His eyes widened with recognition. His body tensed, and his eyes turned guarded. "And my girl, Alana Kennedy."

"Cole Langston."

"Everyone calls me Lani." Her friendly smile lit up her large brown eyes.

"Cole's a paramedic. He took care of the man who fell that I told you about."

"My job," Cole assured the young woman, the look he'd seen cross Dawson's face when he'd first come over still stamped in his mind. As a paramedic Cole was well versed in the art of reading body language, and could discern a lie or an omission when he interviewed victims about their injuries, not necessarily by their words but by subtleties of facial expression and posture. *No, my husband didn't hit me,* or *I just had one drink,* or *I don't do drugs.* Their body language often told a different story, and right now all he saw was tenseness in Dawson's body and panic in his eyes. Cole instinctively knew that Dawson might not have mentioned to his pretty girlfriend about encountering Sloan that day in the ER. He pledged an unspoken "guy pact" to say nothing about Sloan.

"Lani's an RN at WGH," Dawson said.

Cole had no memory of her, but he typically left his patients at the ER and returned to manning his shift.

"I only fill in," Lani qualified. "I help when they're short-handed, mostly in the cancer center."

"Do you know Lindsey Ridley?"

"Lindsey! She's one of my favorites. How do you know her?"

"We're neighbors." Lani snapped her fingers and gave Cole an even brighter smile. "Of course, *Cole*! She talks about you, what a help you are, how you play baseball with her son, Toby. She sometimes brings him to her chemo sessions." Her features softened. "We have a playroom for kids who don't have sitters and have to come with a parent. We have toys and TV, but Toby sneaks out and sits beside Lindsey's chemo chair. It's against the rules for him to be in the room, but . . ." She shrugged, suggesting that she didn't always follow the rules. Cole liked Lani immediately, and nodded and grinned.

"Hey, Cole! Your food's up!" a voice shouted from across the room.

He said his goodbyes to Lani and Dawson and returned to the booth and his sizzling steak, with the image of Toby next to Lindsey in the treatment area stuck in his head. Gloria worked, and Lindsey wouldn't leave Toby alone at the house when he wasn't in school. What a way for a kid to grow up— beside his mother's chemo chair.

He was sliding a knife into his perfectly cooked steak, when a text message dinged his phone. It had come from Sloan and was brief and to the point.

Will ask Lindsey for DNA test. Only way to know the truth.
Returning to LA tomorrow noon.

thirteen

"He seems nice," Lani said after Cole had walked away.

"Yeah. He did a good job helping my worker." Dawson heaved a breath now that Cole was safely on the other side of the room. Cole could have said something about first meeting him with Sloan, but he hadn't. Maybe mental telepathy worked after all, because Dawson had sure been sending out messages. "You've never run into him at the hospital?"

"I'm mostly in the cancer center, and never in the ER."

"So you like this Lindsey?"

"Very much. I think I've worked with every patient who comes through the center, but few as courageous and likable as Lindsey Ridley."

"That's saying a lot." Dawson took a swallow of beer, wondering about the real reason Sloan might have shown up in Windemere . . . and be friendly with a paramedic too. He was hard-pressed to believe that she'd simply driven over for a visit. Sloan hated this town, had fled it twice. What could have possibly drawn her back? Especially now that she was on her way to the fame and fortune she'd always craved?

". . . listening to me?"

Lani's voice intruded into his wayward thoughts. The last person in the world he should have been thinking about was Sloan. He set his glass down, hung his head. "Sorry, love. I got distracted. Tell me again what you said."

Lani offered a bemused smile. "It wasn't important."

"But *you* are."

"Was it me talking about a patient from the cancer center?" He had lost his mother to ovarian cancer in his teens, so she made it a point to not talk about her work around him, and tonight she had. "I didn't mean to make you unhappy."

He shook his head. "No, you talking about your work doesn't bother me. Truth is, though, cancer still kills, doesn't it? No matter all the research, new drugs, gene therapies, and after all the effort, all the money and time spent on curing it, cancer still has its way with us."

A *formidable enemy.* "We're making progress against it every day." Lani brightened, shifted the subject. "Hey, here's an idea . . . let's go to the apartment and have a midnight swim in the heated pool."

He saw in her eyes the offer to stay the night with him, and quickly said, "Race you to the car." She laughed. He stood, tossed money onto the table for the waitress, and held Lani's hand on the walk to the door. He glanced toward the booth where Cole's crew sat eating and talking, and saw that Cole's spot was empty, food untouched. Dawson briefly wondered why a guy would leave a perfectly good steak to grow cold. He shrugged and followed Lani outside, erasing all thoughts of Cole and Sloan from his head.

85

She was running for her life through absolute darkness. Disembodied hands grabbed for her from behind . . . wraiths' hands with grasping fingers, sharp fingernails. Suddenly she felt hot foul-smelling breath on her face. Somehow the creature had circled around and was now in front of her. She skidded to a stop, pedaled backward, struggled to breathe, opened her mouth to scream. Not a sound came from her air-starved throat. She had no voice. The thing that wanted her was only inches from her body. . . . If it caught her, it would hurt her. . . . Bad. From a distance came the noise of someone singing. Her spine struck a sticky wall, pinning her in place. She struggled to break free, but couldn't. The singing grew louder. The voice! She knew the voice. . . .

A terrified Sloan bolted upright in bed, gasping for air. She saw that she was in her hotel room and that the singing voice was hers, the new ringtone she'd downloaded to her cell phone clattering on the bedside table. She pulled cobwebs of fear from her brain. *A dream.* She'd been trapped in an old and familiar dream from her childhood. *Not real. A dream.* She sucked in a lungful of cool air, snatched up her phone like it was a lifeline. "Hello."

"Sloan?"

"Cole?" She felt surprise, then rescued.

"I'm sorry if I woke you. Truly . . . I know it's late, but I have to see you."

She glanced at the digital clock radio on the table. Two a.m. "Now?"

"Please, Sloan. It's important."

Her heart seized. "Lindsey?"

"She's okay. I didn't mean to scare you. . . . Sorry."

Sloan dragged her hair away from her face. "Where are you?"

"In the lobby of your hotel."

This gave her pause. She hadn't remembered telling him the name of her hotel. But she had told Lindsey. She shook her head, again to chase away the last vestiges of her nightmare. "Where do you want to meet?" She didn't want to invite him to her room.

"In the pool area. No one's out here this late, so if you don't mind coming down, I'll meet you poolside."

"It'll take me a few minutes—"

"I'll wait."

She threw on jeans and a lightweight sweatshirt, took the elevator to the lobby, and went out to the fenced pool area, where the cool night air was scented by a blooming honeysuckle clematis. Cole was sitting in a deck chair, but when she stepped from a side door, he stood and walked to her quickly. "I appreciate you coming to meet me."

"It's all right. I'll sleep on the plane," she told him, knowing full well that she never did.

"I got your text sitting in a restaurant, and had to talk to you, especially since you're leaving tomorrow." He glanced at his watch. "Or rather today."

"I thought I'd have another day to visit Lindsey, but my agent wants me home doing promotional work."

After the work of clearing the interstate accident, failing to eat anything but nachos, and driving to Nashville to intercept Sloan, Cole was wiped out. But he'd felt it was necessary to see her face to face to fill her in on what was really happening with Lindsey. He gestured to the poolside chairs. "Can we sit?" He walked her to a lounger and dragged the chair he'd been using closer.

Underwater lights from the pool illuminated a serene watery surface, broken in spots by water bugs. Overhead a waxing moon looked as if a slice had been removed. She settled in the lounger. "You want to talk about the DNA testing, don't you?" The idea was perfectly logical, the procedure simple, so she prepared to defend it. "I'll cover any costs of genetic testing."

"Actually, I'm asking you not to do it at all."

Her guard went up. "Why not? A DNA test is fast and accurate. It will either link us or eliminate me."

Cole braced his forearms on his thighs, allowing his big hands to hang loose over his knees. "There are some things Lindsey hasn't told you, or maybe hasn't gotten around to telling you yet."

Sloan tensed.

"While she was hospitalized, the docs did more scans and tests. Bottom line: Treatments are no longer working. Her cancer has invaded her brain and will continue to spread quickly. She might have five months at best to live. She told me her goal is to at least make it to Toby's seventh birthday in late June. She's opting out of further chemo once this current round is finished, and will move into palliative treatment only. . . . That's end-stage pain management. Hospice will set up a home-visit care schedule."

His words exploded like bombs inside Sloan's head. The moonlight turned her hands ghostly white in her lap, and the wraiths of her earlier nightmare seemed to be creeping around the pool deck, raking her with evil red eyes. Her chest tightened. "We were together all day. She was so happy showing me the scrapbook. . . . She never said a word about . . . about . . ."

Cole leaned closer, trapped her eyes with his. "Except for

her son, you, Sloan, are the only bright spot in her life right now. I've not seen her happier than she's been these few days of believing you're her sister."

Lindsey, taking herself out of treatment. She was dying! Sloan couldn't get her head around it. "I—I can't believe it. I . . . I'm just getting to know her." Another thought struck Sloan. "How will she keep it from Toby?"

"She'll give him the best of herself for as long as possible. Gloria will finish raising him. That's been the plan all along. I should have let her tell you this, but I knew I had to say something to you before you asked her for that test."

An owl hooted from a treetop near the pool, sounding mournful. She pictured Toby, his eyes filled with grief. Despite the sweatshirt, she felt cold seeping from deep inside. She'd known these people for mere days, and yet her heart broke for them. "What do you want me to do?"

"Just wait. That's all I'm asking. After she's . . ." He cleared his throat. "Once Lindsey's gone, do your test. She'll leave plenty of DNA behind. Even Toby . . . especially Toby. A swab from him will also establish your identity and the authenticity of the claim."

She studied Cole, the planes of his face, his sincerity etched in the moonlight. "So you're asking me to pretend we're sisters when we're together even though it might not be true?"

He shrugged, offered a sad but hopeful smile. "You're *somebody's* baby. Why not Jerry Sloan's? What can it hurt for a dying woman to believe you, a famous singer, and she are related? Once she's gone, you can vanish too."

"Somebody's Baby" . . . She had written the song for another but now saw that the words held truth for her too. "I don't know how often I'll be able to visit her." Sloan's tour schedule spun in her head.

Cole pressed his thumbs into his tired eyes. "All that's necessary is to keep in touch with her. Text, call now and again. Any effort you make will mean the world to her with whatever time she has left. And her wish is that all of us don't stand around all gloom and doom. She wants laughter and happiness in her life. We can give her that. Can you help us do that whenever you're around?"

How could she deny such a simple request? "I can do that much."

He'd made his case and believed that Sloan would follow through. He stood and took hold of her hands, and she rose too. With the lounge chair snug against the backs of her legs, they were so close that she saw the stubble of beard growth on his chin, the square outline of his jaw, the dimple crease near his mouth.

Cole saw how moonbeams bathed her face with pale ethereal light, turning her skin milk-white, her eyes as clear as crystal. The image was indelible. "Moonlight becomes you, Sloan Gabriel."

It had been a long time since she'd wanted—truly wanted—a man to hold her. Tonight, right now, she wanted *this* man to take her in his arms and kiss her. His mouth was tantalizingly close. Perhaps his kiss could dull the ache inside her heart, and the sense of déjà vu that had come with it.

Cole told himself it would be easy to bend and touch her lips with his. It was what he wanted—to taste her. Then he thought of Lindsey, of how he'd come to help her, not to kiss Sloan. *Walk away. Danger zone.* He collected his good sense, took Sloan's hand, and walked her to the side door. With trembling fingers Sloan ran her key card down the lock. He pulled the heavy door open, and she stepped into the lighted lobby hallway. He said, "I won't forget this. Have a safe trip and keep in touch."

Sloan turned, rested her forehead against the cool glass, and watched him exit the pool's gate. What wouldn't he forget? Her promise to maintain a charade for Lindsey's sake? Or a moonlit kiss that could have been?

fourteen

"Ready to get to work?" Terri asked as she and Sloan walked through the glass doors of her high-rise office. The reception-ist beamed them both a smile, and Kiley burbled a cheery hello from her desk.

"Isn't that why we came straight here from the airport?" Sloan said.

The plane had landed at LAX, and they'd gone to baggage claim, gathered their luggage, and met their limo curbside. Once in the car, Terri had instructed the driver to drop Sloan's bags at her apartment building and shuttle them downtown through heavy traffic. During the long flight Sloan had told Terri everything Cole had reported about Lindsey, but she'd said that it had been her decision not to ask for a DNA test until after Lindsey's death. Terri had listened quietly and asked, "You're sure about this?"

"It seems like the right thing to do. For now what does it really matter if I'm her half sister or not?"

They'd been sitting in first class, so Terri's tray table had held a glass of chardonnay. She'd taken a sip. "Only a lawyer can answer that question. Want to talk to ours?"

"She's *dying*, Terri. I can't just ignore her."

"I'm not asking you to. I'm just reminding you that you've been paid a nice advance to cut an album, so a hundred percent of your attention is necessary now. We're building a career for you, and that means a lot of hard work."

"I'm *never* going to let anything get between me and what I want, and becoming a singer is something I've wanted all my life. I won't let you down." She'd held back from saying *a famous singer*, her ultimate goal.

Now inside her plush corner office, Terri tossed her purse onto a chair and said, "Come with me. I want to show you something."

Sloan followed her down a carpeted hallway, into a windowless room where long tables were set along three of the four walls, each stacked high with CD jewel cases. "Know what those are, Sloan?" Terri didn't wait for any guesses. "Those are songs from various music publishers, every one of which is looking for a singer. The right singer." She gestured toward two of the tables. "These stacks are hopefuls in the hunt to be plucked from obscurity, hooked up with the right voice, and turned into a smash hit, or at the very least, a song on an established singer's album. Perhaps even on a record by a rising artist.

"Somebody has to listen to every one of those songs. The reviewer's job is to match the song to a particular artist we represent. If one of the reviewers hears music with potential for one of my clients, the CD is shifted to that table and labeled." Terri pointed to the table with fewer well-ordered stacks. "When a new voice, like yours, comes along, it has to be tagged and categorized."

"What do you mean, 'tagged'?"

"It's a broad way of identifying a singer for sales and marketing. We say this artist is 'in the tradition of Reba, or Miranda, or Carrie,' and that helps classify a newcomer for the sales force. Currently you're still riding the wave of winning the contest, so we want to keep you in the forefront until your album is ready to go to market." Terri shrugged. "However, music listeners' memories fade, and if we can't keep someone 'out front,' a singer can have a short shelf life."

Terri's way of reminding Sloan that the music market was fickle. Too long a wait for new material and listeners moved on. After a long pause, Terri said, "Back to these CDs. . . . Since your category is country, those candidates are put into these stacks." Terri pointed. "The choices are further narrowed and sent to a particular artist or producer. The artist gives a listen to decide if a song is right, because artists want songs that work with their voice. Singers often pass over songs that other singers like and turn into hits. It's a collaboration, and also a crapshoot. The magic happens when the right artist finds the right song, the right producer, and the right sound mixer."

Terri picked up a canvas bag and handed it to Sloan. "These CDs have been chosen for you. Give them a listen. Check off the ones you like, and we'll take them into a studio and let you try them out vocally with a few musicians."

Sloan thought back to her band days, how they'd created CDs in small studios, with mikes and a sound mixer on a laptop computer. Music was still made that way, in small studios that catered to pay-their-way singers and bands, and downloaded to social media, where the songs might be heard and "liked." But she belonged to a big-name label, and the steps to success were carefully managed.

Terri glanced at her watch. "Look, how about we call it a day? Car service will pick you up at eleven tomorrow. For now Kiley has a car waiting for you down at the street."

Sloan quickly agreed. The bag in her hand felt heavy, not because of the weight of the CDs but because of the weight of the choices and decisions she would have to make about the songs on them. And because of the monetary advance she'd been given. Enough of her music had to sell in order to repay the advance, while the music built a fan base that would grant her future contracts and albums.

And the bag felt heavy because Lindsey, her possible half sister, was dying hundreds of miles away.

And because Sloan was scared.

Still, as she walked down the carpeted hall with Terri toward the reception area, she dug deep for bravado and belief in herself. "By the way, Terri," she said, shouldering the bag and her purse. "One day producers and agents will be tagging other's voices by saying, 'in the tradition of Sloan Gabriel.'"

Terri tossed back her head and laughed heartily. "That's the attitude I like hearing!"

⁓

Dawson and Lani were driving home from a friend's house when a song began to play on the truck's radio, the singer's voice unmistakable. Dawson reached to change the station, but Lani's hand stopped his. "No . . . don't. I want to hear it . . . all of it."

Lani knew about the song "Somebody's Baby" because colleagues at work were talking about it, but she hadn't yet listened to it. Now, with Dawson beside her, she figured it was time.

"We don't have to listen," Dawson said.

"Yes . . . I want to." Lani closed her eyes as the music touched sore and tender spots still inside Lani's heart, and as Sloan's voice brought every achingly beautiful word to life. On the surface, the verses told a story of love forever lost. Yet Lani heard another truth simmering beneath. Her eyes filled with tears, and she let them slide down her face unchecked.

When the final notes of the song faded, a DJ came on, spouting such phrases as "fast rising" and "most requested."

"She wrote a song about what happened to the three of us," Lani whispered.

"I get *why* she wrote the song, but why did she have to record it? That's the part I resent. Why would she put out a song that's so personal?" The song had sliced Dawson's heart like a razor when he'd first heard it, and now he was just plain angry about it.

Lani sensed his mood, put her hand on his shoulder. "It was how she coped. Just like me working all those long hours at Bellmeade. She had to get it out . . . her pain. She did it with music."

"But it hurts us too! Did she ever once think about you and me?"

Lani stroked his cheek. "Nobody knows it's us, love. To the rest of the world, it's simply a heart-touching song. Only we three understand its true meaning." Lani fumbled in the glove compartment, where Dawson was in the habit of stuffing extra napkins from fast-food drive-through windows. She blew her nose, dabbed her eyes, pushed away sad memories.

Dawson took Lani's hand, squeezed her fingers. "I still wish she hadn't recorded it."

Lani leaned into him, straining against the seat belt's resistance. "I want to make peace with the past, Daw. I want

to wake up every day without a terrible weight on my heart."
She had substituted *weight* for *guilt* because it was easier for
him to hear. For months she'd been climbing out of the mire
of tangled emotions, and she'd made great progress. She loved
Dawson, and he loved her. She was again working as a nurse.
Her sister and her parents were happy for her. Yet every now
and again, she'd get sucked into the vortex of what had happened on one particular and unforgettable autumn day. Hearing Sloan's poignant song had thrown her there this night.

Another song came on the radio, this one upbeat and
raucous. Dawson cranked up the volume, filling the cab with
music from woofers that made the dashboard tremble. He and
Lani joined the singer at the refrain, drowning out the melancholy notes of the former song and the heartache that had
come with it.

———

Sloan spent the next two weeks following Terri's strict schedule of interviews, small-venue performances, and listening to
so many songs that the melodies all began to run together in
her head. She also received texts and snippets from Lindsey,
all cheerful, upbeat, and full of encouragement, with never a
word of complaint about her life and health. A few texts arrived from Cole, just to say hello, but for reasons she couldn't
explain, whenever his texts popped up, her heart beat faster
and her whole day grew brighter.

Late one afternoon, Terri brought Sloan to Tom Jackson's
recording studio, where they all listened to the songs she'd
chosen. The threesome migrated into a small studio, and she
recorded a couple for playback. Then they returned to the
small conference room, where Tom played the recordings.

Sloan heard every ragged breath she took and every weak note she hit, cringed and graded her performance as poor and unimpressive. She cut her eyes to the two people who held her career in their hands, Terri doodling on a yellow pad, Tom leaning back in a chair, staring at a blank wall, his fingers locked behind his head. Sloan squirmed, swallowed nervously. Finally Tom unlocked his fingers, leaned forward, and rested his forearms on the table. He said, "You need better songs."

"I—I can make these work . . . maybe with musicians."

"No need," Terri interrupted. "You're country, and you need a producer in that field. I've got a top-notch man lined up. In Nashville." She made eye contact with Sloan. "Think you'd like to go home to record this album?"

Sloan instantly understood that Terri was offering her a win-win opportunity, to both make her album and check out her family roots. Emotion clogged her throat. "I was born ready," she said.

fifteen

———

"I'm so happy you came with me, Sloan." Lindsey was resting in a lounge chair on Cole's deck, where parents had gathered for a cookout to kick off the summer baseball season for Coach Cole's team after Memorial Day. Sloan had positioned a chair beside the lounger, ostensibly to keep Lindsey company, all the while feeling like a stranger in a strange land. She nursed a glass of red wine, ignoring buzzing chatter from clusters of parents, and raucous shouts from kids playing baseball in the backyard.

"Did I tell you I was a cheerleader in high school?" Lindsey asked. "I wasn't very good at cartwheels, but they never tossed me off the squad." The early-May evening was balmy, but Lindsey wore long sleeves and had a quilt spread across her lap because she said she always felt cold.

Sloan had dressed in capris, an off-the-shoulder top of bright orange, and trendy sandals. "I couldn't do cartwheels either. On an athletic scale of one to ten, I'm a zero."

Lindsey chuckled. "What did you do in high school?

Belong to any clubs? The chorus? With your voice you must have been popular."

The truth was so far away from what Lindsey was describing that Sloan couldn't confess it. "I was in a garage band. Sometimes we performed at football games."

"That sounds exciting. Wish I could have known you then."

The crack of a bat broke the air, and people on the deck leaned over the railing to cheer a blond boy on to second base. Lindsey watched through the railing, smiling. "Toby can't wait to play on Cole's YMCA team. Season starts in June. Maybe you can come to some of the games."

"I—I have a heavy tour schedule this summer."

"Of course. What was I thinking? Maybe you can make it to Toby's birthday party. He's turning seven on June thirtieth."

"*Late June.*" Cole's words returned to Sloan from his poolside visit, an evening she'd replayed in her head many times.

"Maybe." The sad truth was that Lindsey herself might be gone by Toby's birthday, and would certainly be missing Little League games in her son's future.

"Gloria's already making plans and telling me it'll be the best party ever. And, Sloan, I told her you're my sister but swore her to secrecy, insisted you needed your privacy. She won't tell anyone else, but she's sure excited about it." Lindsey's smile turned wistful. "I wish—" Lindsey hiked up the quilt on her lap, cleared her throat. "I'm parched. . . . Would you please grab me a soda?"

"I'm on it."

The cooler, a large galvanized washtub, was at the far end of the deck, where Cole stood over a giant stainless steel grill, spatula in hand, flipping his specialty gourmet burgers, talking to friends, and sipping a beer. Except for greeting Cole when she'd walked onto his deck, Sloan had stuck close to Lindsey. When Sloan had called the day before to say she was in Nashville, Lindsey had insisted that Sloan come to the cookout with her. Sloan had tried to beg off, but Lindsey wouldn't hear of it. "Cole always has a ton of food. Plus Gloria's working, and I'd love to talk to you some more."

So Sloan had come along, and although she'd been sitting next to Lindsey the whole time, every cell in her body was acutely aware of Cole at the far end of the deck. If they'd kissed, she could have stopped thinking about it. But he hadn't kissed her. He'd walked away and left her holding the burden of Lindsey's impending death, and a longing for *more* of him.

Sloan went to the washtub cooler filled with ice and drinks, rooted through the assortment buried in cold water, and dragged out a cola.

"If that's for Lindsey, she likes the orange flavor best."

Cole was flashing his dimpled grin at her. Sloan realized she hadn't even asked Lindsey for a preference. She felt foolish, returned the cola, and fished out a can of orange soda. "Got it."

Cole lowered the lid on the grill, stepped closer. "I'm glad you came."

He smelled of smoke and sizzling meat—in other words, delicious. Her stomach growled, and they both laughed. "Well, I missed the last cookout, and your cooking is legendary, according to Lindsey, so . . ." She shrugged. "Tasting is believing."

His gaze dropped to her lips and sent shivers up her back.

He found her eyes again. "Lindsey tells me you're cutting your album in Nashville."

"Does Lindsey tell you everything that goes on in my life?"

"Only the good stuff. And from where I'm standing it's all good."

Touché. "I'm being sent to Nashville because it has some terrific producers who make magic happen in the studio. I'm meeting with one tomorrow to hash out song selections for my album. And also because my agent knows about Lindsey's claim and thinks I should be nearer to both her and to Nashville."

"So you'll be living in Nashville?"

"Yes . . . at one of those extended-stay hotels not far from the studio where I'll be working."

"I'm hearing your songs played a lot on the radio. Some of the people here"—he motioned toward groups of parents standing or sitting at a large outdoor table—"would like your autograph. You up for that?"

A man leaning on the rail of the deck yelled, "Hey! Langston! Don't let my supper burn while you're checking out a pretty woman." Several others backed up the good-natured request.

Cole waved them off, told Sloan, "I'm glad you'll be closer, not only because I like seeing you, but because Lindsey can't stop talking about you. When you texted you were coming again, it made her day." He winked. "Mine too."

Yells and cheers from the backyard made the people on the deck whistle and stomp. Sloan looked around Cole's shoulder to see Toby running bases and a boy far out in left field racing after a baseball bouncing across lumpy ground. Cole watched, grinned, and gave Toby a shout-out.

When the cheering died down, Sloan said, "I know Lindsey wants her story about me to be true, and I know time's running out for her, so I'm in no hurry for a DNA test."

His smile broadened. "Thank you for that kindness, Sloan. This way she can go on believing and staying happy."

Cole's approval made her feel good. It mattered. *He* mattered.

He returned to the grill, raised the lid, and said, "And for what it's worth, your song 'Somebody's Baby' is amazing. I'll bet it sells a zillion copies. On the CD it says you wrote the music and lyrics. Maybe someday you can tell me more about it."

She clutched the cold drink can so tightly that her fingers, numbed from the cold, dented the can. "Maybe someday," she said, spinning and hurrying back to Lindsey's lounger, knowing full well she would *never* have a reason to tell him that story.

The sun went down, the ball game ended, and everyone ate dessert—fresh-churned ice cream and strawberry cake. Outdoor lights on the deck and in Cole's yard lent the evening a soft gauzy quality. Inside the house, cleanup progressed and an NBA basketball game entertained people who lingered. "I need to go home," Lindsey told Sloan from the lounger where she'd remained all evening. "Don't bother Cole. He still has guests. Just run me and Toby to our house. That's why I drove us over in my car for the party. I knew I'd poop out. You can come right back."

Even in the dim light Sloan could see beads of sweat on Lindsey's forehead. Sloan's stomach tightened. "There's no way I'm not telling Cole." She found him and Toby watching the game. The four of them slipped from the house, and Cole settled Lindsey in the front passenger seat of her car. "I'll drive," Sloan said, sliding into the driver's seat. "Stay with your guests."

"They'll never miss me."

"Go!" Lindsey said, giving him a verbal nudge. "Gloria will be home in an hour."

Sloan's stomach was in knots. "I'll stay there and text you once Gloria arrives."

Toby leaned over from the backseat, put his small hands on Lindsey's shoulders. "I'll help Sloan, Cole. I know what to do."

Cole watched the car back out, turn left onto the road, and drive the quarter mile to Lindsey's driveway, where Sloan parked and the trio went inside. Yet even then, he didn't return to his party flowing with music, laughter, and TV game noises. Seeing Sloan tonight had been unexpected and pulse pounding. He kept reliving his missed opportunity on that other night, when moonbeams had bathed her upturned face inches from his own. He'd kicked himself mentally many times for not kissing her when he'd wanted to so badly. Instead he had choked, lost the chance, which had left him to wish he could rewind time to those lost moments and, instead of backing off, taste her beautiful lips.

Cole shoved his hands into his pockets, gazed up at the night sky, and took deep breaths of air, where the scent of smoke from the grill floated. Stars were sprinkled across the black canopy, tiny pinpricks of light from journeys begun before Earth's creation. Sloan was a star too . . . a beam of light just beginning its journey but destined to cross the sky in a brilliant arc. And how did an ordinary man like himself catch a shooting star?

Cole shook away his introspection, along with his foolish longings, and jogged up the stairs of the deck to return to a world where he belonged.

sixteen

Once inside Lindsey's home, Sloan felt her nerves fraying. What had she agreed to? She knew nothing about helping Lindsey. What kind of care did a cancer patient need? "Sit yourself on the sofa," Lindsey said, motioning to the old couch.

"But isn't there something you want me to do?"

"Just having you in my home is all I need. Gloria should be home soon, and Toby knows what to do for me." Lindsey turned to her son. "Now, you go take a shower, 'cause you smell like gym socks."

"We won!" Toby pumped his fist in the air.

"No gloating." His mother tousled his hair.

"Aw, Mom . . ."

"Shower!" She pointed, and he scampered off. "And use shampoo and soap!" she called, glancing at Sloan with an amused smile. "Sometimes a mama has to remind a six-year-old of washing rituals."

Sloan still stood because Lindsey looked so tired and frail.

Sloan feared she might collapse. "Let me *do* something for you. Please."

Lindsey hesitated, then said, "Maybe help me get into my sleep shirt. By then Toby will be out and he can take over."

Sloan did as asked, undressing Lindsey, consciously ignoring pale and bruised skin, jutting hip bones, the port for administering chemo in her chest, and her bloated abdomen. She eased Lindsey into a long nightshirt and onto the bed, propping her back with a few pillows when she asked. The process had caused Lindsey pain, making Sloan feel guilty. "You all right?"

"Let's not talk about me—too boring." Lindsey patted a spot beside herself on the bed, and Sloan sat. "I saw the way you and Cole worked at avoiding each other all night. What was that all about?"

"We spoke."

"For all of ten minutes when I asked for a soda. I know you two see something special in each other, but you're both fighting it. Whatever for?"

"Are you a matchmaker? I can go to any online site if I want a date." She smiled to brighten the serious look on Lindsey's face.

"He *is* a good man, Sloan, in a world where good men can be few and far between. Believe me, I know quality when I see it, and Cole is quality. Don't you like him?"

Lindsey's earnestness stopped Sloan cold. She'd never had a best friend with whom to share her secrets, her crushes, her good times and bad times. For Sloan, growing up had never been about confiding or belonging—it had been about keeping secrets and surviving. Lindsey's best friend, Gloria, had moved across the state to help her, while no one had ever clung to Sloan. Perhaps Dawson had come the closest . . .

but that was over with now. Sloan's habit was to shut down closeness. Life was safer that way. And hearts were better protected.

Still she thought Lindsey deserved an honest answer. "I'm not about dating and becoming involved with anyone, Lindsey. Music has always been my life story. It's all I ever wanted, and now I have a shot at the brass ring. Can't let anything or anyone hold me back." She offered a wistful grin. "Not even a good man."

"So you'll never fall in love?"

"I won't say never, but I sure don't have time for it now. Besides . . . love is complicated. Who needs the pressure? Music is the one thing that's never let me down."

"Well, that song you wrote sure made it sound like you understood what it is to love someone."

She couldn't discuss, *wouldn't* discuss, the song with anyone. She deflected with a comeback question. "Were you in love with your ex-husband when you married?"

Lindsey picked at her coverlet, took time before answering. "More afraid of him than in love with him."

Her answer surprised Sloan. "Afraid? What do you mean?"

"That answer will have to wait for another day. The only thing I can say for sure is that our son was the only good thing Bo Ridley ever did for me."

Just then Toby scooted into the room wearing soccer shorts and a too-large Hulk the Avenger T-shirt, and carrying a lidded tumbler of ice water. "I brought your water, Mama." He set the tumbler on her nightstand.

Sloan stood, Lindsey opened her arms, and Toby carefully slid into her embrace. "Thank you, Little Man." She buried her nose in his hair. "Now you smell like my sweet son."

"I smell like a girl," he grumbled. "I used Gloria's

shampoo—stinky flowers. She never remembers to buy the stuff I like."

Sloan had moved away to stand near the door. Watching Toby and Lindsey's hug made her heart take a stutter step as she imagined the weight of his child's arms around her neck.

"You mean that bubble-gum-scented shampoo?" Lindsey asked, running fingers through his damp hair. "I'll ask her to buy it next time she goes to the store. Now be a sweetheart and get Mama her pills. I need some rest."

He hopped up from the bed. Sloan started forward, but Toby frowned up at her. "I can do it. Don't need no help."

"He does it all the time," Lindsey assured Sloan. "He knows what he's doing."

He went to the dresser, stood on a step stool, and sorted through the numerous prescription bottles. Sloan noticed that every bottle was banded with a strip of either dark blue or yellow tape. Some bottles wore both colors. For day and night, Sloan imagined. Toby carefully popped caps off and shook pills into a small dish, stepped off the stool, and carried the dish to his mother. It looked like a bowl of confetti. Lindsey took each pill with a sip of water from the tumbler, and when all had been swallowed, Toby walked the empty dish back to the dresser.

"Now you two go on," Lindsey said. "I'm sure Gloria will be here shortly."

In the living room, Toby and Sloan sat on opposite ends of the sofa. She felt awkward, unsure what to say or do. She'd just watched a six-year-old boy give his mother a dishful of cancer drugs as if it were a common ordinary event performed by every six-year-old.

Toby said, "You don't have to stay, you know. I can stay awake until Gloria comes. I do it all the time."

Sloan knew there was no way she'd walk out the door and leave Toby and Lindsey alone. LaDonna had often left Sloan when she was a child growing up, and Sloan remembered feeling afraid of every sound, every imagined bump in the night. She also saw that Toby's eyelids were drooping. She glanced at the TV and saw a video game box. "You play games on that?"

"Course! Mama used to play the games with me . . . not so much anymore. Gloria doesn't like to play, so Cole plays when he's got time."

"How about playing a game with me?"

Toby looked surprised. "You can play?"

She sometimes resorted to gaming boxes in hotel rooms when there wasn't anything to watch on TV or if she couldn't sleep. She also thought back to her high school days in Dawson's basement bedroom, where the two of them passed hours on cold or rainy afternoons playing video as well as other games. Sloan told Toby, "I'm pretty good. Show me what you got."

Toby tucked a game CD into the box and brought both controllers to the sofa, then handed one to Sloan. "My favorite game is *Alien Space Invaders*. . . . You know how to play it?"

"No, but you can teach me."

The game was simple. Flying saucers hovered in a blue sky and dumped blobs of invaders onto a grassy field where Toby, a figure dressed in laser green, and Sloan, an image robed in bright blue, popped up over brick walls to shoot down the aliens that were blasting fiery streams from their guns. The more Toby and Sloan shot down the invaders, the more rapidly the aliens flowed from the saucers. Toby's face was a study in concentration. "Know what I pretend?" he asked as his thumbs flew on the control buttons.

"Tell me."

"I pretend the invaders are Mama's cancer cells, and so every time I take one out, it dies and can't hurt her." The words were so honest and touching that Sloan forgot to fire, and her protective virtual wall got a hole blown in it. "Watch out!" Toby yelped, firing at the black-robed enemy storming Sloan's wall. "They almost got you."

"Sorry . . . thanks for the assist."

They were still playing when the front door opened and Gloria shuffled into the room. "Sorry I'm late." She dropped into the recliner, gave Sloan an exhausted look. "One of our dementia patients got out of his ward and put us on lockdown. No one could leave the nursing home until we found him. He was hiding in a cabinet under the kitchen sink." She shook her head. "Cole texted me that you were staying with Lindsey."

"And me!" Toby said, exasperated.

"Well, of course, *you*."

"I had good company," Sloan said, standing and smiling down at the boy. She started for the door.

Toby rushed after her. Gloria stayed put in the chair. At the door Toby tugged on Sloan's hand. "Will you come back soon?"

She peered into his exotic-colored eyes, almost gold, tinged with green, and teased, "So you can beat me in *Alien Space Invaders?*"

"Naw . . ." His smile was sheepish, but his brow quickly furrowed. "Because when you come, it makes my mama happy."

Emotion balled in her throat. She nodded, left, and walked swiftly to her car, where she stopped and took deep breaths of the night air, unable to release the image of Toby's upturned face. What was it Cole had told her? *"Toby's way too old for his age."* She understood the comment now. Toby was an old soul—as she had been—a player in a world where childhoods were contaminated, his by cancer, hers by alcohol. Visions of grasping hands formed in her mind, making her gag. She glanced across the dark distance to Cole's house, where the party was long over. And for an instant she saw a figure on the deck, a man resting forearms on the railing. She closed her eyes, and when she opened them, the figure had vanished. Sloan turned, yanked open the car door, got in and started the engine, revved the motor, and sped away.

seventeen

"Five months! Are you serious, Lani?"

"Almost six," Lani said, remembering she'd have a few weeks of clinic duty once classroom work ended. "But Memphis is only five hours away. I—I thought you'd be happy for me."

"I'm glad about the offer, but you'll have to move if you take it, and I can't move with you. I have a job and school and a new project starting."

Lani hadn't been prepared for Dawson's reaction. "There's a stipend for an apartment included with the fellowship, and I'll get a paycheck, plus learn a whole new discipline. It's the opportunity of a lifetime. I don't want to turn it down."

"And I'm guessing Melody thinks it's a great idea for you to go."

"I haven't told her, Dawson. I'm telling you first because you're always first in my life."

Dawson felt a flare of regret for his initial reaction, and stopped pacing his living room floor. May sunshine pooled through the sliding glass balcony doors and puddled on the carpet, leaching the gray color from the fibers. "And you're first in my life, and I can't imagine us being apart until December."

Lani stood on the kitchen side of the freestanding counter that divided the cooking space from the living room and acted as a physical barrier, much as her news acted as an emotional one. Days before, Mrs. Trammell, head of nursing, had called Lani into a special meeting, where Lani had heard about an addition to be built onto the Arie Winslow Cancer Center—a children's wing, specializing in pediatric cancers. Thanks to a generous donation from a benefactor, ground breaking and construction would begin in June. Mrs. Trammell was offering Lani a fellowship to St. Jude's, a premier children's cancer hospital in Memphis. The fellowship would pay Lani's way so that she could study cutting-edge procedures in childhood oncology, while also getting hands-on clinical training as a nurse for children with cancer.

"Don't you know I'll miss you too?" she said. "Being with you is my dream come true, but *this* is my dream too. I've always loved pediatric nursing, and you know that."

"Windemere hospital has a pediatric floor." He said the words softly, not meaning to bruise the tender spot on her spirit.

"I—I don't want general pediatrics. I've learned so much working in adult oncology, and this fellowship is a gift, a way to help children diagnosed with cancer, and *I'm* the nurse Mrs. Trammell has selected for it. Once I come back, I'll be in a position to help build the new program. I don't like the idea of moving away either, but if I'm going to advance my career, I *must* go. I'll drive home every chance I get, and you can come to Memphis whenever you can break free. The time will fly—I promise." This fellowship offer seemed golden to her. She loved Dawson, but starting fresh in a new place, in a challenging learning environment, was her final hurdle to overcoming all that was holding her back.

She stepped from around the counter that separated them, went over, put her arms around him, and laid her cheek on his chest. He stood stiffly, rejecting her overtures. What Dawson saw were long lonely weeks without her. Selfish, he knew, but he loved her, and hated the idea of not having her close to him. Moments passed, but she didn't let go, and soon, despite his resistance, he felt the turmoil within begin to calm and his heart soften. The fellowship would mean separation, loneliness, and isolation for them both. The distance between them was only geographical. Their plans and dreams were not lost, merely deferred.

Sloan's nerves were piano-wire tight. She waited with Terri in a small kitchenette of a recording studio for a producer, a man who would help her create an album that could be life-changing. Terri had taken a red-eye from LA last night, picked Sloan up in a rental car this morning, and driven them to an inconspicuous small brick building in a seedier part of downtown Nashville. Terri had talked nonstop about the producer, telling Sloan, *"He doesn't take just anybody, Sloan, but the minute I mentioned your name, he said yes to an interview."* A receptionist had shown them to the kitchen area, where she had asked them to wait. Sloan had been in several recording studios, many small, but this one was totally lacking in charm. Sensing Sloan's uneasiness when parking, Terri had said, *"What matters is the equipment inside and the genius of the producer you're going to meet. Believe me, some of the top talent in the country record here."*

The room, painted yellow and in need of a fresh coat, reminded Sloan of a cheap deli. She took a sip of water from her water bottle, trying to block out the smell of coffee left too long sitting on a warming plate near a portable microwave oven. Her mouth felt bone-dry.

A man breezed into the space, and Terri jumped up, her face lit with a smile. "Conner! Good to see you."

The man was tall and thin, wore faded jeans and scuffed boots, had a face deeply lined by too much sun, and wore his gray hair in a long ponytail tied with a rawhide cord. His brown eyes took in Sloan, and he held out a roughened hand. "Conner Callahan. Sorry to keep you waiting. Had a horse emergency at my ranch."

Sloan shook his calloused hand, feeling unimpressed.

"So you're the gal with that knock-'em-dead voice and a song rocketing up the charts. That song has legs, lady. It's gonna be around for some time, I'm betting. Pleased to meet you." His voice held a thick drawl and sounded gravelly, but his smile was a force of nature. He poured himself a cup of what looked like sludge from the coffee carafe and sat across from Sloan and Terri in an old metal kitchenette chair.

"So far, since winning the contest, my *life's* been a rocket ride, Mr. Callahan."

"Call me CC . . . everybody does." He sipped the coffee, locked his fingers around the cup. "Frankly, I'm not a fan of singing contests, Sloan. Mostly because they turn into popularity contests, and the best singers don't always win." She braced herself for criticism. "But in your case, they got it right." Again, his smile. "My wife's a fan of the show, and toward the end, close to the finals, she says, 'Conner, sit down and listen to this girl.' Now, we been married almost fifty years, and she's a gem, but bless her heart, she can't carry a tune in a bucket." He took a mouthful of coffee, swallowed. "But what she can do is peg good talent, so when she says 'Listen,' I do."

Sloan figured he was making a point, but he hadn't quite gotten to telling her what *she* needed to hear—that he would produce her album. Neither had Terri interrupted with hyperbole about her client, which was a sign of reverence for an agent like Terri Levine, who always had something to say.

Conner asked, "You know what makes a great singer?" Unwilling to venture a guess, Sloan gave a demure shrug. He said, "There are three things, in my opinion . . . a great voice, the right song, and a singer's delivery or interpretation of a song. A lot of singers come and go. Plenty are one-hit wonders. They have a song that grabs the public's ear, and it zooms to the top of the charts." He scooted one hand up in the air. "But, unfortunately, these same singers can't seem to do it time after time. And that's what I look for in a singer, one who can do it more than once or twice."

Sloan's heart sank. Was he warning her that she might not be able to repeat a success?

"Know why?" Conner asked. Again, her shrug. "You know Patsy Cline's song 'Crazy,' don't you?" She nodded, hummed some of it, making him break open another grin. "Did you know that Willie Nelson wrote that song?" She didn't. "Willie couldn't find any of his buddy singers to take it. He sang it in a fast tempo, but still no takers. Finally Patsy got hold of it, slowed the tempo, reinterpreted it, put her voice brand on it, and turned it into a classic."

Sloan thought the information interesting but didn't understand how it applied to her.

Conner leaned forward, his eyes on Sloan's. "First time my

wife brought me 'Somebody's Baby,' I got chills up my spine. That's one hell of a song, little lady."

Sloan felt moisture skim her eyes, blinked it away. "Thank you." She hastily added, "But I usually sing others' songs." She hoped Terri had told him she wasn't a lyricist.

He shook his head. "Lot of the top voices don't write their own music. But they sure know how to deliver a good song that people like to hear. When Terri called me and asked me to take on your album, I knew I had to do it."

She had been unprepared for the ease of his acceptance. "I—I appreciate—"

He held up his hand. "You got two things going for you—two things that come with top-tier singers—talent and an ability to connect with an audience. What you need are the right songs. So I've already talked to some of my best songwriters and got them working on songs for you."

"Really?" Sloan felt breathless, as if she'd been riding a roller coaster.

"Fair warning. You will work harder than you ever have in your life, Sloan. You'll hate me and you'll love me, but when we're finished, I predict we'll have an album that will make its mark on the country music world. And if it makes enough of a mark, it'll cross over to other charts. Best of both worlds."

Now Sloan grinned and eyed Terri, who gave Sloan a *Didn't I tell you so* wink. "Conner's the best."

He added, "We're calling the album *Somebody's Baby*, 'cause the single's already a hit. I have a CMT video in the works for the song too."

Sloan swallowed hard, felt her insides quiver, and told herself she could distance herself from the song and perform it for video. Her emotional specialty was disconnecting on the inside from the things she didn't want to deal with. She would do this from now on when she performed the song. *Push away. Forget.* "I look forward to working with you."

Conner stood and stretched. "I want you here in the studio at four tomorrow afternoon so we can get to work on one of those songs you picked out in LA. Only one I want to use. Now come on, and I'll show you the studio where we'll be working and introduce you to a few people you'll be working with." He stopped, hung his head slightly, let out a sigh. "I'm acting like a charging bull. . . . My wife says I get too carried away, and I forgot to say that Terri's told me about your sister, her cancer and all."

Sloan sidled a sideways glance at Terri, who shrugged, but Sloan trusted that Terri had her reasons for telling the producer. To Conner, Sloan said, "Her name's Lindsey, and she's very sick."

"I won't be insensitive to that pull on your time, Sloan. I lost a brother to cancer, and I know what it feels like to watch someone you love dying and you not being able to do anything about it. You just have to tell me when you have to cut out of here. But until you do, we work."

"I won't let you down."

"Come on now. Let me show you off. Everybody working here wants to meet the gal who sings the song that makes 'em cry."

eighteen

"So how are things going between you and my sister?"

Lindsey's question caused Cole to turn his attention from the road to offer her a long stare. "What are you talking about? There's nothing going on between me and Sloan." Cole was taking Lindsey to her two-hour chemo infusion appointment at the hospital, before heading to the firehouse for his shift. She liked to go while Toby was in school, get home, and recover somewhat before his school bus dropped him in the afternoon.

Lindsey gave him a smug smile. "Not sure I'm believing that, Cole Langston." Lindsey crossed her arms. "You better look where you're driving, or you'll put this truck in a ditch and both of us with it." He turned his attention toward the road, adjusted his steering. "I have cancer, Cole, but I'm not addled. I see the way you two look at each other."

"How's that?"

"Like you were two ice cream cones that each wanted to lick." She laughed at her own clever wording.

Cole felt his neck and ears turning red. "Colorful way to put it, but I haven't seen her since the cookout. Not sure she'll remember my name."

"Don't pretend that what I said isn't true."

He shook his head. "She's a beautiful woman but way out of my league, Lindsey. I'm walking away."

"You shouldn't." Lindsey's teasing tone turned serious. "Sloan's got a world of hurt knotted up inside her. She could use a friend like you."

He turned into the hospital's parking lot, glanced at Lindsey. "She tell you she was hurting?"

"Not in so many words . . . but I know what suffering looks like. I see it all around me up there in the chemo unit. I see it in my own mirror every day. Just 'cause somebody don't talk about it doesn't mean it don't show. My sister has hurts, and she's buried them deep."

He thought about that as he parked, killed the engine, and walked around to open the passenger door for her. "You have any thoughts on what you think she's hurting about?" He helped Lindsey out of the truck, walked her inside the hospital.

"Been trying to figure it out. I see the signs whenever we talk, but there's no way to know without asking outright, or unless she volunteers telling. Maybe it's something from her childhood, growing up without our daddy, or maybe a love thing that didn't go right." They stopped at the elevator, and she pushed the button for the chemo floor, waited, shivering from the air-conditioning.

Cole couldn't deny he'd felt those guarded undercurrents when he'd been with Sloan too. "From my line of sight Sloan Gabriel is sitting on top of the world."

"Not everything's what it looks like on the surface, Cole."

The door slid open, and she stepped inside, but when Cole started to join her, Lindsey held him back. "No need for you to come. I know how you hate going up there. Go on to work. I've already made you late."

"How will you get home?" he asked as the door began to slide shut.

"My sister's picking me up. Too bad you're working the next twenty-four hours, or you could stop over this afternoon." She flashed a mischievous smile as the door sealed shut.

Cole stood staring at the stainless steel doors and mulled over what Lindsey had said. He blended her comments with Sloan's hit song. She'd written that song for or about someone. Then he remembered watching Sloan and Dawson as they'd stood together in the ER lobby, the look on their faces, and the tension in their bodies. Cole had been convinced they had a past with each other, but after meeting Lani, it was clear that Dawson had moved on. Perhaps Sloan had not.

He shook his head to clear away the jumble of emotions crowding in on him, and knew his desire to hold her, kiss her mouth, had not abated one bit. Yet to crave Sloan was a luxury he couldn't afford to pursue. He gave a rueful smile, turned, and rushed off to work.

⌣

"How's my favorite patient?" Lani asked as she hooked Lindsey, stretched out in a chemo chair, to a machine that would deliver measured doses of a pharmaceutical stew into the central line port in her chest.

"'Bout as good as you can expect for someone getting

poisoned to death by chemo drugs. But I show up mostly to visit with you anyway, not this old machine."

Rows of heat-resistant windows designed to fill the room with natural light filtered morning sun into the space. The architect had thought of everything to make the room welcoming and mask what it truly was—a battlefield between life and death. There were only two other patients under Lani's care this morning, both attached to pumps, one woman reading, another knitting. Sometimes patients wanted someone to talk with, while others wanted to crawl inside protective shells and not be bothered. Lani tried to be sensitive to each individual's needs.

"Instead of poison, how about thinking of it as a military force flowing through you, armed and ready to take out the enemy?"

"Like predator drones?"

"Exactly!"

Lindsey shrugged and gave a half smile. "They've been stalking my bad guys for years, and they haven't gotten them all yet, only made them retreat into another part of my body."

Lani crouched beside the chair, put her hand on Lindsey's shoulder. "I know it's been a long war, but don't give up hope."

"I like having you on my side." She patted Lani's hand.

Lani had not yet told many people about taking the St. Jude's fellowship. In general, chemo patients tended to become attached to their caregivers, and Lindsey, who usually wore a smile and rarely complained, was one patient Lani would truly miss. Maybe now would be a good time to tell her—

"How's that good-looking man of yours?" Lindsey's sudden shift in topic and a cheerful smile pulled Lani away from her intention.

"Dawson's fine. Working too hard, but doing what he likes to do." Lindsey had never met Dawson, but Lani had shown her photos of the two of them on her cell phone. "How's that good-looking young man of *yours?*"

Lindsey's whole demeanor softened. "Toby's still the love of my life."

"He'll be getting out of school for the summer soon, won't he? You going to bring him to the playroom so I can pamper him with soda and candy?"

Lindsey shifted her gaze, knowing she couldn't tell a bald-faced lie to Lani concerning the decision she'd made about her cancer treatments. She was leaving the unit for good after today, and would begin hospice care at home. She wanted one last summer—if she could manage it—with her son without the drugs and paraphernalia of these last few years. Just medications for pain control. Her doctors had been forthcoming weeks before when they'd showed her MRIs of her brain and pointed to the dark spots . . . her cancer's final frontier. Only Cole and Gloria knew she was abandoning treatment. She wanted Sloan to know too. . . . Next time they were alone, she'd tell her.

Answering Lani's question, Lindsey said, "School's out a week before Memorial Day, but I registered him for a summer camp program at the YMCA, so he can have some fun. And Cole's coaching baseball at the Y in his spare time, so no need for me to drag him here."

"Sounds like a perfect fit for you both." Lani stood as another patient entered the unit. "I'll come check on you soon."

Lindsey closed her eyes, performed deep breathing exercises, and focused her mind on an image of Toby grinning to show he'd lost a second front tooth.

"Mom, look what the tooth fairy brought me! Five whole dollars! She must really like me!"

"She loves you, Little Man."

The next thing Lindsey knew, Lani was gently shaking her shoulder, unhooking her infusion pump, and offering her an orange-flavored soda. "I guess I fell asleep," she said with a yawn. She stretched, took hold of the cold cup, and sipped through the straw. The sparkling sweetness revived her.

Lani asked, "You need a ride home? I'll call you a cab."

Lindsey craned her neck toward the room's entrance and broke into a big smile. "Not necessary. I have a ride. Someone I want you to meet. Why, here she is now."

Lani had been busy with the pump and pouring Lindsey's drink, but she turned toward the doorway, and felt her knees almost buckle. Coming straight toward her and Lindsey was Sloan Quentin, like a blond sorceress stepping out of a past Lani wanted to forget. The moment felt surreal.

Sloan's gaze shifted from Lindsey's smile to the nurse beside her chair, and she stopped walking. The clench in her stomach was reflexive, a reaction that came whenever confronted by the unexpected. The fight-or-flight reaction, scientists called it. If Lindsey hadn't been beaming her a smile and holding out her hand, Sloan would have turned and fled.

"Sloan, come meet my favorite nurse, Lani Kennedy."

Sloan and Lani locked guarded gazes. Lani offered a tentative smile. "You look good, Sloan."

"You two know each other?" Lindsey asked, then did a finger snap. "Of course! You both grew up in this town. Bet you went to school together. Were you friends?"

"No," Sloan and Lani said in unison, making Lindsey call out, "Jinx!"

The three of them laughed aloud, and that broke the tension.

"I was a year ahead of Lani," Sloan said, coming closer, eyes only on Lindsey.

Lani's head swam with questions, but before she could say anything, Lindsey clasped Sloan's hand to her cheek and said, "Lani, I'm pleased and excited to tell you that Sloan Quentin Gabriel is my long-lost sister."

nineteen

Lani went mute. Sloan shifted uncomfortably. Baffled, Lindsey glanced between them in the ensuing silence. "Hello—anybody hear what I said?"

Lani found her voice first. "I—I didn't know you had a half sister, Sloan."

"It was a surprise to me too, but Lindsey contacted me while I was in Los Angeles and made a pretty compelling case for us being related."

"We had the same father," Lindsey added, glancing between the two. "Jerry Sloan. I think that's why her mother named her Sloan—after Daddy."

Sloan silently pleaded with the universe for Lani to not turn inquisitive over Lindsey's announcement, or worse, start spouting off details from their shared past. A few words from Lani could be her undoing.

Lani sensed Sloan's unease, one that matched her own. At the moment, she didn't care how Lindsey had come to call Sloan sister. Lani's personal history with Sloan was much too difficult to handle, and she'd come too far over the past year to fall into the abyss that had once almost consumed her.

Lindsey quickly realized that Sloan and Lani were not pleased to see one another, and she backpedaled. "It's a long story and I'll tell you sometime," Lindsey said. "Bottom line . . . I figured out our connection months ago. I wrote Sloan, and was blown away when she came all this way and listened to my proof. I always wanted a sister, and now I have a famous one!" Lindsey added, "I know *you* have a sister, so you get how excited I am to discover I also have one."

"How is Melody?" This from Sloan, in an effort to redirect the conversation.

"She's doing well. Mr. Boatwright retired, and she's in charge of his office these days."

Sloan felt her tension easing, realizing Lani didn't want to revisit the past either. Relieved, she asked, "So you got your nursing degree?" She swept the treatment room with a look— the chairs, equipment, the spotless new floors and walls.

"I did. And you're a singing star. I guess we both landed upright, didn't we?"

"It seems so."

Lani pushed ahead with, "Our whole town rooted for you during the contest."

"So I've been told . . . sort of surprised me too."

Lani sorted through the chaos of emotions inside her, wanting to convey to Sloan that she was all right about Sloan's returning, no matter the reason. "One thing about this town: It rallies around its own, and you're counted as a true daughter of Windemere. We're proud of you, Sloan. Truly."

Sloan offered a nod of acquiescence, a tiny smile. She remembered that kindness was one of Lani's virtues.

"Once word gets around that you're here, people will want to see you. Newcomers will want to meet you," Lani said.

Sloan had hoped that the isolation of Lindsey's house in a rural area would shield her comings and goings, but she should have realized that the town was too small for her *not* to be noticed. "My plan is to stick close to Lindsey, so I hope word doesn't get around."

Lindsey heard Sloan and Lani sharing a subliminal conversation, and Lindsey realized that she, without meaning to, had been the one to unearth it. To smooth over her faux pas, she jumped in with, "Well, now that the two of you have become reacquainted, maybe you both can come visit me at home. You're two of my favorite people, you know."

Lani's gaze drifted to Lindsey's upturned face, her expression innocent and guileless. Lani glanced again at Sloan, standing in a pool of sunlight spilling through a window and turning her hair white-gold. Sloan was beautiful, and more polished and softened than in high school. Sloan Quentin had been a counterpoint to Dawson's dark hair and eyes, while Lani usually felt plain and ordinary beside him. "Will you be here long?" she asked Sloan.

"I'm cutting an album in Nashville, so I have a place rented near the studio, but I'll come visit Lindsey when I can, especially with her being sick and all."

Lindsey said, "Seeing Lani has been the only perk for me coming to chemo." She pushed up from the chair. "I should get on home. Don't want Toby coming into an empty house." She wobbled slightly, and Lani and Sloan both reached to steady her.

"You should eat some lunch," Lani said.

"I've got her," Sloan said, a firm grip under one of Lindsey's arms. "I'll make sure she eats something."

"She likes milk shakes," Lani called as they shuffled toward the door. She wondered what Sloan must have felt, to have learned about a long-lost sister, only to face losing her to cancer. Life didn't play fair.

"Vanilla," Lindsey said. "With lots of whipped cream. I never have to worry about what I eat these days. Just have to worry about keeping it down."

Sloan frowned over Lindsey's dark humor. They took a few steps, and then Sloan turned. "I'm glad you got your RN degree, Lani. Nursing suits you." Then, recalling Lani's initial reaction at seeing her, Sloan added, "I'm a little surprised Dawson didn't tell you he'd run into me weeks ago."

Lani felt as if the wind had been knocked out of her. Not trusting her voice, she shook her head to confirm that Dawson hadn't.

Puzzled by Dawson's omission, Sloan concentrated on holding on to Lindsey until she was steady on her feet, and walked her through the doorway.

After they were gone, Lani stood paralyzed. *Dawson knew Sloan had returned and kept it from me.* She struggled for equilibrium as a chime went off, alerting her that another patient was finished with chemotherapy. She hurried across the room.

Waiting for the elevator, and seeing how pale and weak Lindsey was, Sloan asked, "Why don't we hit a drive-through for that milk shake on the way home?"

"Yes . . . that would be best. Chemo sucks me dry." Lindsey glanced back momentarily and said a silent final farewell to the unit, its machines and drugs, knowing this was the last time she'd set foot in it again. "I feel like celebrating, so make sure the shake has a cherry on top, all right?"

"You should have told me! Why didn't you *tell* me, Dawson? We just ran into each other. It was awkward! Embarrassing! And with Lindsey, of all people." Lani stood at the sink in his apartment, rapidly scraping skins off potatoes and tossing them onto a growing heap they'd be unable to eat in a week's time. Lani had finished her shift in the cancer unit and had left instead of helping the afternoon nursing crew, always busier with patients. Peeling the five-pound bag of potatoes kept her hands busy while her mind replayed the encounter with Sloan.

Dawson, still dressed in his construction clothes and heavy work boots, leaned against the counter, his lower back pressed into the hard stone. "I was blindsided too, but she said she was leaving town real quick, and I didn't see any reason to mention it to you and stir things up." He crossed his arms and watched her flail at the hapless potatoes. All he wanted was to shower, grab a cold beer, and chill out with Lani after dinner—and *not* talk about Sloan.

"Did you *talk* to her when you ran into her? Ask *why* she'd come back?"

"I wasn't interested in why. I was in a hurry, and she was with that guy, Cole, we met at the restaurant weeks ago. She and I said a few words, and we went our separate ways." He slapped construction dust off a leg of his jeans.

"Don't withhold information thinking you're protecting me. *Talk* to me!" Lani stomped her foot, gouged out an eye of the potato she held. "I know why she's back."

Dawson sagged, saw his peaceful evening disappearing into Lani's anger. "I give up. So, why did she come back?"

"Well, my patient Lindsey Ridley, my sweet *favorite* patient, told me she and Sloan are sisters . . . half sisters, because they had the same father. Did you ever know that Sloan might have had a sister? You *lived* with her, Dawson!"

He straightened, more surprised by than interested in Sloan's familial connection, but he knew that the unexpected meeting had been traumatic for Lani, and therefore, he had to tread carefully. "We never talked about her family. All she wanted was to be free from her mother."

Dawson reached down and unlaced his boots, kicked them into a corner. "Baby, we watched her sing on that TV contest together. We both voted for her. You told me you were all right with her winning and her name change and her song that's playing every time I turn on the radio. Give me some head room here, Lani. I didn't mean to 'withhold information' from you. I just want us to move on."

Lani knew she wasn't being fair, because Lindsey, not Sloan, had told Lani about a shared father, but right now she was so angry—not just at Dawson, but at everything, at life, at what had happened years before. She struggled to regain self-control.

Dawson rubbed his eyes, feeling beat. "Look, can we talk later? I'm going to clean up."

He fled the kitchen area, and Lani stopped whittling on a potato that now looked shredded and pathetic. *Poor potato.* She set it aside, stared down into the sink piled with brown potato skins, as depression engulfed her. She shook her head, did deep breathing exercises to hold the dark emotions at bay. What had the counselor at the hospital told her? *"Fight your dark moods. Don't let them get a foothold. Exercise. Endorphins are your friends. Change your habits and patterns. Depression hates that. Don't fall into its rut of negativity."*

Without telling either Dawson or Melody, Lani had sought out a psychologist in the hospital, a woman on staff hired to help employees deal with burnout and other work issues. She'd helped Lani immensely over the weeks to take control whenever dark memories threatened her.

She had planned to ask Dawson to come with her to Memphis this weekend to check out the apartment space where she'd be living for the coming months. The paperwork said the rooms were partially furnished, but she needed to see exactly what *partially* meant and what furniture she'd need to bring with her. And now they'd fought over something that, when she thought about it, she knew was truly trivial. *My fault.* Through the glass doors she saw the sun going down, turning the sky pink and gold and lavender.

Taking the fellowship in Memphis was the right thing for her to do. She needed a reboot of her career because nursing had been her dream since age thirteen. She didn't want to retreat. Dawson and Sloan had moved forward. So would she. Lani *had* meant what she'd said to Sloan. . . . Lani was glad for Sloan's success. Sloan's and her shared ordeal and its damage would never completely vanish, but Lani knew from her work as an RN that scar tissue thickened and formed over all wounds—on the flesh and inside the heart. And Lindsey? Well, her future was darker. Lani recalled the joyful expression on Lindsey's face when she'd introduced her to Sloan, her half sister. *All* of them deserved some joy!

Dawson took his time in the shower, letting the water soothe tired muscles while he chastised himself for not telling Lani about running into Sloan. Determined to apologize, he went into the kitchen. Lani was gone. He groaned, hating that she'd left without them settling things. He knew how shocked he'd felt running into Sloan out of the blue . . .

like walking through a time warp into a place that he never wanted to revisit. He should have told Lani on the day it happened. "Rookie mistake," he told himself with disgust. Now Lani was hurt.

Then, on the granite countertop next to the sink, he saw the word *SORRY* spelled out in battered potatoes. He grinned, felt a knot rise to his throat, and reminded himself that the same spirit that made Lani ache so profoundly also allowed her to love unreservedly. It was one of the many reasons why he loved her so much.

Dawson opened a drawer, dug out a pot, filled it with water, and threw in the pile of wounded spuds. He grabbed his cell phone and texted: How about a dinner of mashed potatoes and take-out chicken tonight?

Seconds later, her text chirped: On my way.

twenty

Cole entered the Windemere Public Library a day and a half after dropping Lindsey for her chemo treatment, his twenty-four-hour shift having stretched into thirty-two. The city council simply *had* to increase the EMT hiring budget. Windemere's population was growing, and all the shifts and crews were overworked. And yet in spite of his physical exhaustion, he was at the library because an idea had burned a hole in his willpower, and he was following through on it.

"May I help you?"

The librarian's voice from behind caused him to jump. He turned to face a woman, asking, "Um . . . do you keep old yearbooks someplace in here? You know, from the local high school."

"Certainly. We're digitizing the older editions but still have many in print form. It's a slow process. Is there a particular year you would like to see?"

"Not exactly sure . . . maybe six or seven years back."

"I'll take you to the stacks where the books are shelved, and you can look through them."

That suited Cole. He wanted to be alone when he searched the books' pages for the time when Sloan had attended Windemere High. It wasn't in his nature to snoop, but Lindsey's text about Sloan and Lani running into each other at the cancer center while he was at work had eaten a hole through his brain. Not a happy reunion. Something going on between them, and I'm totally confused.

He'd had that very same feeling when he'd run into Sloan talking to Dawson Berke, but now Lindsey had witnessed tension between Lani—Dawson's girlfriend—and Sloan. When Cole had met Lani and Dawson in the restaurant, they'd looked happy together. At least until Cole had come to their table and said hello. Dawson had been friendly, but had been tense and uneasy the entire time Cole had chatted with the couple. So today, as soon as he'd finished his shift, Cole had showered, changed into fresh clothes at the fire station, and come downtown to check out a hunch.

Sloan had said she and Dawson knew each other in high school, and Cole was betting that Lani also had been a student at WHS. In high school, she'd been Sloan Quentin, so he figured she'd taken the name *Gabriel* for the sake of her career. Lots of professional singers, actors, and actresses changed their names.

The yearbook collection was aligned on metal shelves in a far back corner of the building bordering a concrete wall, with a student desk close by, and not a solitary person anywhere near the area. Alone and private. Just what he wanted. He scanned the spines of the shelved yearbooks, paused, and did some mental calculations. Lindsey had told him Sloan was seven years younger than her, so Sloan was now in her early twenties.

He counted backward, chose books according to his best guess, sat at the desk, and began reading through indexes for her name. He hit pay dirt for what had been her junior year. Apparently, she'd missed the eleventh-grade photo day, so only her name was listed, but he did find a shot of her on a school stage with four guys, in a band called Anarchy. He laid the book aside and picked up the one for the following year, where he found her senior picture, and also a photo of Dawson. Cole saw in a glance that Sloan hadn't been a joiner. Under Activities only the name of the band was listed. Under Dawson's name was *Cross-Country, All City, All County*.

Cole lingered over Sloan's picture. She was pretty but looked edgier, with more eye makeup than necessary, in his opinion. He leafed through various yearbook sections ... Sports, where he saw Dawson in a group shot with his team-mates, Senior Days, where there were several pictures of Anarchy performing for crowds of students. The caption named the lead guitarist as Jarred Tester, and he and Sloan looked pretty cozy in the montages. Cole skimmed a section called Student Life. It had no captions but only grab shots of kids walking hallways, clustered in a courtyard, gathered at lunch tables, seated in classrooms. There he found Sloan and Dawson, arms entwined in three photos and looking like a couple. So they had dated. Maybe it hadn't ended well.

Cole flipped to the Senior Prom section, with photos of couples standing under a trellis of fake flowers, but none of Sloan with Dawson. Cole couldn't find them in a jumble of pictures of dancing couples either. Cole eased back in the hard library chair, reminded himself that not all seniors went to their proms. Cole had attended his, but with a girl who was a buddy, not a love interest.

Lani. Where was she? Dawson had introduced her as Alana Kennedy. He turned to the index and found that she'd been a junior during Sloan's senior year, which surprised him. On the Homecoming pages, he found Lani in a group shot of a committee of junior girls who'd helped decorate the gym for a homecoming dance following a football game. The page also held a large photo of the Anarchy band playing on the field during halftime, with Sloan center stage, holding the mike in a death grip.

Cole flipped to photos of the junior class and located Lani, along with a laundry list of school activities beneath her picture. The contrast between Lani and Sloan and their involvement with their high school was striking and only served to pique his curiosity. He tossed pages back and forth among the three images—Sloan, Dawson, Lani.

He'd seen the strained civility between Sloan and Dawson with his own eyes, and the genuine happiness between Lani and Dawson. And now there was Lindsey's report of what she'd witnessed between Sloan and Lani. What was going on with these three? A love triangle? A bitter breakup? Something that had happened after high school was over?

He rubbed his face, felt the stubble of his beard, and blinked, blurry-eyed and brain-fried. He was too tired to think now. Plus it really wasn't any of his business. Why should he invest time and energy researching the past of a woman so far out of his life sphere in the first place? *Idiot!* Disgusted with himself, he stood, re-shelved the books, and left the library, no closer to solving the mystery than when he'd come.

Sloan worked two weeks and often late into the night with CC in the small recording studio, sometimes with musicians, sometimes with only prerecorded musical tracks. The going was slow at first, with CC offering her songs penned by his favorite songwriters. Sloan sat wearing headphones to hear renditions of songs, and flashed a smile when she heard one she especially liked.

CC had told her, *"You're the singer, Sloan, and you get to choose the songs you like best. We'll compile a list, let you do a vocal run-through with just the music portion, and then you can decide if it's right for you."* She liked that about CC. He never pushed her toward a song. He let her find the lyrics, the tone, and the mood that worked best with her voice. He would work his magic after the tracks were laid, but she retained artistic control.

CC said pacing in the album was important, so together they created a list of tunes with varying rhythms—fast, slow, saucy, a redo of some other singer's popular song—and built what CC called her vinyl identity, anchored by her hit single, "Somebody's Baby," which was still climbing the charts.

Terri flew in from LA for a few of the sessions, including today's. "You're booked into a Memorial Day event in Dallas," Terri told her. "Onstage with some rising newcomers, along with two name bands. And last week your song had record-setting downloads. This is all very good, Sloan."

Sloan was sitting cross-legged on her bed, her back padded with pillows against the headboard. The best thing about working long days and evenings was that deep sleep held on to her, and she had no nightmares of clutching hands. "Give me a list of my competition."

Terri pulled papers from her briefcase and laid them on

the table beside the chair where she sat, while Sloan nibbled her way through some chicken nuggets from a fast-food drive-through window. "Already done."

"Soon as you return from Dallas," Terri said, "you'll begin filming your video."

Sloan thumbed through messages on her cell while Terri told her about the upcoming video shoot—the director (one of the best); the locations (still being selected, but there would be several); and the time set aside for postproduction, when the clips would be strung together into a scripted visual story line and readied for MTV and CMT launches.

Sloan half listened as she read through texts from Lindsey that kept her linked to Windemere. . . . Toby couldn't wait for the school year to be over, Gloria was working too hard, Lindsey herself was feeling pretty good further out from chemo, and missing Sloan. Sloan had received no messages from Cole, and was surprised to feel disappointed about it. What was it about the man that tugged at her? For starters, she couldn't understand why he hadn't even tried to kiss her that night by the pool. He'd wanted to. She'd seen it in his eyes. And she would have let him too. True she was attracted to Cole physically, but also to his persona, his skill set, cooking expertise, rapport with kids, and most of all the way he looked out for Lindsey. He was strong, independent, and certainly didn't seem to *need* anyone in his life. Or even want anyone—

"Are you listening to me?"

Terri's question startled Sloan away from her wandering thoughts. She slid her phone aside, looked contrite. "Of course. Um—what did you say?"

"I asked if you're going to Windemere this weekend."

"Maybe. Toby has a baseball game, and Lindsey wants me to come with her and Gloria."

Terri offered a rueful smile. "So you've accepted her narrative of you being her sister?"

"I—I guess I have."

"Even without proof positive? Because this can't stay a secret anymore. The more you hang in Windemere, the more it will be noticed. Yours and Lindsey's connection is going to come out. Are you ready for that?"

Sloan furrowed her brow and thought of the people who already knew . . . more than she'd ever intended. "I don't talk about it to others. *You're* the one who told CC."

"Because I don't want you torn between your career and what's happening to Lindsey. I was busy career building when my mother died. I could have been there with her in the hospital, but wasn't. I've always regretted that."

Terri's confession surprised Sloan, but it also acted as ballast for her own choices. "I—I like Lindsey. She's sister-worthy," Sloan said wistfully, "and life's dealt her a bad hand. I don't think I can walk away from her now. It would be cruel, and she doesn't deserve that. But I don't want to hurt myself either."

"Yes, she doesn't deserve cancer. However, trust me that the media will come sniffing around, and probably put you under a microscope." The idea sent a chill through Sloan, and it must have shown on her face, because Terri quickly added, "But you have me on your side, and it's my job to put a positive spin on everything you do, especially if you've been honest with me."

Sloan ignored Terri's invitation to say more. She yawned and slunk down into the pillows. "I'm being a real good girl, Terri. Never fear."

Terri scooped up her purse and briefcase. "Okay, then. I have to catch an early flight." She turned off the desk lamp, adding, "Have a good time with your family."

My family. The words replayed in Sloan's head as she drifted into sleep.

twenty-one

Lani found Ciana in the main barn grooming one of her many horses, and when Ciana looked up, she welcomed Lani with a sunny smile. "How are you? I thought you'd be gone by now. Memphis, isn't it?"

"Dawson's packing the rental trailer at my sister's place now. We'll drive over this afternoon, move everything into my new place and get me settled. Classes start Monday."

"You excited?"

"Yes, but nervous too."

Ciana put down the curry brush and walked closer. "You're going to do fine. And it's for just a few months, right?"

"Five, but three extra weeks for clinic duty," Lani said, unable to express how much she was going to miss her life in Windemere. And Dawson. "I should be home for Christmas."

Ciana swept Lani with a gaze. "You're not dressed for riding Oro today."

"I was here last weekend. No, I'm here to talk to you." A lump clogged Lani's throat, and she swallowed it down. "I—I want to sell Oro, *need* to sell him, and thought maybe you or Jon could handle it for me."

Ciana looked shocked. "You've had Oro since you were thirteen."

"I know . . . but I can't take care of him anymore."

"If you're worried about winter feed money . . ."

Lani shook her head. "That's an issue but not the main one. It's . . . it's time . . . for me to let go of him." A tear trickled from the corner of her eye, and she swiped it aside. "He helped me through a lot of hard times growing up, but . . . I need to move on. If you handle the sale, I know he'll go to somebody who'll love him. He's a wonderful horse."

Ciana squeezed Lani's shoulder. "I doubt Jon will sell him. Oro's old but a perfect saddle horse. He'll have a home here for the rest of his life."

Lani buried her face in her hands and broke down crying. Ciana wrapped her arms around the girl who'd been her best friend, Arie's, cousin. "It's all right, sweetie. You were a wonderful owner, and when you move back, you can ride him if you ever want to."

"He helped heal me." Lani's words were muffled against Ciana's clothing.

"And now it's time for you to go heal others."

———

"I just don't think I can finish watching the game. I want to more than anything, but . . ." Lindsey let the sentence trail with a labored breath.

Sloan had driven over on a Saturday morning to see one of Toby's YMCA baseball games. The metal bleachers under a hot sun were hard and uncomfortable, and in spite of their holding umbrellas to shade themselves from the heat, Lindsey looked sickly and in pain. "We should leave," Sloan said, jumping up.

"Please stay, Sloan," Lindsey said. "Toby knows I sometimes have to leave early, but it'll mean a lot to have someone in the family stay and finish cheering for his team till the end of the game."

"I'll run her home," Gloria said firmly. "I know what needs doing once we get there."

"*Someone in the family . . .*" Sloan regretted her first judgment of Gloria, because without Gloria's care and devotion, Lindsey and Toby would be much worse off. Gloria folded two umbrellas and scooped up her and Lindsey's stuff. "I'll be here for your Little Man. No worries," Sloan said.

"Win or lose, Cole will take the boys out for pizza, and most of the parents tag along. I know Toby would like having you come too."

Sloan nodded and watched the two women walk to the parking lot and drive away, as she mulled over the idea of eating pizza with kids and strangers. And with Cole. She adjusted her sunglasses and old ball cap and hunkered down. Ever since she'd arrived, people had been staring at her. Their looks and elbow nudges had thrust her back to the days when gossip had followed her in the town, and although these young mothers and fathers, many with toddlers in tow, were total strangers, she felt self-conscious, misplaced without Lindsey and Gloria on either side of her. She stepped down off the bleachers and wandered along the fence, closer to the dugouts. She'd rather stand than sit anyway.

It also gave her an opportunity to concentrate on Cole as coach. He appeared to enjoy the job and the boys, offering encouragement if they struck out, or if their hits turned into easily caught fly balls, or if they were tagged before getting on base. By the time the game ended in a tie and the two teams lined up and slapped hands with each other, all disappointments were forgotten. "Who wants pizza?" Cole shouted to his players.

A chorus of "Me, me, me!" went up.

He turned and saw Sloan at the fence, and grinned, as if he'd won an unexpected prize. The sight of her made the already sunlit day sunnier. "Well, hey!" He thought she looked gorgeous in shorts and a tee, her blond hair pulled through the back of her ball cap.

Sloan felt her pulse kick up a notch, and returned his smile, explaining, "Gloria took Lindsey home and asked me to stand in for them at the pizza party. I rode with Gloria, so I'll need a ride."

"That can be arranged. You ever been to Pizza World?"

"Never heard of it."

"Then you're in for a real treat, city girl."

Toby hustled over, dragging a sack of bats through the red dirt. His happy expression faded when he saw that Sloan was alone. "Mama get sick?"

"I think the sun got to her," Sloan said, feeling a heart tug and not wanting to dampen his spirit. "May I come with you today in her place?"

Toby shrugged, kicked a clod of dirt with his shoe. "Sure."

Cole took the bag, tossed it over his shoulder. "Come on, buddy. I'll race you to the truck."

Sloan watched them run across the now empty parking lot, the bats clattering in the bag. Toby reached the truck first, and his childish squeal of "I win! I win!" echoed through the still, hot air. And inside Sloan's head, ghosts stirred of another sunny day in a park near a set of swings. She took a sharp breath and pushed the phantoms aside, then quickly jogged to the truck, where Cole and Toby waited for her to catch up.

⁓

Pizza World lay within a sprawling strip mall on a newer side of town. In the years since she'd been away, Windemere had grown considerably, with clusters of new homes and shopping centers, parks, schools, and playgrounds. The changes amazed Sloan. "This was farmland when I lived here."

"Well, it's still rural on my side of town, and that's the way I like it," Cole said, parking the truck.

Stepping inside the pizzeria was like entering a gigantic cafeteria. There were rows of long tables and benches for seating, plus cafe tables hugging walls that were covered with pennants, posters, and framed photos of Little League baseball teams. The aromas of yeasty crust, tomato sauce, and pepperoni made Sloan's tummy growl, unheard over the noise of laughter, shouting, and kids' voices.

"Yep," Cole said, watching her check out the space. "Every team who plays in a sports league comes here after Saturday games. You up for it?" He pointed. "Over there. They saved us a table for two."

One of the dads waved. Cole gave a thumbs-up and grabbed trays for Sloan and himself. Toby barreled ahead, shoveled pizza slices onto a plastic plate, and hurried away to join his teammates already seated on benches. Cole ushered Sloan along a long cafeteria-style counter of hot sliced pizzas slathered with every imaginable topping, including dessert toppings. He paid with a credit card for the team, and when he and Sloan reached their table, she again saw people eyeing her. "Am I the first girl Coach has ever brought to a pizza party?"

"The *prettiest* girl he ever brought," he said around a mouthful of toppings and sauce.

Two girls materialized beside their table, staring wide-eyed and pink-cheeked, the shorter girl clutching a pen and two Pizza World napkins. She held out the napkins. "Can we have your autograph?"

Sloan smiled, signed the flimsy tissue, and handed them back, and the girls scampered off, squealing.

"Toby's told everybody you're his aunt. No harm in that, is there?"

There was nothing she could do about it, so she said, "That's fine."

Cole and Terri were the only ones who knew the complete story, and both wanted to protect Lindsey, and also Sloan's privacy. Cole took another bite of pizza, spoke around the mouthful. "I've seen your car parked at Lindsey's house more often lately."

"My part of the album is finished. It's in the final stages of production, then will go out to retailers. These days I'm taping a video." She rolled her eyes. "Pretty boring work, lip-syncing phrase by phrase to please a cranky director. Feels like I'll never be done because of lighting issues, and set maintenance, tech glitches, and rain delays. But when we wrap up every day, I don't want to sit alone in my hotel room, so I come here. I like Lindsey. Very much. And Gloria says Lindsey looks forward to my visits . . . a win-win."

"I'm glad you're getting to know her better."

The unspoken lay between them. . . . *Lindsey's time is short.* "I'm spending this weekend at the house," she volunteered. "Toby gave me his room. Says he'll sleep on a blow-up mattress in his mom's bedroom. He told me it's like 'camping.'"

Cole chuckled. "Yeah . . . we went camping once. Last summer in my backyard. He made it till midnight, then told me he should check on his mom. I was never so glad to see a camping trip end, so I could finish the night in my bed." Sloan laughed over Cole's expression. "Toby still talks about it, though, says he wants to camp some more. My back hurts just thinking about it. You ever camp?"

How did she tell him that for her *camping* had meant being shut into her tiny trailer bedroom if LaDonna brought a "friend" home? "Never tried it. Not sure I want to be out in the wild with 'lions and tigers and bears, oh my!'"

"Okay, Dorothy, I get it. You're happier in Oz."

Toby edged up to the table, pizza sauce circling his mouth, a serious look on his face. "Cole, can we go home? I want to see Mama."

Cole's eyes softened. "Sure can, buddy. Why don't you wash up, and Sloan and I will wait for you on the sidewalk."

Toby scampered off, and Cole and Sloan walked out, leaving the racket of voices behind. Cole said, "You know Toby's birthday is at the end of the month. I'm doing a cookout bash, and Gloria's bringing all the stuff for Toby and his friends. It's only hot dogs, ice cream, and cake—homemade by me"—he bowed slightly—"but if you want to come . . ." He paused, leaving the invitation hanging.

"Soon as the video wraps, I head out on tour. What's left of June through most of July," she said, genuinely regretful. "I would if I could."

He was disappointed. "Okay, how about you let me know when you'll come back, and I cook you a special dinner?"

Her pulse quickened with the offer and the look in his eyes. "It's a date."

Their gazes held, an intricate web of desires untouched, of promises untapped. The door opened, breaking the spell, and Toby pushed between them. "You ready?" Cole asked.

He was talking to Toby, but Sloan imagined he also meant the question for her.

twenty-two

Classroom studies at St. Jude's and ongoing clinical work were the kind of mental and emotional stimulation that Lani thrived on. The classroom work challenged her brain, and the clinical, her heart. She soaked up the long hours like a sponge, never even saw it as work, saw it simply as an extension of the life she wanted. Time flew by. She made friends with other nurses in the fellowship program—Janette (everyone called her Netter) from Iowa, Tracy from Florida, and Kesha from Chicago. They would often gather in Lani's living room, drink wine, and talk about their days, the work, and the children in their care. The only hole that the experience couldn't fill was Dawson's. She missed him terribly . . . his smile, his arms, his presence. They texted, talked on their phones late at night, but still it wasn't the same as having him close enough to touch.

"Miss me?" she'd ask when he called.

"Like a fish misses water. My crew avoids me because I'm so snarly. You miss me?"

"Only when I'm awake or asleep."

That made him laugh. "So that would be all the time?"

"All the time, every day."

"So let me ask . . . what are you doing Fourth of July?"

"Some of my nurse friends want to go to Beale Street and hit the jazz clubs, then watch the fireworks over the Mississippi River. One of them has a cousin with a condo overlooking the water. How about you?"

"I was thinking of driving over and seeing if we could make some fireworks of our own."

Her heart leaped. "*Please* come. They're a great bunch, and we'll have a good time." She didn't add that when she'd showed her friends his picture, they'd asked, "*What are you thinkin', girl? Leaving that hunky-looking guy alone at home.*" And said, "*Hope you got a mean old guard dog around him.*"

"Gee, me hitched up with a group of pretty nurses. Let me think about it. . . ." Dawson teased. "So if I should have a heart attack and need mouth-to-mouth—"

"*I'll* be the nurse who'll resuscitate you."

Their group for the Fourth grew in size when interns from the hospital heard about the get-together. On the night of the Fourth, Beale Street was packed with people partying in the body-drenching humidity. The group crammed into bars and clubs, toasted the night, danced, and shared hospital war stories, and although Dawson was familiar with their medical jargon, he was content to sit on the fringes observing Lani. Her eyes sparkled, her laughter bubbled. With her peers, she was the Lani he'd first fallen for, effervescent and outgoing, totally different from the Lani of those dark months in Windemere. He was happy for her but fearful for himself. She was in her element here, doing what she loved to do, with people who spoke the same language—medicine. What if she didn't want to come home?

No matter how many beers he drank that night, or fireworks explosions they saw, not even the night and morning they shared in each other's arms could drive the fear of such a possibility out of his head.

———

Sloan zipped along the interstate in her rental convertible, the mid-July sky sliding from twilight to darkness in a slow fade. She glanced at her dashboard gauges and noticed that the gas tank needle pointed to empty. She was near the off-ramp for the rural back roads that would take her to Lindsey's house, so she exited, pulled into a gas station, refueled, went inside to pay. She waited in a short line, heard the attendant's radio playing in the background, and her own voice singing. She held back a self-satisfied smile. *"Your album opened at number five on the country Billboard charts,"* Terri had told her two days before on the phone, *"and 'Somebody's Baby' has crossed over to the pop charts. That's a big deal, and the label is very happy."*

Sloan was happy too. She'd just come off a blistering tour in the northwest and was taking some overdue and necessary R&R. While waiting in line, she glanced around the station's mini-mart, swept clean, and glowing with fluorescent lighting, at shelves stuffed with road food, refrigerated cases of water and soda, and countertops crowded with last-minute grab-and-go items. Her eyes hit a dead stop on a large glass jar near the register, partially filled with money. The label read: PLEASE HELP! UNPAID MEDICAL BILLS. Underneath the label was a photo of Lindsey Ridley. When it was Sloan's turn to pay for gas, she nodded toward the jar. "Friend of yours?"

"Sad story," the woman behind the counter said. "Poor gal's dying from cancer and has bills stacked up to the ceiling. No insurance. Not a lick."

Sloan's eyes widened in disbelief. "How do you know?"

"I know her friend, Gloria, and she's set these jars all over town so folks can donate. Every penny matters." The attendant handed Sloan her change, and Sloan stuffed it into the jar and hurried to her car. Could this be true? Why hadn't someone told her? She gunned the engine and shot down the two-lane road, and by the time she'd reached Lindsey's, she was angry. The porch light was on, casting yellow light outward, and moths were flapping helplessly at the fixture. Sloan knocked, and the screen door was flung open by Toby, who hugged her around the waist and pulled her inside. "Thanks for the games!"

She patted Toby's upturned face. "Did everything get here in time for your birthday?"

"Yes! Everything's awesome. I got more games than all my friends!"

She'd sent him a new state-of-the-art gaming console, a TV just for game playing—the new set was positioned beside the other television—and a stack of the newest games for his age group.

Cole, sitting on the sofa with a game controller, stood awkwardly. Their eyes met, and he saw instantly that Sloan was upset. "Everything all right?"

"Where's Gloria?"

Cole thumbed toward the kitchen doorway. "Making popcorn. Can I help you?"

"Not yet," Sloan said, stepping around the furniture groupings, "but I want to talk to you later."

Cole eased down onto the couch, and Toby bounced down beside him and pushed the button to un-pause the game. Cole played, his mind no longer on the cartoon characters but on Sloan and her angry expression. Whatever had happened, she was wearing it like a signboard. He hoped Gloria could handle it.

Gloria turned from the microwave with a bag of popcorn when Sloan swept into the kitchen. "Welcome back! Lindsey's on the back porch in a lounger—" Gloria's smile faded. "Is something wrong, Sloan?"

"I stopped at a gas station and saw the contribution jar for Lindsey."

Color splattered Gloria's face. "Oh, Sloan . . . don't say nothin' to Lindsey about the jars. Please."

"She doesn't know?"

"No, she doesn't. I took it on myself to set up the jars. But people are helpin', giving money for her bills. She didn't want you to know about the insurance stuff. Not ever. She made me swear to never tell you."

"Does Cole know?"

Gloria's head bobbed. "He put a big jar at the firehouse, and those guys stuff it regular. We got over a thousand dollars already in three weeks. Isn't that wonderful? Don't be mad at me, Sloan. . . . I'm just trying to help."

Gloria's sincerity and pleas softened Sloan. "I just wish someone had said something to me about it."

With eyes downcast, Gloria tore open the popcorn bag and dumped the contents into a plastic bowl. "You was on the road, and she didn't want you knowin' how bad off things were with money. She ain't got much left 'cept pride, so leave her some of that when you talk to her. Not her fault." Gloria drizzled melted butter onto the snowy white kernels.

"You said Lindsey's outside?"

"She likes to sit out most evenings stargazin'. Says it's good for her soul." Gloria clutched the bowl and stepped around Sloan, and Sloan opened the solid wood back door and stepped into the night. "I best take this in to Toby and Cole."

Lindsey lay in a lounge chair, wrapped in a cotton quilt, and turned toward Sloan with a smile for a greeting. "Thought that might be you when I heard the car engine. You look lovely. . . . Here, come sit with me. Excuse the quilt, but I still get cold, even in July."

Sloan pulled over a lightweight lawn chair, her irritation evaporating into the star-riddled sky. "How you doing?"

"Not much new. But I made it to Toby's birthday and now every extra day is a gift." She reached out her hand, and Sloan clasped it. "You were too generous to him, you know."

"A guy only turns seven once." Her mind flashed a backward glance to her own birthday events. Gifts never took priority over her mother's love of gin. Sloan had slept one such birthday night away in the backseat of the car while LaDonna had partied inside a bar.

"How'd your concerts go? Wish I could go to one, but those crowds." She shook her head. "Too much for me. You staying long this visit?"

"Concerts were fine. And I have to go back to LA in just a few days."

Lindsey rubbed her temples. "I'm glad you came tonight, and I'm glad we're alone. I need to talk to you." Sloan stilled. "I don't have much time left. . . . Pretty much running on empty now. I'm on morphine, big doses of it, but the headaches . . . none of the pain drugs are helping much. The hospice people take care of me during the day, and Gloria at night, but it's wearing her out after working all day."

Hearing Lindsey speak of her impending death, on this starry summer night, with only the sounds of katydids and tree frogs, felt surreal. This wasn't right. This wasn't fair!

Lindsey's voice grew stronger. "I've made a will with a lawyer, so it's all legal and everything. What little I have I'm leaving to Toby. I bought this house for cash, and it's deeded to Gloria, so they'll have a place to live after I pass. I want you to take all my scrapbooks and records of our daddy." Lindsey cupped her hand over Sloan's. "Gloria has my power of attorney, and guardianship of Toby. She can make decisions for him, and raise him up. I'm trusting her with my most valuable possession."

Lindsey's reality left Sloan subdued and shaken.

"Gloria's had a hard life, in and out of foster homes from the time she was ten, but she's my dearest friend, and I know she'll take care of my Toby. I wanted you to know my plans so that you won't worry about Toby after I'm gone. You have a wonderful life ahead of you, and you don't need to go worrying about things in Windemere."

She didn't want to unravel in front of Lindsey, but felt torn, not wanting to disappear from Toby's life, but she had a career to navigate. "How can I help, though . . . after . . . ?" She couldn't bring herself to finish her sentence.

Lindsey helped. "From time to time, maybe you can look in on them. You know, just keep in touch . . . birthdays,

Christmases . . . that kind of stuff." She leaned closer. "I've bought cards ahead to his eighteenth birthday, and asked Gloria to be sure he gets one every year. I love my boy with all my heart, and he's the hardest thing to leave behind."

"His memories of you won't die. I've been told that love never dies." Sloan spoke around the thickness in her throat and the unspoken pain in her heart. She knew firsthand the truth of those words. *Love never dies.* She composed herself. "Does Toby really understand what's happening to you?"

"We've had some talks. When he was three, we buried his goldfish together, and he seemed to understand then that the fish wasn't coming back."

There was a huge difference between losing a goldfish and losing a mother. "I'll keep in touch with him and Gloria, Lindsey. Maybe I can fly them out to LA and take them to Disneyland."

"He'd love that. What am I saying? They'd both love that." Lindsey gazed skyward, sighed. "Look at all those stars. Know what I'm looking forward to? Seeing those stars up close and from all sides, because I'll bet they're awesome."

twenty-three

Cole stood on his back deck, forearms resting on the top railing. He watched Sloan walk the distance between his and Lindsey's homes in the dark of the night, with only starlight and a sliver of moonlight to guide her steps. At the foot of the stairs she looked up, and he straightened. "I've been expecting you."

She froze for a moment, knowing it was one in the morning and wondered how long he'd been waiting on the deck. He'd left Lindsey's at nine. Despite the late hour she reminded herself of her mission and came up the steps quickly, then halted with several feet of separation between them.

"Want to go inside?" he asked.

"No. This is fine."

He felt the air between them fairly crackling, some because of her determination to have a showdown with him, some because he wanted to shorten the distance between them to perhaps toe to toe. Yet he didn't move.

And neither did she.

"You want to talk about the collection jars," he said matter-of-factly. "Gloria wanted to put them out. Made her feel like she was helping." He shook his head. "Like she was doing something worthwhile because it isn't easy to stand by and watch your best friend die."

"Not easy for anyone else either," Sloan said curtly. "Gloria told me Lindsey doesn't know about the donations."

"True. How could she? It isn't as if she gets out much these days."

Sloan had rehearsed a speech, but now, under the canopy of stars, the words fled. "What happened to her insurance?"

"She had insurance, but the premiums skyrocketed, until it became impossible for her to keep up, and her insurer dropped her."

"Is that why she stopped medical treatment?"

"She stopped because there was no hope for recovery. Not because of insurance."

"I would have liked to have been told about her inability to pay her premiums." She felt renewed anger rise. "Who's paying for her medications and that pain pump now?"

"There are medical programs helping out, and hospice costs her nothing." He offered a rueful smile. "And of course, the donation jars."

"What happens after she—" Sloan couldn't bring herself to say the D-word, finished with, "Well, to Toby and Gloria, later? I mean about money and all?"

"They'll get by on what Gloria earns. Been doing it so far. Toby will grow up here, go to school, play baseball, all the usual things kids do, just like Lindsey wants for him."

And they have you, she thought, but didn't say it. "Why didn't Lindsey want me to know about her insurance problems?"

"She wanted a sister, not a money tree."

His comment went all over her. "I *have* money, Cole, and I can stuff those collection jars with hundred-dollar bills if I want."

"It's your presence she wants, Sloan, your company, but as you've said, you have a career schedule to keep."

Her hot anger turned to cold fury. "I'm a singer, Cole. Do you know what people see when they look at me? They see a girl standing onstage basking in the limelight. They buy music from websites, maybe an album in a store. What they *don't* see is how hard I've worked. They don't see the years of singing in bars, the friends I lost along the way, the hard scrabble it took to become who I am on the stage. I've wanted to be a singer all my life . . . and you have no idea of the price I paid to get here."

He listened, not just to her words but also to her subtext . . . of hurts still knotted inside her, her past still draped in shadows. "I get it, Sloan. You've had a hard slog and you're in a place where you can help Lindsey financially. That's excellent. She needs the money, and you have it. A simple fix. My point is that you've already helped Lindsey when you accepted her story of your being her half sister. You befriended her. That's your real gift to her, Sloan."

"Gloria and Toby can't spend gratitude."

Cole chuckled, stuffed his hands into the pockets of his jeans. "You and Lindsey are very different people. She leads from her heart. You think through every move before you make it. Not a criticism," he quickly added. "Just an observation from an outsider."

"Leading from the heart is unsafe," she snapped while moving backward, wanting even more distance between her and this man who seemed able to see inside her. She didn't want to be under his microscope. "I'd better get back." She stopped their conversation cold. "Don't want anyone to wake up and find me gone."

"Understood." He watched her hurry down the stairs, jog to the patio next door, and let herself in. He watched her, knowing that she had deliberately sidestepped any kind of intimacy with him, and knowing that, regardless of how long she stuck around at Lindsey's, Sloan Gabriel was already gone.

———

"I want to do this, Terri, so don't try to talk me out of it." Sloan paced the carpet in Terri's office, pleading her cause.

Terri steepled her fingers, her gaze following Sloan's quick, determined strides. She listened to Sloan's plan and her arguments for it, patiently waiting for Sloan to run out of steam. When Sloan finally took a breath, Terri motioned with her eyes to a bright orange leather chair, urging Sloan to sit. "You do know this event can be run online. It doesn't have to be 'in person.' You've heard of crowd sourcing?" Terri asked.

"That's not the way I want to raise the money. I want a real in-the-flesh, bona fide performance concert."

"Donations only? If you do the concert for free, as a charity event, be warned. People often pay as little as possible, so you might not raise as much money as you'd like for Lindsey's cause."

Sloan hadn't considered that. "She has no money, Terri, and Gloria is committed to raising Toby until he's eighteen. What if he wants to go to college? I'm telling you I want to do something to help my sister."

"Your half sister."

"My *dying* half sister," Sloan snapped. She'd been unable to get her conversation with Cole out of her head. She thought that giving a fund-raising concert might help him see her in a better light, not as someone able to write a check but as someone who cared. And she did care about Lindsey and Toby very much. "What do you suggest I do to raise the money?"

"Give a concert and charge admission. That way you can do whatever you want with the money, pay off her medical expenses, set up a trust fund . . . whatever."

Of course Terri's suggestion made sense. Sloan nodded. "Let's do it."

"And where are you going to have this concert?" Terri asked.

"Windemere. The town has a rodeo arena at its fairgrounds that can hold lots of people. We can announce it on social media. You can publicize it. One night, one event."

Terri shifted thoughtfully. "It will cost money to set this up. The sound and lighting people don't work for free. Plus the cost of the space you choose, cleanup crews, security . . . the list goes on. And how about musicians? You'll need a few. Your label may offer to help, but not necessarily."

"I'll pay for all that myself. I have the money, and I'm earning more." A chart-topping song and an album earning royalties were adding up. Sunlight filtered through the floor-to-ceiling window and fell across Sloan's chair and Terri's desk, sending jeweled sparkles off a cut glass candy dish perched at the desk's corner. Sloan watched as Terri mentally calculated the pros and cons of Sloan's plan.

"Actually, I don't think it's a bad idea, Sloan. It will garner some good publicity."

"That isn't why—"

Terri held up her hand. "I get why you want to do it, but there're a lot of pieces to pull together. When do you want to do this?"

"Quickly. Lindsey's really sick."

"Are you ready for reporters digging into your personal garden? 'Dying Long-Lost Sister Meets Love Child of Jerry Sloan.'" She created a headline with her finger in the air. "Are you prepared for the intrusions, because I know you like your privacy?"

Sloan stood, walked to the window, and stared down on traffic crawling along the boulevard. "I can handle interview questions. I'll talk about Lindsey, not me." Since her win on *American Singer*, the press had been kind to her . . . "girl from trailer park makes good" stories. There was plenty in her past that she didn't want in the tabloids. One day everything would come out, but until it did, she would continue to sing and perform, and keep her mouth and her heart shut tight. "You already know my story. . . . My mother drank, and I got out as soon as I could. I traveled with a band for a while, worked on my solo style in Nashville, moved to LA so I could try out for the show." She turned to face Terri, crossed her arms. "And I won."

"So DNA doesn't matter?" Terri asked, her eyes challenging but kind.

"If I'm going to play the part, I'm going all in," Sloan said, with more bravado than she felt. "In the end, Lindsey will get the money she needs. I don't want this to be a memorial concert either. I want Lindsey alive when it happens. I want her to know that Toby will have some money after she's gone. She deserves that much from her 'sister.'"

Terri spun her chair to face a computer screen, and tapped

a few keys. "You have a pretty full schedule through October. A Christmas special to record in August . . ."

Sloan headed to the twin mahogany doors that sealed off Terri's personal office, where she paused and announced over her shoulder, "Well, please clear the way, because I'm going back to Windemere so I can spend some time with Lindsey."

Before Sloan could step through the doorway, Terri said, "This *is* a kind thing you're doing. Lindsey's fortunate to have you on her side."

A flood of memories from unhappy years washed through her mind, followed swiftly by images from her days in Windemere when she was called the singing lady by someone who had mattered more than she had ever thought possible. With great effort she stemmed the flow from the past. "I would do as much for a complete stranger in dire need, and whatever else Lindsey is, she's not a stranger."

twenty-four

Whenever she entered a child's hospital room, Lani could easily distinguish the parents of "newbies" from parents of "veterans." Newly diagnosed children's mothers and fathers wore frightened, bewildered, and grief-stricken expressions, and were often suspicious of every staff member or tech or doctor who floated near their sick child. Kids who had "been here, done it before" had relatives who looked settled in, cautious, and resigned to again walk the path of hope that this time their child would be made well. The kids fell into categories too. Younger kids screamed whenever anyone they didn't recognize came close, because strangers might mean needles and shots and bags of fluid hung by their bed that often made them deathly sick. Readmissions knew the ropes, navigated the courses of new treatments with attitudes of resilience or defiance.

St. Jude's treated all kinds of childhood cancers, but Lani had always known that treatment of blood cancers would become her specialty—in particular ALL—acute lymphoblastic leukemia, the form that had stalked her cousin Arie until it had metastasized to finally claim her life years before. The irony was that if Arie had contracted it as a child these days, she might have lived. With new medical wizardry such as contemporary chemotherapies, stem cell implants, and gene-targeted therapy, 90 percent of ALL victims could be considered "cured" after ten years if they had no intermittent relapses. Huge progress. Too late for Arie.

Lani also knew the warnings about not becoming emotionally involved with patients, as did all medical personnel, but that wasn't the way Lani was wired. She made friends with her patients, and one girl, ten-year-old Sara Beth, and her mother, Pam, had quickly fallen into her "favorites" category. They were from a Mississippi town about the size of Windemere, with deep Southern roots and honey-thick drawls, the husband and daddy in the military, far away from family and, by confession, *"Awful bad lonesome."*

Whenever Lani came into Sara Beth's room, Pam would light up and talk nonstop about family and home. This morning Sara Beth was sitting up in the bed, wearing earbuds plugged into an electronic port in the side rail, immersed in a movie on the television mounted on the wall. Pam chattered while Lani worked. "Me and Jimmy fell in love in the eighth grade. I felt on fire every time I saw him, and turned out he felt the same way too. We got married the week after we finished high school. We were so happy when we had Sara Beth, but work was hard to come by, so Jimmy joined the army. We've lived in North Carolina and Arkansas and Louisiana." She ticked off the places on her fingers. "Then our baby girl got sick." She glanced tenderly at Sara Beth.

The child had been diagnosed at four and a half, had been

treated, and had achieved remission at age six. Now, a few years later, she had relapsed. Second remissions were more complicated to achieve. "Four is young," Lani said, checking Sara Beth's vitals. "I'm sure she was scared."

"She sure *was* scared. Me and Jimmy too. She had all these bruises on her arms and legs, and when we took her to the hospital, them doctors thought we'd hit her. The idea!" Pam huffed. "But in the end she was properly diagnosed."

There were counselors in the hospital, available to parents, but Lani was here in the room, and Pam felt a bond with her, so Lani listened sympathetically, pushing away thoughts of the one case that had broken her heart and almost made her give up nursing.

"Everything went fine that first time. The chemo done its job, but now her cancer's come back. And Jimmy's yonder in Afghanistan. We sure miss him." Pam stared at the floor, her chin in her palm. "I promised Sara Beth I'd never leave her alone in any hospital, and I haven't!"

The room was L-shaped, with the hospital bed in the room's center and a sleeping bed in an alcove so that a parent could spend the night. Depending on the length of a child's hospitalization, some parents slept in the room, some stayed in a nearby Ronald McDonald House, and some families couldn't stay throughout their child's hospitalizations. Pam surrounded her daughter with pink girly blankets and pillows, books, and stuffed animals that starkly contrasted with the medical equipment.

"And the doctor keeps telling me about treatments, and I don't know what to do. Jimmy's so far away." Pam's voice was riddled with indecision.

Sara Beth pulled out her earbuds. "Is Daddy coming?"

"No, sweetie. You know he would if he could."

Sara Beth's face fell. "I want Daddy."

"He'll be calling soon, honey." The army had excellent support systems in place overseas for their personnel, but the nine-and-a-half-hour time difference between Memphis and the soldier's location made his Skype calls to his family erratic.

The movie forgotten, Sara Beth asked, "Do you have a daddy, Lani?"

"My mom and dad live in Alaska. . . . It's far away, and really cold." Lani recalled the long, frigid months of seemingly endless night she'd spent there in self-imposed exile.

"I know! I bet you have a *boyfriend!*" Sara Beth snickered, and Lani winked at her.

The girl pointed at the TV screen, where a cartoon character dressed much like a prince was holding hands with a cartoon girl dressed in rags. Cinderella . . . a little girl's benchmark of true love.

"Now, don't you go getting nosey," Pam chided, yet they both looked at Lani expectantly.

Lani laughed. "I *do* have a boyfriend. And he's as handsome as a prince."

Sara Beth giggled, covering her mouth with the hand not attached to the IV line. "So are you gonna be his princess?"

"Well, then who'd be your nurse?"

Sara Beth considered the question thoughtfully. "Okay," she said with a sigh. "I guess if he's a real prince, he'll wait until I get better."

Lani understood Sara Beth's odds of another remission. She quickly put on her busy nurse expression and said, "Watch your movie, and I'll see you two this afternoon."

She left the room, her mind on Dawson. The distance between them was more of an obstacle than she'd thought it would be. She hadn't seen him since July Fourth because he was swamped with work. They texted and talked, but she missed his touch, his presence, especially on long hot summer nights spent alone. She volunteered for extra shifts rather than face the loneliness that left her in a state of suspended animation. Lani never doubted her love for him, but with so much time and distance between them, would this separation send him into the arms of another?

Terri Levine became a miracle worker as she quickly and completely pulled together Sloan's concert. The fairgrounds became the venue, and Sloan would play on a platform stage within the rodeo ring, under the arena's bright lights, with colorful spotlights splashing color and special effects over the stage. Her band would set up in the center, allowing her to move in a circle and give the audience full sight lines to her live performance. The early-August event was set for eight p.m. "I've had a chat with the weather service," Terri told Sloan when she chose the date, "and they've promised the skies will be rain free, under threat of my eternal wrath."

"A frightening thought," Sloan said, amused, knowing she'd give the concert regardless of bad weather.

Publicity began on social media, and the concert was sold out in less than twenty-four hours, with all earnings going into a special trust set up for Lindsey, Sloan's newly discovered half sister, and for Lindsey's son, Sloan's nephew. People who remembered Jerry Sloan from "the good old days" posted their memories about him, and online music sites saw an immediate uptick in sales of his old music. The news thrilled

Lindsey but delighted Sloan, because royalties from the old music would deposit into Jerry's estate, left to Lindsey.

However, Terri lured bigger money through fees that bought entrance into a VIP tent that would offer food and drinks and the chance to meet Sloan in person following the concert. What surprised Sloan was how many well-known country music musicians and performers wrote sizable checks to the concert event. In the final tally, her label covered all the costs to hold the event, and both the arena and the VIP tent promised to be packed with donors and stars.

The news of the concert also came with a benefit to Lindsey that no one had anticipated. As Lindsey's spirits soared, so did her health, the divide between the body and mind breached to offer a magical zone of temporary healing called the bounce back. "I won't miss this," she promised Sloan, with a glow on her face that hadn't been seen during the many weeks of her downward spiral.

"And you won't have to. We're installing a closed-circuit TV in the house, with cameras on-site so you can see the show without risk." Lindsey needed the layer of protection—no crowds, no excess exposure to the outside world.

"But Gloria should go! And Toby—"

"Covered," Sloan assured her. Terri had arranged for a local RN to stay with Lindsey and a sitter to accompany Toby to the concert and bring him home, in order that Gloria could have a good time "stargazing" in the VIP tent.

A week before the concert Sloan was in her Nashville room when Terri, in the city to handle last-minute details, handed her a manila envelope. "Here are the tickets and VIP badges you asked me to set aside. Are you sure you only want *three* besides Gloria's? You can have more. You're the star."

Sloan peeked inside the envelope. Certainly Cole would get a ticket and a name badge. FedEx would deliver the other pair, although she was unsure they'd be used. She hoped they would be. "Terri, I cut ties with this place years ago, so yes, three is enough. Now let's go to dinner. I'm ravenous."

twenty-five

Sloan rehearsed for her concert in Windemere, with the same musicians who'd worked with her on the album. With three days remaining before the event, feeling prepared, nervous, and antsy, she drove to Lindsey's, determined to decompress. Dark rain clouds chased her all the way from her hotel to Lindsey's front door, where Gloria met her, looking distraught. "It's gonna rain, Sloan! Pour. Don't want *nothing* to spoil your concert."

"Nothing's going to spoil it." Sloan tugged her roller bag inside, where the smell of home-cooked biscuits made her mouth water. "Weather's supposed to be clear by Saturday night. And maybe the rain will cool things off a bit too." August was forever hot and steamy in Tennessee. "How's Lindsey?"

"She's restin'."

"Toby?" She glanced around, having expected him to meet her at the door as usual.

"He's camping with Cole."

"In *this* weather?"

"For his birthday, Cole bought Toby some real camping gear . . . a tent, lanterns . . . a bunch of outdoor stuff, and he's been promising they'd camp out tonight in his backyard, but with the rain and storms, they've moved the campsite into his living room."

"Well, fun for Toby. I'll put this in his room and wait for Lindsey to wake up."

She reached for the handle of her bag, but Gloria grabbed hold. "I'll put it away if you'll take Toby's toothbrush over to Cole's. I think the boy forgot it on purpose." Gloria hustled off, and returned with a ziplock bag of toothpaste and a toothbrush. At the sight of the Spider-Man colors and Spidey symbol, a memory crept out and caused Sloan's chest to tighten. Gloria asked, "Can you take it now before the sky opens? So I don't have to leave Lindsey alone?"

Sloan stuffed down the memory, accepted the plastic bag. "Glad to help."

"And hurry back. I'm cookin' up chicken and dumplings and buttermilk biscuits."

Sloan drove to Cole's and had almost made it to the front door when the rain clouds let go.

Cole heard his doorbell, opened the door to see Sloan wet with rain on his welcome mat. A surge of pleasure shot through him. "Hey! Come in. Don't get soaked." He tucked her inside the foyer. "Great to see you."

"I thought I could make it before the rain hit. Sorry." She shook rainwater onto the tiled floor, warmed from head to toe by the voltage of his smile.

"I'll get you a towel."

"Don't bother. . . . I can't stay. I come bearing toothbrush and toothpaste for a certain camper." She held out the bag.

"Toby, it's for you," Cole called over his shoulder, then, leaning closer to Sloan, whispered, "I thought he was traveling light when all he showed up with was pajamas and his baseball glove."

Cole's warm breath fluttered wisps of her hair and sent goose bumps skittering along her skin. She shied away.

Toby ran into the foyer. "Sloan, we're camping! Come see, come see!"

"One towel on its way," Cole said.

Sloan followed Toby into Cole's great room, where a dome-shaped tent of bright green stood in the center of the floor, looking very out of place and giving the room a new-out-of-the-package smell. Cole's sofa had been shoved against one wall, chairs to another. The edges of his nine-foot colorful area rug peeked from beneath the tent. "Wow. It's . . . *huge*. I thought I'd see a pup tent."

"Yeah," Toby said, "ain't it neat!" He pulled her toward an entrance flap. "You gotta come inside. We got sleeping bags, lights, a TV, *everything!*"

Cole returned and handed her a towel. "Almost everything. We left the sink in the kitchen."

She blotted her hair and arms while staring at the tent. Metal poles came together to form a dome in the center of the structure, holding it upright and in perfect symmetry. "You think it's big enough?"

Cole's grin widened. "It sleeps four, just in case he wants to bring a few of his friends along sometime."

"I can stand up in it," Toby announced proudly.

"I can kneel gracefully," Cole said, making her smile.

Toby tugged on Sloan's hand. "Come inside, see our stuff. It's supercool."

Just then a jagged brilliant streak of lightning shot through dark clouds, and a boom of thunder shook the window glass of the great room. "That was close," Cole said, frowning.

Too close. "I should go before it gets worse."

"Not a good idea," Cole said, and before she could insist, the wail of a tornado warning siren cut through the roar of the rain. "That's it. We're all going down to the basement."

"What about Mama?"

"Gloria knows to get down to your basement. It'll be okay."

Sensing the boy's reluctance, Sloan held out her hand. "Come on, Toby. Cole's right. We'll go down together."

They descended the stairs with Cole in the lead, and walked into an inner room with a solid steel door. "My safe room. I built it when I updated the house." When he shut the door, the room went silent. And very dark. Sloan gave an involuntary gasp.

Cole heard her, felt her recoil standing next to him. "Hold on. I've got this." He flicked on an LED lantern and turned the room blue-white.

Sloan took deep breaths, attempting to mask the cold fear that had snaked through her in the darkness.

"Awesome!" Toby whispered.

His word broke the spell of the darkness's hold on her. Feeling childish about her reaction to the dark, Sloan inspected the room and the comforts Cole had stashed for emergencies—floors cushioned with rubber mats, a cluster of LED lanterns, stacks of blankets, pillows, and two plastic containers of food and water.

"This is even cooler than my tent," Toby said, dropping down and rooting through a tub holding food.

"I'm impressed," Sloan said.

But Cole had seen her reaction to the darkness, *fear*.

Maybe the tornado warning had spooked her. "Sit, make yourself comfortable." He set the lantern along a cement wall, turned on another to fill the space with more light. Sloan propped a pillow against the wall next to the light source and sank to the floor. Cole retrieved a battery-operated weather alert radio, fiddled with the knobs to search for information, and sat cross-legged beside her. "I heard that a tornado hit the town a few years back. Were you living here at the time?"

"I was in middle school, and the tornado cut a path right through downtown." An instant image of the trailer where she and her mother had spent so many miserable years flashed in her mind. She had stayed home from school that day and had been alone, and she would never forget the coppery color of the sky, the stillness of the air—like nature was holding its breath—and the feeling of foreboding, just before a funnel cloud touched down and ripped parts of Windemere apart. "We were lucky. It missed us, just intense wind and rain, but downtown and a few farms were hammered." She cast Toby a glance, watched him dig into a box of crackers. "I wouldn't want to go through another one, that's for sure."

The radio crackled, and a robotic voice issued barometric pressures and other numbers. Cole leaned forward. "Sounds like it's passed north of us, so the town caught a break this time." Minutes later, the radio announced an all clear for their area.

"Awww. Is it over?" Toby sounded disappointed.

Cole, grateful they'd dodged the worst, got to his feet. "Come on, we have a campout upstairs. You still want to camp, don't you?"

Toby scrambled up, and Cole led them upstairs by the lantern's light to the great room, where vanished electricity had left the room shrouded in darkness. Toby grabbed a flashlight, and Cole set the lantern on the floor. Sheets of rain still stung the windows, sounding like waves crashing on a shoreline. Sloan shifted, unsure what to do. "I guess it's okay for me to leave. I mean, the danger's over and it's just raining."

Cole's eyes bored into hers. "No way. Trees will be down, roads flooded. Little Man, it seems like we're having company tonight. How about rolling out another sleeping bag for our guest?"

"I can't stay here all night."

"You can't leave either. Extenuating circumstances." Cole's face, lit by the upward glow from the lantern on the floor, made him look otherworldly.

"Yeah!" Toby inserted. "That'll be cool. Like we're rescuing you." He dropped to all fours and crawled inside the tent, then stuck his head out momentarily to say, "And in the morning, Cole's gonna make 'camp pancakes' with chocolate chips and whipped cream!"

"But there's no electricity."

"Gas stove and gas fireplace," Cole said, thumbing over his shoulder. "We know how to camp, don't we, Toby?" They slapped high fives, and Toby scooted backward. As soon as the boy was in the tent, Cole led Sloan into the kitchen area by lantern light. "I know this is awkward for you, but I'm not kidding about it being too dangerous for you to leave tonight. You're safe here."

The storm wasn't the only reason she wanted to leave. Being close to Cole was unnerving, the whisper of his voice, the feel of his warm breath on her face. How could she possibly sleep next to him all night inside a tent? "I can go back to Lindsey's."

"Don't think so. Let me show you something." He walked her to the back door. "Land's low in our area, so it always holds water in heavy rain. The yard's underwater, and so is the driveway and front road." Her safety was primary, but he wanted her to stay, and any reason to keep her with him would do. "I'm playing my paramedic card. Sorry . . . you're stuck here tonight."

"I should call Lindsey." She reached for her cell phone, before remembering it was in her purse, which was—where?

"You can try, but I'm pretty sure the cell towers are jammed this far out. They usually are in any emergency."

"But . . . Lindsey—Aren't you worried about her? She and Gloria are in the dark too."

"Watch," he said, turning her toward the door's windowpanes. He raised the flashlight and flipped it off and on so that the light shone across an expanse of standing water between his and Lindsey's houses. Seconds later another flashlight beamed a staccato pattern. "That's Gloria telling me all's well. I taught her some Morse code, basic stuff. *SOS* and *A-OK*, because electricity and cell phones can fail."

He lowered his flashlight. They were so close, he could smell her rain-damp hair mingling with the scent of her floral perfume. *Intoxicating.* "Plus, I'll need you to stay here with Toby if I get called out on the job. Four-wheel drive, high cab, off-road tires," he added with a grin before she could point out the discrepancy between her staying and him leaving.

Toby was her reason to stay. She gave an involuntary shiver. "My clothes are wet. I—I have nothing to sleep in."

"I have a shirt I'll be glad to loan you, and we'll toss your jeans over a chair to dry."

"You think of everything, don't you?"

"I *don't* think of everything. Otherwise I'd have something besides one of my old work shirts for a pretty woman to wear when she gets stranded in my house on a stormy night."

The absurdity of the whole situation and his good humor made her laugh and lower her defenses. "Well, okay then. . . . Why don't you show me my wardrobe choices? I have standards, you know."

twenty-six

Cole lay listening to Sloan's and Toby's rhythmic breathing from the bedrolls beside him in the tent. The rain had passed, but not the electrical outage, and without AC, the house had become stuffy. He'd brought in a large auxiliary battery from his garage and wired it to a string of twinkle lights, along with a small fan. The tent was too big for the fan to be much help with cooling, but it kept the air moving. All three of them had chosen to sleep atop their sleeping bags . . . too warm to crawl inside. Toby was in between Cole and Sloan, to act as a barrier because Cole knew he might be unable to cope with lying beside her, desiring her as he did.

He rose up on his elbow, watched her as she slept, her flawless face, the tangle of her hair on the pillow, the blond strands catching and holding light like the sparkle of stardust. She wore one of his softest denim shirts, the shirttail long enough to reach her knees. When she'd put it on, Toby had giggled and said, "You look funny."

Cole thought she looked gorgeous and enticingly sexy.

He'd also given her a pair of his running shorts, but she'd had to use a safety pin in the waistband to keep them up. And now she slept, a few feet away in proximity, a world away in reality. *Out of your league,* he reminded himself, and hunkered down, turning his back to her and knowing it was going to be one *helluva* long night.

He must have dozed, because whimpering and soft crying alerted him. Cole flipped over, sat up. "Toby?" But the boy was sleeping. The sounds came from Sloan, soft sobs, but she wasn't awake. Her head tossed from side to side, and the lights reflected her look of pure terror. *A nightmare?* Cole scrambled around Toby, watched Sloan writhe and twist, and was unsure how best to wake her. She looked to be in agony. He straddled her, gripped her shoulders, leaned close, whispered, "Sloan . . . wake up. You're dreaming, honey. Wake up."

Her body arched, her eyes flew open, and he heard her take a deep ragged breath. "It's okay, Sloan. You're safe. I'm right here." It took a few seconds for her eyes to focus. She shuddered, turned her head, wept quietly. He drew her to him while she cried. When her trembling slowed, he whispered, "Let's get out of here so we don't wake Toby."

They crawled out of the tent, and once in the open room she gulped in air. He led her to the sofa pushed aside for the tent, lay down on the cushions, and with her spine pressed against the length of his body, he locked his arms around her in the embrace he'd been trained to do for patients in emotional distress. He stroked her arms to calm and soothe. "You're safe now. I've got you. Nothing can hurt you."

Sloan, awake, turned into him, weeping and balling his T-shirt into her fists. Cole felt the wetness on his skin, and wished he had a wad of tissues, but he wouldn't have moved for all the world. "Bad dream?" Silence. "Tell me, baby, get it out. Let me help." Slowly he felt the tension in her body loosen, her tears lessen. "You had a nightmare. . . . It's over now and you're safe."

"Hands . . . almost . . . got me." Her voice was muffled and sounded childlike. He realized that while she might be awake, the dream still held her captive.

He pressed his lips to the crown of her head, damp with sweat and smelling of fear. "Talking often helps a dream to lose its power. Will you tell me about it?"

"Always . . . same dream . . . years . . ." Her voice, childish and singsong.

He righted her, lifted her chin so that their faces were inches apart and on the same plane. Her eyes were wide, not yet seeing him but instead seeing some distant past. He lightly brushed away a clump of hair stuck to her cheek. "Go on. I'm listening."

"Mama brought men home. Some were nice. But one . . . not very nice." Her voice kept its little-girl cadence. "He—he came into my room at night when Mama was asleep." This in a whisper.

He felt like a rock had settled in his gut. "How old were you when the man came to your room?"

"Five."

He held himself perfectly still, deciding against asking *What happened?* "What did you do when he came into your room?"

She perked. "I hid under my bed. He tried to reach for me, but I lay on my side and made myself very straight and flat against the wall."

"That was smart of you." Cole's mind raged, wanting to tear the unknown guy apart with his bare hands.

She cast her gaze downward, shook her head. "I could hear

his hands scratching on the floor. I held my breath, sucked it all inside me to make me really small. If he couldn't reach me, I didn't have to come out like he kept telling me to."

He imagined the man's hands scraping in the dark, like rats' feet, her tiny body flattened, with nowhere to go. The image made him want to puke.

"Then one night—" She looked up and straight into Cole's eyes.

In the gloomy shadows of the room, so close to her, he watched her eyes begin to clear, and return her to the here and now. He knew that Sloan was fully with him, and silently willed her to finish her sentence, but allowed her to take all the time she needed.

Sloan held Cole's gaze, the child replaced with the grown-up version of herself. She couldn't hold back. "One night he grabbed me. He dragged me from under the bed. I guess I'd grown some and wasn't small enough anymore."

Her voice was stronger, in control. His pulse pounded, and he steeled himself for what she might say. "Did he hurt you?"

On her face, was a sly smile. "I bit him so hard, I tasted his blood. And I screamed and kicked, and he yowled and called me names, and we woke up LaDonna and she came to my room."

Her finish to the story left his insides watery. "Clever girl. You were brave and smart." He ran his thumb under her eye, absorbing tears and perspiration. "Rest now."

Sloan snuggled down again to his chest. "She made the man leave, but she was mad at me, and let me know it. You see, the guy had money. She'd let him buy me toys and give her stuff she wanted. She let me know I'd lost her a good meal ticket."

The words were matter-of-fact, said in a monotone. Cole

cringed. "The guy was a disgusting creep. She should have called the cops. Why didn't she report him?"

Sloan had fallen sound asleep in his arms. He kissed the top of her head. "You got out, Sloan. You made it." He understood her better now, her dedication to making it in the music world. Her devotion to that goal had probably saved her from a life like her mother's. He shifted, careful not to disturb her, scooted down far enough to rest his head on the arm of the sofa, and, cradling her, whispered, "P.S. . . . I love you."

Cole slept fitfully, startling awake from time to time to see that Sloan, still tucked in his embrace, was sleeping soundly. When the first streaks of dawn fell through the arched windows, he carefully inched himself off the sofa without waking her, stretched his cramped muscles, smoothed his hand along her cheek. The room was stifling, so he didn't bother to cover her. He crawled inside the tent, only marginally cooler from the fan, and checked on Toby. The boy slept, but Cole knew he'd soon be up, because Toby's internal clock seemed set for six a.m., and sure enough, the minute Cole stretched out on his sleeping bag, Toby began to stir.

Cole had hoped for time to process what Sloan had told him, and what he'd felt with her curled in his arms all night. He wanted her in all her complexity. He wanted to drive away her demons, comfort her. Love her. But reality struck, and he reminded himself that they lived in different universes. She was riding a rocket to the stars, and he was plodding along on planet Earth.

Cole heard Toby come over, but kept his eyes closed.

"Hey, Cole! You awake?"

Cole opened one eye. "I am now."

Toby tittered. "Come on, wake up. I'm starving!" He glanced back at Sloan's empty bedroll. "Hey, where'd she go?"

"Sofa is my guess."

"She'd never make it camping all night in the real woods, I bet."

Cole sat up. "She's tougher than you think, Little Man. Don't think the real woods would be a problem for her at all."

———

Sloan woke to the smells of frying bacon and maple syrup, blinked at sunlight filling the room. She saw Toby sitting at the kitchen table wolfing down pancakes, and Cole standing at his fancy stove, flipping more pancakes on a griddle. She sat up, and Toby caught her movement. "Hey, Sloan! We're already up."

She cleared her throat. "So I see."

Cole's eyes met hers. "Good morning. I have a stack hot off the griddle."

"I'm not much of a breakfast eater." She was embarrassed this morning, remembering how she'd clung to him sobbing during the night, telling him about the past that she'd never shared with another living soul.

"Mama says breakfast is the most important meal," Toby chirped. "These are yummy!" Reluctantly she sauntered over, took a seat. Toby made a smiley face with a stream of whipped cream on his oversized pancake already swimming in syrup.

"Chocolate chips?" Cole asked.

"Just a couple of plain ones."

He dropped two onto a plate and walked it over to her.

Outside the bay window she saw yard puddles reflecting

morning sunshine. The outdoors looked laundry-day clean. "Water gone down?"

"Mostly. Ditches are full and tree branches lying around." He set hot coffee beside her plate, took the chair next to hers so that she was in between him and Toby.

She sipped the coffee, found it excellent.

"It'll be muddy at the fairgrounds, but it won't ruin your concert."

The concert. She hadn't given it a thought since the day before, after arriving with so much enthusiasm. Time to get back on track.

Just then the electricity hummed on, blasting cool air from an overhead ceiling vent and turning on lights that had been shining the night before. Toby let out a whoop, sopped up a last bite of pancake. Cole grinned. "Toby, go get your gear together, and don't forget that a good camper always cleans up after himself."

The boy put his plate in the sink with a clatter and disappeared around the half wall, and presumably into the tent. Sloan, alone with Cole, felt nervous and edgy. Cole recognized her unease. "For what it's worth, I don't believe you'll have that dream again. You banished it when you talked about it."

"I used to have it when I was a kid, but it went away, and came back months ago. I don't know why."

"Stress dream. You're under a lot of pressure."

"*That's* not going to change."

"What happened back then can't hurt you now, Sloan. You handled it with amazing courage."

The look in his eyes turned her mushy. She stood abruptly. "I better get my gear together too."

"Your clothes are dry, and I laid them on the bed in my

guest room, down the hall." He pointed toward the opposite end of the house. "Next to my bedroom."

Their eyes met, held, and she felt herself flush like a schoolgirl. "I'll find it."

"And thank you for the concert ticket and VIP badge. Your concert will be great, and a real help for Lindsey and Toby. You're a hero."

She didn't want him thinking more of her than was true. "My motives aren't totally pure, Cole. Windemere was never kind to me, and I wanted to make it big so people would be sorry they hadn't been nicer when I was growing up. In truth no one ever really cared in the first place. I'm just a girl from the trailer park who made good. To me, Lindsey is the real hero."

twenty-seven

"We didn't have to come, you know."

"I took time off and drove from Memphis. We're staying." Lani kissed Dawson's cheek, and he reluctantly handed his keys to the valet parking attendant. Only special guests received such special service. All others were parking in the outlying lots of the fairgrounds. "And the note she sent with the tickets was kind and thoughtful. She *wants* us here, Dawson."

They were shown to the front row of a section of padded chairs, set on thick artificial turf, the only seating on the ground facing center stage, and except for lighting, sound techs, and a cameraman on a dolly, the audience in the chairs would have a perfect sight line to the guitarists, keyboard player, and drummer. And also to Sloan, when she stepped onstage. More than a thousand people packed the rodeo arena, built for cowboys and bucking broncs, but the audience seated front and center were "favored" attendees, men and women, strangers he assumed were important in Sloan's music sphere. However, this first row, his and Lani's row, was cordoned off with a red rope, underlining that they were Sloan's *very* special guests.

Dawson balked over sitting in the front row, but Lani tugged his hand, and he followed her to their assigned seats. He fidgeted, wary about the night ahead. True, he and Sloan had buried their past, but he was concerned about Lani. In the few months she'd spent at St. Jude's, she'd turned a corner emotionally. Her move to Memphis had been hard on him, but right for her, and he didn't want this evening showcasing Sloan to set her back.

As if sensing his thoughts, Lani laced her fingers through his. "It'll be all right. Tonight's her gift to us, to what we went through together. Music is how she communicates."

He gripped Lani's hand, not as confident about Sloan's motives but willing to rely on Lani's belief in the goodness of people. And after all, Sloan's purpose for the concert was altruistic, all about helping Lindsey Ridley.

Lani peeked down the row of chairs, saw Gloria and, beside her, Toby. He looked adorable, wearing new jeans and a bright blue polo shirt, and his reddish hair was slicked down. She caught Toby's eye and waved, leaned forward, elbowed Dawson. "Isn't that Cole sitting at the end of the row? You remember, the guy from the restaurant?" She waggled her fingers at him, and he gave her a thumbs-up.

Dawson nodded a greeting to Cole, while realizing that Cole's seat in the front row spoke of his importance to Sloan. *Interesting.*

The stadium lights dimmed, and an announcer stepped forward, followed by the band members. The crowd stomped and whistled. The emcee welcomed everyone, gave a short reminder of the concert's true purpose, and then said, "Here she is—country music's newest star, and Windemere's own."

Sloan ran from under the raised stage and up a short flight of steps into a blaze of spotlights, and launched into a fast-paced number from her *American Singer* win. The crowd let out a deafening roar. She wore gold and white, head to toe, a tank top that glittered with sequins, white fitted jeans, and gold leather boots dusted with rhinestones. Her amplified voice rocked the arena.

Cole couldn't take his eyes off her. She dazzled, sizzled, never stopped moving on the stage, rounding the platform, sliding lightning fast from number to number, singing songs from her album, and songs made famous by others. And when the crowd screamed for her to sing "Somebody's Baby," she stood center stage in a single spotlight, held up her hand until a hush fell. "This is for Lindsey, my sister." And Sloan sang the words with such emotion that the whole arena held up lighted cell phones in tribute to a woman they had never met but who lay dying a few miles away. When Sloan took a bow and started to exit the stage, people screamed for an encore.

Sloan said something over her shoulder to the band and walked to the edge of the platform. She looked down at the first row, in Cole's direction, raised the mike, and announced, "This is dedicated to all you shy people, you who stand with someone special in the moonlight and don't know what to do!" Behind her the band erupted into a driving-fast tempo, and she belted out the song "Passionate Kisses," made famous by Mary Chapin Carpenter. When Sloan hit the lyric *"Give me what I deserve, 'cause it's my right. . . . Passionate kisses, I want passionate kisses from you. . . ."* she pointed at Cole and blew a kiss.

The crowd went crazy.

Cole threw his head back and roared out a laugh. From a few chairs away Dawson Berke watched the interplay between

Sloan and Cole and remembered what it had felt like when Sloan Quentin had sung to him. *High school.* She'd been dressed more biker-chick than country-glitter. Another time and place, dark times that had almost wrecked his soul. Lani squeezed his hand. Assurance. He leaned into her ear. "I love you."

She turned her head, and he saw her smile. *"I love you too,"* she mouthed.

He gave Sloan a measured look, watched her waving to the audience on its feet and screaming her name as she was blowing them goodbye kisses. She was beautiful, possessor of a stunning talent, and now she owned the dream that had driven her ever since childhood. And driven her away from him. She was a star. Without a second thought, he took Lani in his arms, and while people surged around them, and with him oblivious to time, place, and social propriety, he kissed her . . . passionately.

———

Inside the VIP tent, Cole felt like a fish out of water, engulfed in a flood of humanity he didn't know and didn't belong to. He had hoped to at least tell Sloan hello, but she was constantly moving from group to group, propelled by her agent, giving attention to all the high rollers who'd paid for badges to enter the tent and meet her. Toby had been taken home, and Gloria was somewhere in the mash of rich and famous people. He navigated around groups and couples like a swimmer avoiding rocks and shoals, to make his way to the buffet tables, where he stopped and grabbed a plate. He was picking his way through mountains of appetizers when from behind him, a woman's voice said, "I saw the way Sloan aimed that last song straight at you. You think she's pretty hot stuff, don't you?"

He turned to face a woman he'd never met, who was wearing too-tight jeans and a too-low-cut blouse, and whose eyes broadcast that she'd also had too much to drink. "Are you speaking to me?"

She gave a sloppy smile. "I was sitting a few rows behind you, and I saw her shtick, and trust me, I've seen her do it to lots of other guys. It's her trademark . . . hanging over some poor schlep, making him think he's special."

Cole disliked the woman instantly. "Have we ever met?"

"I'm Kathy Bosch. That's my husband, Marvin, over there." She waved vaguely with her wineglass toward a group of men, and red wine splashed over the rim. "I live in Miami now, my husband's in shipping, but I grew up in this sorry-ass little town. Went to high school here. I was Kathy Madison then. You didn't go to school here, did you? I would have remembered a man who looked like you, honey."

Cole took a step back. "Ma'am, would you like something to eat?"

She snickered, continued as if he'd not spoken. "You know, the minute the news went online that Sloan was givin' a concert, I said to Marv, 'I want to go to that one, sweetie. Just write a nice fat check that'll get us into that after-concert party, 'cause I went to school with her.' . . . She was Sloan Quentin back then. And she may call herself Sloan Gabriel now, but back then she was just trailer trash."

Cole felt as if he'd been shoved. "Now, wait a minute—"

Kathy went innocent. "Just sayin' people don't really change who they are down deep."

"Why, Kathy! What an unexpected surprise." The sudden

rescue came from Lani, who inserted herself between Kathy and Cole.

Kathy looked flustered, quickly regained equilibrium, and offered Lani a sanguine smile. "I *thought* that was you in the front row, but from the back, I couldn't be sure, with your hair longer."

"In the flesh," Lani said, her gaze cool and challenging. Without taking her eyes off Kathy, she said to Cole, "Kathy and I were friends in high school."

Cole heard her emphasis on *were*. "That's what she was telling me." The venom in Kathy's voice talking about Sloan was unforgettable. "She says she lives in Miami and that her husband's in shipping."

Lani pinned Kathy with her brown eyes. "And yet here you are. You came all this way for Sloan's concert? I'm surprised."

"I came to visit my mama. She's been sick," was Kathy's petulant defense.

Different story to a different listener, Cole thought.

"Sorry to hear about your mom," Lani said. "So, you doing well in Miami?" There was no way for Lani to miss Kathy's diamond chandelier earrings and the diamond rings on her left hand, with stones the size of a bird's eggs.

"My husband's real good to me. All I have to say is 'Sweetie, I want . . . ' and he buys it. Best thing I ever did was get out of this place. Horrid little town." She plucked a grape from a fruit platter on the table and popped it into her mouth. "You're doing well, I reckon?"

Cole noted that the longer Kathy dialogued with Lani, the thicker and syrupier her voice became. *You can take the girl out of the South, but not the South out of the girl* took on meaning for him.

"Really well. I have my RN degree, and I *work* for a living . . . spend hours *upright*."

Cole winced at Lani's slam while silently applauding her, and was glad to be on the sidelines.

Drunk or not, Kathy caught it too, because bright spots of color appeared on her cheeks. "And I recognized the guy you were sitting with tonight. . . . You *finally* got Dawson Berke away from Sloan. I surely remember how you used to moon over him when he was in Sloan's clutches. How'd you manage that after—"

"Good night, Kathy." Lani hooked her arm through Cole's, spun on a dime, and walked them both away from the buffet table.

"She's a nasty little piece of work," Cole said. He felt Lani trembling on his arm.

"Yes, she always was."

"Hard to believe you were friends."

"It took me a while to catch on." Lani smiled up at him.

"Thanks for the rescue." Cole scanned the ocean of people. "Where's Dawson?"

"Out front getting the valet to bring his truck."

Cole's head was buzzing with questions he wanted to ask. He was struggling to form one that wouldn't be too invasive when Lani's phone buzzed. "That's him texting me now." She peered up at Cole. "Pay no attention to Kathy. She disliked Sloan because Sloan was with a guy Kathy crushed on."

"Already forgotten." He kept Lani's arm inside his elbow. "Let me walk you out. I wouldn't want you to step on a snake on the way."

"I'll take your offer."

Minutes later Cole stood outside watching Dawson's taillights disappear. The muffled sound of music and chatter came from behind him, and with no desire to return inside, he handed his ticket to a valet for his truck to be brought around. While he waited in the muggy August night, he revisited parts of the evening—Sloan, holding hundreds of people in her musical spell, her voice and body language sending the song "Passionate Kisses" straight at him. He thought of the nasty woman Kathy, poised to spill dirt about Sloan all over him. Of Lani coming to Sloan's defense. Sloan. Dawson. Lani. Whatever had happened years before had forged a union that somehow bound them together, like it or not. Cole was an outsider, an observer unable to see through the fog of their yesterdays and penetrate the meaning of their triad.

twenty-eight

The day after the concert Sloan parked her rental car in Lindsey's driveway, jumped out, and hurried to the door. She was booked on a six o'clock flight to LA and knew she couldn't stay long, but she hadn't wanted to head off without telling Lindsey goodbye. She glanced toward Cole's place, had hoped to see him before she left, and felt a keen edge of disappointment to see that his truck was gone.

Inside she smelled food being cooked, and in the kitchen she discovered Toby standing on a chair in front of the gas stove. A flame under a cast iron pan burned bright blue. "What are you doing?"

"Making Mama's lunch." He grinned and waved a spatula. "She likes my grilled cheese. It's her favorite."

"And you cook all by yourself?"

"I'm not a *baby*." He looked insulted.

Sloan saw that the countertop was strewn with blocks of cheeses, an open tub of butter, a loaf of bread, and several sharp knives. "Where's Gloria?"

"Grocery store."

"Does she let you cook when she's gone?"

He wouldn't meet her eyes. "She cut the cheese for me before she left, and I know how to do the rest. Cole taught me. I use three different kinds of cheeses, buttered bread, and a hot fry pan."

She was certain Cole would have supervised any cooking Toby did. "Can I help?"

He slid the spatula under the sandwich and flipped it over. "I got it. See? It's perfect!"

She saw that it was, and thought back to when she was a kid making meals out of anything she could find because LaDonna was out partying. "Looks tasty."

Toby placed the sandwich on a paper plate beside the stove, turned off the gas, and hopped down from the chair. He held up the plate, smiling broadly. "Told you I could do it."

Sloan followed him into Lindsey's room, where she was propped up on several pillows. Oxygen cannulas stretched from her nose to a bedside oxygen tank. Dark depressions made half circles under her eyes, and her cheeks looked as if they had melted away. Just the day before, Lindsey had looked rosier, her face fuller, and she hadn't been on oxygen.

Lindsey held out her hands for the plate and gave Sloan a wan smile. "I'm so happy you stopped by before going home."

LA, home? Sloan had never thought of the city that way. She lived in an apartment leased from a real estate management company.

Lindsey hugged Toby. "Baby, run on now and let me eat in peace and talk to Sloan." Once Toby was gone, she set the plate aside and took Sloan's hand, urging her to sit on the bed. "Your concert was amazing. I can't thank you enough for setting everything up so I could 'attend.'" Lindsey moved and winced. Sloan winced in empathy. "Anyway, getting to watch you perform was one of the highlights of my life. Oh, how I wished Daddy could have been here to see you. You were so pretty up there, and you had people eating out of the palm of your hand."

"Show-biz hype." The concert had raised a large amount of money to pay off Lindsey's medical expenses and also to create a trust fund for Toby's future.

"I was hoping you'd stay around a few more days," Lindsey said.

"Me too, but Terri has a load of interviews lined up for me. I have to leave, but I promise to come back for Labor Day."

"Cole's doing his annual Labor Day cookout, a barbeque, so you have to come."

"I won't miss it." Her phone chirped with a text message. Sloan read it, sighed. "The airline reminding me of my flight." She still had to drive back to Nashville, turn in her rental car, and navigate through TSA to her boarding gate. "I hate to rush off, but I must."

"Thank you from the bottom of my heart." Lindsey cradled Sloan's hand on her cheek. "I need to ask a favor before you go."

"Anything."

Lindsey's gaze drifted to the paper plate. "Would you please take this sandwich with you? I can't swallow a thing, and I don't want to disappoint my Toby."

***

Sunday morning sunlight splashed across Dawson's balcony and the café table where he and Lani ate a leisurely breakfast, both postponing her leaving for Memphis as long as possible.

199

Dawson shoved back from the table, stretched his long legs out in front of him, and continued listening to Lani tell him about her encounter with Kathy and Cole the night before, what she'd overheard before stepping between them. "I don't remember Kathy," he said, "but from the sound of things, I wouldn't want to." He took a swig of coffee. "Question . . . why did you feel the need to defend Sloan to the woman?"

Seeing guarded coolness in Dawson's eyes, Lani settled her fork on her plate. "Because I thought it was wrong for Kathy to trash Sloan, spread gossip from old days in high school just because she never liked Sloan . . . and especially after all she's done to help Lindsey. It was just plain wrong to say hateful things about her to Cole."

"How do you think he fits in?"

"He's Lindsey's neighbor and friend, and I'm pretty sure he's crazy about Sloan."

"His mistake."

"Don't be that way. We all saw how she sang that last song right to him. He means something to her too."

"Sloan already has everything she ever wanted—her name in lights, people all over the world playing her music, adoration by the masses." Agitated, he cleared his dishes and went inside, where he dumped the plates and utensils into the sink.

Moments later Lani was behind him, her arms around his waist, her cheek resting against his back. "We're not fighting, are we? It's not the way I want to leave you, Daw."

He heaved a sigh, turned, and wrapped her in his arms. "Sorry, didn't mean to get all wound up. It's just that it's August." In tandem they turned their heads to stare at the calendar hanging on a nail in the wall, one particular day circled in black ink and marked with Dawson's hand-drawn balloon.

August had been the month when Sloan and Dawson had fractured and split apart. Three years later on a cold February day, Lani had stepped into the picture and changed it forever.

Tears swam in Lani's eyes. "Did you think I'd forgotten what's special about that date? I could never forget! I purposely worked double shifts that day at the hospital. I was so wiped out, all I could do was fall into bed at midnight, so I understand how hard August is for you." Grief was like that, two steps forward, one step back. It lurked in the background, and on some level owned its victims for the rest of their lives.

"Not all of it . . . like right now," he said, placing a kiss on her forehead. He rocked her gently while they stood without a hairsbreadth between them. "I'm all right, baby . . . just wishing you didn't have to go." He closed his eyes to shut out the sight of the ink-stained date on the calendar, and the memories that always came with it.

———

"Congratulations. Your album is number one on the Billboard country charts and number seven on the pop charts. The concert was a success in every way . . . money for Lindsey, and *you* in the public eye. Huge success, Sloan. Good news. Enjoy it."

Sloan had slept in and was coming into Terri's office on Monday afternoon when her agent met her at the door with news of her album. "You got coffee?"

"I thought you might be a little more excited about your numbers."

"Jet lag." Sloan sauntered to the familiar orange chair in front of Terri's desk and poured herself a cup from the silver carafe sitting on a silver tray. "Of course it's good news. My mind's still on Lindsey, that's all. She didn't look very good when I left."

Terri scooted behind her desk, swiveled her chair to stare quietly as Sloan sipped her coffee. "Honey, you've done everything you can for Lindsey. You've given Toby a future and his mother peace of mind. I'm not unsympathetic here, but you need to start living your life again, and let me tell you, it's a beautiful life."

"I hate that little town and the hold it has on me."

Terri steepled her fingers. "I felt the same about Hoboken, New Jersey, when I moved out bag and baggage. Couldn't get far enough away fast enough. I came here with nothing but determination, and for the good weather, of course. So, let me give you some news to lift your spirits. What are you doing on Labor Day?" Sloan, who'd been staring into her coffee cup, looked up. Terri gave a Cheshire cat grin. "I got a call this morning. How'd you like to open for the Rick Searle Band in Atlanta's Mercedes-Benz Stadium?"

Sloan shot out of the chair. "Rick Searle! Are you kidding? They're the biggest band in country music!" The band had shot to the top of the music charts a few years before, and every album they produced went to gold and platinum, one to triple platinum.

"Yes, they are, and their fan base is rabid. And the band wants you to open for them."

Sloan paced, her head spinning. She stopped, whipped around, ran to the desk. "I thought Lauren was opening for them." Lauren was a well-established singer already.

"She was, but polyps on her vocal cords started hemorrhaging. She had surgery last week, and she can't speak for a month, much less sing. Don't worry, she'll be back in six months better than ever, but she's out for Searle's Labor Day show. And Searle wants *you* in her place. I know this is last-minute, but it's huge. I accepted on your behalf."

In the blink of an eye, Sloan's priorities shifted and turned her world upside down. Windemere and her Labor Day plans were whisked away and quickly shelved. "What do I have to do?"

"On Wednesday, you're going to Sondra's studio for a wardrobe tweak." The atelier was one of Hollywood's most famous, with creations worn by many a star on Oscar night. "I'm having new outfits designed for you, head to toe change-up. I want you looking like the star you are onstage . . . gowns with lots of glamour that show off all your assets. At the end of the month you'll go to Atlanta for rehearsals with the band. Rick's a taskmaster, but he knows what his audience likes and wants, and he always delivers. Sound like a game plan you can embrace?"

The opportunity was golden, beyond her wildest imagination. Her spirits soared, and she thought of what climbers must experience when reaching the top of a mountain. She offered a self-satisfied smile. "Embracing the plan with arms wide open. Wouldn't miss it for all the world."

twenty-nine

The first time Sloan stepped inside the Mercedes-Benz Stadium, the sheer enormity of the place took her breath. A stunning wall of glass soared upward in a spacious lobby where banks of escalators led to upper levels that could seat eighty thousand people, all with a clear view of the main attraction—the Atlanta Falcons football field. Three hundred feet above the green patch of exquisite turf, a hundred-foot 360-degree LED video board encircled pinwheel metal panels that could retract and allow daylight to flood the arena. She was standing at a railing, gazing in awe at the field, when a woman came to stand alongside her.

"Impressive, isn't it?"

"Words can't express." Sloan turned to see a pixie-sized brown-haired woman who offered a warm smile.

"A modern day marvel to the gods of football. I'm Kathryn Searle, and you're Sloan, aren't you? Pleased to meet you."

"My pleasure, for sure."

"Our tour bus just pulled up and the baby's asleep, so I

thought I'd take a peek while I could. The guys will be coming along in a minute. I threatened their lives if they woke our baby."

Sloan had flown into Atlanta the day before and checked into a downtown hotel room Terri had reserved. A driver had picked her up around noon and brought her to the stadium, where security guards had been told to expect her. "I've watched games on TV, but even the overhead photos from a blimp can't really do justice to the place. It's *huge*." She again looked upward at the vast number of seats.

"Those far upper tiers will be closed off for our show. Our audience will be in the lower two. Based on ticket sales so far, we're expecting around forty thousand. The Falcons are on the road for the next two weeks, or we'd have never been able to get this space for our show."

Sloan's biggest live audience to date had been five thousand, in the late spring and early summer days before her album release. As if sensing Sloan's apprehension, Kathryn said, "Ten thousand of those tickets were sold after it was announced that you'd be performing too. We're pleased to have you on board."

Just then six men, the Searle band, barreled in noisily, Rick the tallest and most recognizable. After a round of introductions, some horseplay, and verbal banter, Sloan felt less like a stranger on the sidelines. Rick settled everyone down. "Our crew's in the bus behind us, to start setting up. What about your musicians?"

"Coming from Nashville tonight."

Rick put his arm around his wife and said to her, "The girls on the bus want to shop. You want to go with them?"

"Not much fun taking a cranky baby. I'll stay on the bus with him, maybe get some sleep."

He kissed her. "We'll wrap the tour in October. Then we'll stay home. I promise."

Kathryn gazed out at the empty stadium, a wistful expression on her face. "Until the road calls you back."

Sloan understood. She'd felt the exhaustion of touring herself, of sleeping on planes and grabbing catnaps on buses, of eating a diet of road food and giving shows in cities she couldn't even recall. Must have been even harder with a baby. Still it was the life she'd planned. Fame came with a price, and she was willing to pay it.

"The hospice people says it's nearin' the end for Lindsey. She's had a couple more brain seizures, so they're keepin' her heavily sedated."

Walking to his truck parked outside the fire station, Cole heard a tremble in Gloria's voice through his phone. "Just getting off from my shift. I'll swing by the house."

"I—I told my supervisor that I wouldn't be coming in for the rest of this week. I just think I should hang here at the house with the hospice folks. I want to be here . . . be *with* her as much as I can."

Cole closed his eyes, pressed finger and thumb into his closed lids, fighting exhaustion. "Okay. But I don't think we should say anything to Toby yet."

"I won't, but Monday's Labor Day and there's no school, so he'll be home, and I'm not sure I can keep myself together in front of him."

"I'll keep him busy. Stay calm."

Cole disconnected and climbed inside his truck, where he sat staring out the windshield at green trees that would soon dress in the colors of autumn, colors Lindsey would not see again. His thoughts drifted to Sloan in Atlanta rehearsing for a concert, and he wondered if he should let her know. The Searle appearance would make her star shine more brightly, shoot ever higher. Yet the campout night lingered in his head. Sloan, scared by nightmares. His arms around her, holding off the dark. Her story of a scarred childhood. Then came images of her concert, where she had stood onstage, a sparkling vision of a woman in total command, a princess reigning over a kingdom that adored her.

He'd read that the Searle show was breaking ticket sales records for a country band concert. Cole realized there was nothing Sloan could do for Lindsey now, nothing more anyone could do. He forced away thoughts of Sloan Gabriel and his desire for what he wanted but could not have. He cranked the truck's engine and exited the lot, heading not home but to the house next door, where death crouched.

"You coming to the after-party?"

The question came from Tate, the band's bass guitarist, who'd been flirting with Sloan since the first day of rehearsals. "I'm not one to miss a party."

Tate's grin widened. "Good, 'cause I'm looking for an excuse to stay close to you after the show." He winked and strutted off. Sloan watched him go, a good-looking guy with a hard body, a killer smile, and a glib line for women. Most of Rick's band and crew either were married or had girlfriends. Tate had let her know from the start that he was unattached and interested. She'd met men like him—one-nighters, *Good night, good morning, goodbye.*

This was concert night, and she'd be onstage in less than two hours. As the stadium filled, her nerves were tighter than a steel drum. Through the glass wall she saw the buildings of downtown Atlanta cut sharp lines into a red-and-gold sunset sky and streaks of pink clouds. *Beautiful night*, she told herself. She was ready. The band was ready. The fans were ready. A trifecta.

Her life was moving at breakneck speed. CC had sent three new songs for her to evaluate for her second album, scheduled to begin recording in January. Another video was in the works, and her fall tour schedule was full—certainly not as big and grand as Searle's, but one day, she told herself, it would be.

Terri had sent roses to her hotel room to celebrate her big night, compliments of the agency and Sloan's record label. Sloan swore not to disappoint either. *Labor Day* . . . it would be the beginning of a whole new chapter in her life.

———

"I think it's time to gather the family, because it won't be long now," the hospice worker told Gloria, who was curled up on the sofa with a box of tissues.

Cole was standing on his deck grilling hamburgers with Toby, knowing that people at Lindsey's had to eat even if they insisted they weren't hungry. His plan was to bring the cooked burgers to Lindsey's, but then Gloria texted—Come now. He shut off the gas tank on the half-done burgers, closed the lid on the grill. "Time to go," he said to the boy.

"Is it happenin' now?"

"Soon." There'd been no hiding the truth from Toby so

close to the end. Cole took the boy's hand. "What say we walk over?"

Toby slipped his hand into Cole's, and they went down the deck steps and across the grass and clods of red dirt that separated their houses. "Will leaving our house and going to heaven hurt Mama? . . . You know, like the cancer hurts?"

"No . . . all her hurting is done now. Her soul just steps from one place to the other, like when you fall asleep in the dark and wake up in the sunshine."

Toby looked up at a red-and-gold sunset sky and streaks of pink clouds. "Does the sun shine in heaven?"

"Always. Forever."

"That's good. Mama likes sunshine."

———

Sloan couldn't come down from her adrenaline high. The rush she'd felt from forty thousand voices chanting her name, stomping, cheering, shouting after every song, had been exhilarating but had left her feeling as restless as a caged cat. The wrap party was being held in a plush VIP lounge on a secluded upper deck of the stadium, with cushy furniture, a fully stocked wraparound bar, and a panoramic plate glass window where Sloan was looking down on the stage. Lights and sound equipment were waiting to be broken down, boxed, and carried to trailers and buses that would take Rick's show to the next scheduled concert tomorrow, after a night's rest in a hotel.

She was sipping her second margarita when Tate came alongside her, a drink in one hand and a plate of food in the other. "I brought this for you, pretty woman. Been watching, and haven't seen you take a single bite. I'm way different. I can't eat a thing before a show, but after? Starving! Rick always gets the best caterers in a city for his crew, so try a taste." He proffered the plate, along with a devilish smile. "You won't be sorry."

"Why do I think you're talking about more than the food?"

He laughed heartily. "A guy can dream, can't he? You were dynamite onstage tonight. Crowd was feeling it, and so was the band."

"I was glad to be a part of it."

"Been hoping you and me can carry some of that good feeling forward."

Behind them people chattered, laughed. Bartenders mixed and poured drinks, and servers whisked away used plates and glasses. She nibbled on a shrimp from the plate, glanced at him through thick eyelashes, realizing they'd been on this path moving toward this moment for days. "What feeling would that be?"

He set the plate and his glass on a cocktail table, put her margarita glass next to his, and leaned into her. "Let me show you."

Tate kissed her, lightly at first, and when she didn't pull away, the kiss deepened. She tasted the smoky flavor of whiskey on his tongue. Blood rushed hot in her veins. It had been a long time since she'd been with a man. Her arms encircled his neck, every nerve end throbbing.

He broke the kiss. "Lordy, you taste good." He pressed her closer, and she felt the hardness of his body. Desire burned through her like a forest fire. He trailed kisses along her throat, nuzzled her ear. "Come back to my room with me. You won't regret it."

What could it hurt? One night, and then both of them going their separate ways.

The last time she'd spent the night in a man's arms, Cole's arms, she'd been a blubbering mess, dumping some long-ago fears and hurts on him. There would be none of that tonight with Tate. Just heat and passion, and pleasure. "I have to grab my purse."

They waited for the elevator, him bouncing on the balls of his feet. She rooted for her cell phone on the ride down. "I haven't checked messages since this morning."

"No problem." The elevator dinged its arrival on the ground floor, where a lone security guard called a cab for them.

While they waited, she scanned the list of text messages . . . several from Terri and CC, one from Cole. Her heart kicked up a beat. She tapped the phone's surface and opened Cole's message.

Lindsey passed away tonight, 10:40. Funeral on Thursday. Come if you're able.

thirty

Cole was standing at the front window in Lindsey's living room when a black town car drove up the driveway. Sloan exited the car, wearing a scarf and large round dark sunglasses that covered half her face. The driver followed with her bags. She had texted Cole at seven in the morning that she was on her way. The sight of her never failed to lift his spirits— even now in his sorrow over Lindsey. Sloan faltered at the front door, but he quickly crossed the room and flung it open. "Come on in. I've been waiting for you."

Earlier she'd showered, thrown on an old pair of jeans and a tee emblazoned with the word *Nashville* and stuffed everything she owned inside two roller suitcases, including the thousands of dollars' worth of new costumes. She had washed her face clean of the stage makeup, hadn't bothered to do anything more constructive than put on lipstick, and paced until the bellboy had arrived to take her luggage to the lobby, where a car and driver waited curbside. Of all the things she'd been thinking of the night before, Lindsey's dying had not been on her radar. Now all she wanted to do was throw herself into Cole's arms. Instead she stepped into the silent house, tossed off her sunglasses, and gave him a repentant look. "I didn't get your message until two-thirty this morning, and by then it was too late to schedule a car."

Her eyes were red, puffy, and swollen from crying. He longed to take her in his arms. "You're here now. That's what matters."

The house smelled of bacon and eggs, burnt toast. Sloan's stomach went queasy. He opened his arms, and she caved into him with a gush of tears. "I should have . . . been here. . . ." Sloan hadn't slept well in more than twenty-four hours, not the night before the concert—too hyped before her performance—not in her hotel, not on the long drive from Atlanta. She felt light-headed from exhaustion and sorrow. "I'm so sorry, Cole. So sorry I didn't know . . . sooner."

"It wouldn't have mattered. Believe me, Lindsey would have wanted you to perform, and me too. She slipped into a coma and never woke up. Last night she left us, gently and without pain." In his job, Cole had seen enough people die to know Lindsey's death had been a "good" one. "I hated to send you the news in a text that should have been communicated personally with a phone call, but your phone just went to message every time I tried."

"My phone was turned off, and I didn't look at it until I got back to my hotel room. You did the right thing. I wouldn't have wanted you to wake me up this morning to tell me she was gone. I want to be *here*." Sloan couldn't confess that the text also had stopped her from making a big mistake with Tate. When she'd burst out crying, and saying that her sister had died, Tate had hastily put her into the cab and sent her to the hotel alone. And now, with her ear pressed to Cole's chest, listening to the rhythm of his heart, strong and steady, her jangled nerves calmed, as if a balm had been spread over an open wound.

Cole could have held her forever, but she stepped away, and reluctantly he let go. "Would you like anything? . . . Coffee? Food?"

She had eaten nothing since the lone shrimp the night before but wasn't hungry. "I had a cup of coffee on the car ride." She took a ragged breath. "Cole, can I see her room?" She thought maybe the room would bring her closer to Lindsey's spirit.

He led the way, and when she entered, fresh tears filled her eyes. The bed had been stripped to the bare mattress, all the pill bottles swept from the dresser, everything made tidy. Made as hollow as the feeling inside Sloan's heart. *Empty . . . vacated . . . gone.*

"Gloria and the hospice worker did this last night. Gloria said that's how they do things at the place where she works . . . strip beds and pack up everything. She was about to squirt air freshener, but I told her no. I didn't want Toby coming in here, with every trace of his mother erased."

Toby. "How . . . ? Where . . . ?"

"He and Gloria are at the florist, choosing flowers for the funeral. Gloria thought it would be good to involve Toby, and I agree. As soon as they return, we'll go to the funeral home and choose a casket."

She shuddered. Caskets came in every color. *And in every size.* A wound in her heart reopened as she remembered another's casket, small and ice-blue in color. "Cole, let Gloria buy anything she wants. Don't compromise."

"Understood."

Sloan shook off memories, said, "Now tell me more about last night. I want to hear everything."

"Gloria, Toby, and I were in the room, sitting around her bed, talking to her, watching her breathing stop and start. Toby held his mother's hand until she took her last breath, and even then he wouldn't leave." Cole patted the mattress. "He curled up like a puppy at the foot of her bed, and once he fell asleep, I carried him to his bed. After he was tucked in, I called a funeral director I know and he took over. This morning Toby refused to come into her room, but kids grieve differently than adults, so I think that will change over time."

Sloan struggled to block a haunting memory of herself once opening a bedroom door and peeking inside to see rumpled bedding and clothes on the floor, and scattered drawing paper, a room where the air was stamped with the scent of wax crayons and candy mints and fruit-flavored gum. She shut the door on the image, whipped around to face Cole. "I think we should make up Lindsey's bed with her coverlet and her pillows. The room should smell like her for Toby. He—he needs to feel her presence, not her absence."

Her suggestion surprised Cole, but he liked it, well aware that mourners often found comfort in familiar things. Gloria's training might have been all right for a care facility, but not for a child's home. "Fresh linens are on the closet shelf." He swiftly walked to the closet's accordion door. "The coverlet's in the laundry room waiting to be laundered."

"I'll get it."

They swiftly worked in tandem, and in no time the bed was neatly made. Cosmetics long banished to a drawer to make room for pill bottles were replaced on the dresser top, and Sloan found a dog-eared Bible inside a bedside table drawer and put it where Lindsey had always kept it. In a final act of bringing the room back to life, Sloan spritzed Lindsey's favorite perfume into the air and onto the pillows. "There," she said with a satisfied look. "This is better."

"Remarkably better." Cole took the perfume bottle from Sloan's hand and put it atop the bureau. He cupped her face with his hands. In this moment she wasn't a star. She was a soft and amazing woman he wanted to kiss, *needed* to kiss.

She read the intention in his eyes. And *now* he wanted to kiss her? When she looked frightful, puffy-eyed and burdened with grief? "I—I look—"

"Beautiful," he finished, and kissed her softly, then more deeply, his tongue exploring, tasting, absorbing her essence into himself. He took his time, never moving his hands, letting the kiss rise and fall to the rhythm of her beating heart and his every breath. The kiss coalesced inside her, reaching deep into her core, transforming from tenderness into desire and then into something else entirely. She wanted to soak into his flesh, become a part of him, the skin and bone of him. He was fire and ice. Life and breath. And when the kiss broke, they were both left shaken, her trembling, him wordless.

He touched his forehead to hers and took in gulps of air like a man coming to the surface of the water after a near drowning. He had wanted to kiss her for the longest time but hadn't expected the avalanche of emotion pouring through him now. *You can't have this woman*, his mind warned. Loving Sloan was folly, a burden too heavy for his heart to carry.

She felt dizzy, faint. *What had just happened?* Her legs felt rubbery. Her heart skipped beats. She had erected walls all her life to keep others out, and this man had breached her barriers with the touch of his lips. She told herself that it had to be lack of sleep and food that had made her vulnerable.

"Sloan? Are you here? Where are you?" Toby's voice.

She remembered leaving her bags just inside the front door, quickly stepped away, her eyes locked on Cole's, and called, "In your mama's room." *It had been a kiss, a simple kiss. Move on.*

The boy skidded to a stop at the doorway. "Me and Gloria picked out pretty flowers for Mama."

Sloan swept to the doorway, knelt in front of Toby. "Tell me about the flowers."

Toby cocked his head, glanced past Sloan and Cole to the things within the room, and finally back to Sloan. "It's pretty. Like Mama used to have it before she got sick. Did you fix it up?"

"We did it together." She gestured to Cole, who'd come to stand behind her.

"I like it."

Gloria joined Toby in the doorway, peeked into the room. "Oh, it's so *nice!* Just like—" She stopped herself.

Sloan stood, hearing what Gloria had almost said. . . . *Just like Lindsey was coming back.* She offered Toby her hand, and the four of them walked into the living room. Gloria looked ready to collapse, and said, "Cole, we should go now."

"I'll stay here with Toby," Sloan said, and as soon as they were alone, she smiled and stroked his cheek. "Hey, you know what? I haven't eaten all day and I'm really hungry. Could you make me one of those awesome grilled cheese sandwiches of yours? And while you cook, please tell me all about the pretty flowers."

On the day Lindsey was buried, the promise of coming autumn turned into threats of summer rain. Low gray clouds held the sky hostage, and the air felt thick and smothering. The vases of flowers at the gravesite seemed drained of color, and the cemetery grass was a smear of brown. The only pop of green was the fake grass surrounding Lindsey's casket. The graveside gathering was small, only immediate family. And Lani and Dawson.

Sloan hid behind big round dark glasses, eyes forward, afraid that Dawson might catch her eye and she would break apart, shatter like glass. She wanted to run, but couldn't. She refused to sit, so she stood, stiff and unmoving, forcing herself to stare at the jumble of vases and flowers, most from neighbors and medical people, her record label, and Terri's firm. Rick and Kathryn had sent a small tree to plant in Lindsey's yard. After.

Toby and Gloria sat in chairs facing the casket draped with white and pink and yellow roses, Toby, glassy-eyed, in a tan suit a size too small, Gloria in a shapeless black dress, weeping into a wad of tissue.

Cole, wearing a navy-blue suit, stood beside Sloan, acutely aware of her rigidity. He didn't miss the way she and Dawson went out of their way to avoid one another, even eye contact. A weeping Lani had spoken to Sloan, offered condolences, a squeeze of hands, but not Dawson. And during the service Lani kept her arm looped through Dawson's, like a tether grounding him. Cole had witnessed grief many times on his job, and certainly burying Lindsey was sad, but deeper shadows hung around these three, like dark smoke in a conspiracy of silence. Caught in the turmoil of his thoughts, Cole missed the minister's "Amen."

Sloan nudged Cole. "I'll wait in your truck. Let Toby and

Gloria take their time." She darted off, and he watched her flee, feeling defenseless against an anguish that he knew existed but could not fathom. The ghost of their kiss days before ravaged his mind, tormenting him. She was vapor. Now he saw her . . . now she was gone.

Sloan hurried toward the truck parked on a gravel path behind a line of pine trees. Today in the breathless air, their needles couldn't whisper. She needed to get as far away as fast as possible from this place. She was nearing the pines when a man stepped from behind a tree, startling her.

"Excuse me, ma'am."

She tried to sidestep him, but he moved with her.

"Are you Sloan Gabriel, the singer?" He was dressed in a black Western shirt, black jeans, and black cowboy boots, and he spoke with a thick drawl.

What the—? "Please go away! I'm at a funeral. Leave me alone!"

He ignored her plea, grinned. "I just come by to say thank you."

Confused, she measured him. "Thanks for what?"

"Let me introduce myself." His grin turned wolfish. "I am Beauregard Ridley, but everyone calls me Bo, and I've come to fetch my son."

thirty-one

Sloan stepped backward. "Get out."

"Not gonna happen. *That* woman"—Bo pointed toward the casket—"she stole my kid from me, run away with him, and I been lookin' for him ever since."

"I doubt that," Sloan snapped. "Lindsey saved Toby and herself from you. She had a restraining order against you, something the courts don't just hand out for no reason."

An angry Bo moved toward her. She stood her ground, dared him with her eyes to touch her. He never got a chance, because suddenly Cole was standing on one side of her, and Dawson on the other. "This guy bothering you?" Cole asked. They must have looked intimidating, because Bo backed away, glaring.

"He says he's Toby's dad and wants to take him with him."

"Toby's not leaving with you," Cole said.

Gloria rushed up, breathing hard from exertion. "You get out of here, Bo Ridley. Right now!" She grabbed Cole's wrist. "Make him go away, Cole! Please!"

"Well . . . if it ain't Gloria." Bo made the name sound like a dirty word. "You ran away with her. . . . I thought as much when I couldn't track you down either. You *cow*."

"Shut up," Cole said through clenched teeth.

Gloria's face flamed, but she didn't move. "I see you're the same charmin' jerk you always were. Leopard don't change his spots. Why'd you come here today?"

"You askin' how'd I find you after three years? Four years if you count the time her daddy, Jerry, run me off." He pointed at Sloan. "Her concert—that's how I found my boy. News was all over the Internet 'bout how she's raising money for some sick woman named Lindsey. I just followed the music."

Sloan flinched. Bo finding Lindsey was on *her*?

"Then when I read Lindsey's obituary, I got in my car and come to get my son."

The news had reported that Lindsey had died, because that was how the media worked—broadcasting everybody's business, no matter how personal. Sloan felt Toby squeeze between her and Cole, and wrap his arms around Cole's leg.

Bo's eyes darted to him. "Would you look at *that*. My boy's half grown! She took him! That bitch took him from me! I'm your dad, Toby, and I'm takin' you with me. Come here!"

Toby cowered, and Sloan knew the boy had little memory of the man. If any. She put a protective hand on Toby's head. "He's not going anywhere, except with me and Gloria."

Dawson stepped forward, his jaw clenched, his body coiled spring-tight. He gave Bo a shove that made him stagger and almost fall. Lani had told him about Lindsey's troubled marriage and Bo's abuse. Bo showing up today to snatch his little son was unacceptable. Fathers should love and protect their children. "You heard the lady. Leave before I make you."

The threat was a low growl, and Bo moved farther away

but clenched his fists. Cole unwound Toby's arms from his leg, stepped beside Dawson to present a united front. "You don't want to go there, Bo. You can't take both of us, trust me."

The menace must have seemed believable, because Bo unfisted his hands and let them drop to his sides. "This ain't over. Lindsey's dead and I'm Toby's father. I got rights."

"We'll see about that. Our attorney will be in touch," Sloan bluffed. They had no lawyer, and she certainly had no idea about his parental "rights."

Gloria said, "And she left me guardian of Toby before she died. She had a lawyer draw up the papers naming me his guardian, and told me I was to take care of him till he's all grown up. That's got to count for something."

Bo's eyes narrowed and darted between Sloan and Gloria. "You two ain't winnin' this. I'm taking my boy home to Memphis. Maybe not today, but real soon. That's a promise!" He fairly spat the words, and then stalked off between the pine trees to the far side of the gravel road and got into a massive red truck sporting monster tires and a fog light bar atop the roof of the cab. He took off, throwing gravel and breaking the graveyard's silence.

Toby began to cry, and Cole knelt. "I don't like that man," Toby said.

Sloan was frightened too. What if Bo *could* take Toby away? What kind of life would the boy have with a father like Bo? She lifted her sunglasses to nestle on her head and looked Dawson full in the face. "Thank you."

Lani huddled beside him, and he draped his arm around her shoulders, pulling her closer. "You're welcome."

They held each other's gazes for long seconds, speaking in a code that Cole didn't understand, but with the simple exchange, he felt a tectonic shift in something that had settled between them in the confrontation. Cole resigned himself to never knowing, and at the moment, what did it matter? They still had Toby. Cole scooped up the exhausted, sniffing boy, and Toby laid his cheek on Cole's shoulder. "What say we go back to my house? I'll fix us some lunch."

"I'll meet you there." Gloria headed to the parked hearse and its driver, who had driven her and Toby and the casket to the cemetery for the service. Sloan had refused to get into the hearse and had ridden with Cole, but Gloria's car was parked at the funeral home.

Lani said, "We'll bring the flowers back to the house in Dawson's truck."

Customs. Rituals. Routines. Cleaning up after the dead. Dry-eyed, head high, still shaking with anger and fear for Toby, Sloan walked with Cole as he carried Toby to his truck.

"Glad that's over." Dawson threw off his suit coat and undid his tie, tossed them over the arm of a chair the second they stepped inside his apartment.

"Thank you for going with me. You didn't have to, and I know how hard it was to go, but I appreciate it." Lani rose on tiptoes and kissed him lightly. She had requested a two-day leave from her job and had driven to Windemere the day before to attend Lindsey's funeral. "She was a special lady. She'll be missed."

Dawson dropped onto his sofa and, with a pat on the cushion, invited her to join him, and she did. "I go to that cemetery off and on, you know. To visit. Leave flowers."

Lani feared he'd fall into the darkness of that cold November day from the past, that terrible day that neither of them should revisit right now. Burying Lindsey had been hard enough without facing that other time. Lani herself had barely escaped with her sanity from that day. She slipped her arm between his torso and the back sofa cushion, and settled against him lovingly. "Good thing you were there and made Toby's awful father go away," she said in an effort to redirect Dawson's thoughts.

Dawson stroked her hair. "Cole would have done it if I hadn't. I saw how attached he is to the boy."

"True. Lindsey came to depend on him. I think she had a serious crush on Cole, but what was the point? She was dying, and he only thought of her as a friend."

Dawson shrugged. "Well, he's a stand-up guy and I like him. I don't think he's going to let anything happen to Toby if he can help it."

Lani was hesitant to bring up Sloan's name, but she was sure that it wasn't just Toby whom Cole loved. Lani had seen the way Cole looked at Sloan. He was in love with her, sure as day follows night. And Sloan Quentin was a powerful lure on a man's psyche. Lani straightened, shied away from thoughts and memories that could twist and wound. "Hey, let's fix some lunch, and then I'll get on the road."

Dawson tipped her backward on the sofa and leaned over her. "Do you know that I think of you as way more than a friend?" His dark eyes held the look that spoke of a more primal hunger and never failed to make her body catch fire.

She traced his lips with the tip of one finger. "Who needs to eat lunch? Overrated meal, to my way of thinking."

Sloan and Gloria sat at Lindsey's kitchen table, a pot of coffee and a pile of doughnuts between them. Comfort food. They were both on their third sugary indulgence. Gloria said, "It don't seem right . . . her not being here. I keep listenin' for her little bell to ring, so I can go to find out what she needs. Mostly she wanted company, someone to sit and talk till she fell asleep."

Cole had said the same thing that night at the pool. Had it only been April when he'd come to Sloan with his request? Tonight it felt like a lifetime ago.

During lunch Cole had been called to a house fire with injuries, and Sloan, Toby, and Gloria had returned to Lindsey's house, where Sloan and Toby had played an endless stream of video games all afternoon, Toby flopping between mopey and angry, and by bedtime he'd been frightened and withdrawn. Toby was sound asleep in his room now, and night had pitched its black tent outside. The fridge and freezer were stuffed with enough food for an army—casseroles from neighbors and Lindsey's church fellowship. The living mourned the dead.

Sloan reached for another doughnut, chocolate with sprinkles. Gloria wiped her eyes with a tissue long past its prime. To keep Gloria from another crying jag, Sloan said, "Tell me how you and Lindsey became friends."

"High school, ninth grade. I was a foster child from age ten, so I moved around a lot and I was the new girl at Lindsey's school."

"Lindsey told me. How'd you end up there?"

Gloria looked at her shyly. "My parents left me with my grandma when I was six and disappeared. When Nannie died, I was ten, and had no place else to go except child services."

Sloan remembered all the times LaDonna had threatened

to give *her* to child services, how fearful she'd been of the system. Living with LaDonna had been difficult, but she'd feared the unknown even more. "What was that like?"

"Some people were real nice. Others, not so much. I stayed with an older single lady for a while, and she had a garden and we grew vegetables. That was my best home." She smiled with the memory. "I was a shy little fat girl." She heaved her shoulders, took a bite of her doughnut. "I did okay growing up, but it was hard to make friends. But in ninth grade, I met Lindsey, or rather she met me. She just sat down at the lunch table and started talking to me." Gloria shifted her gaze to a spot on the table. "Girls would do that sometimes, pretend to be nice to me, then make fun of me behind my back." Her gaze shifted to Sloan. "You were born pretty, Sloan. Person can't help what she looks like. And boys? Don't get me started. But Lindsey treated me nice." Warmed by memories, Gloria's face glowed. "Lindsey was never mean to me. She was my best friend ever. And she took real good care of me all through high school."

Sloan felt her eyes stinging with tears. She wanted to tell Gloria that being pretty was no guarantee that other girls would be nice to you. "And you took care of her after high school."

"But now she's gone and left me. Gave me her home and her child. Her treasures. They're my treasures too. And now that awful man Bo Ridley's gonna take my sweet Toby away. How can I keep Toby from his daddy? At least you're kin. You're blood."

Sloan felt a knot form in her stomach. Everyone believed Lindsey's story. Only Cole and Terri knew there was no positive proof. At the moment Sloan felt more related to Gloria than to Lindsey, the both of them survivors of shipwrecked childhoods.

"What am I gonna do, Sloan? How can I keep Toby from his own father? Tell me, please."

Sloan took a swallow of coffee grown cold. "I don't know, Gloria. I haven't a clue. But I think I know someone who might."

thirty-two

Melody heard a commotion outside the door of her inner office, and her receptionist's voice demanding, "Hey! You can't go in without an appointment! Stop! Come back!"

Melody's door was flung open, and she bolted to her feet. Her eyes widened when she saw her intruder. "*Sloan Quentin?* I—I mean, Gabriel?"

"In the flesh." Sloan pulled a second woman in behind her. "And this is Gloria Harrold. Can we talk?"

From behind Sloan and Gloria the flustered receptionist said, "I told them they needed an appointment."

"It's all right, Celia. I'll take over." Celia shut the door, and Melody motioned toward chairs in front of her desk. "Please sit."

Sloan took one chair, Gloria the other. "Sorry to make such an entrance, but I have to fly back to LA in three days, and we have to see a lawyer, and you're the only lawyer I know in Windemere."

Just that morning Terri had called to say that Sloan had

been nominated for awards by the Country Music Association in two categories, Best New Artist, and Best Song, "Somebody's Baby." Nominations were in September, the awards show in November. *"You need to be here, Sloan. I know you just buried your sister, and I'm holding off the media as best I can, but I can't for much longer."*

"Give me three days, Terri . . . please. Something important's come up."

Melody put elbows on her desk and folded her fingers together. "First, some niceties. Congratulations on your career. I was out of town and missed your Windemere concert, but I wrote a check for Lindsey's fund. I know she was your half sister. It was all over the news. You have my condolences. Lani thought the world of Lindsey."

Sloan hadn't meant to barge in like a bull in a china shop. She'd had little interaction with Lani's sister while living in Windemere, meeting once at a party—another memory that she was forced to turn aside. Sloan was also certain that her history with Dawson didn't add to her likability either. But being unsure if Melody would have taken her phone call or an appointment, barging in seemed the best tactic, because time was essential. "This is very important, so I'm sorry about the entrance."

She launched into her story, while Gloria sat looking shell-shocked. Sloan had gotten to the part about Bo Ridley's appearance at the funeral, demanding his son, when Melody held up her hand. "Whoa, stop. I'm an attorney, Sloan, but I do tax and real estate law, trusts and property rights. My expertise doesn't apply to custody cases."

Sloan felt her face drain of color, and her fisted hands went white-knuckled in her lap. "So you won't help us."

"I *can't* help you. But," she quickly added, "I know an

attorney who probably can. She works for the Tennessee Department of Child Services. She's busy, so it might take some time to set something up with her. When will you return from LA?"

Sloan drew a blank. She had no idea what lay ahead for her in LA. She had a touring schedule already arranged, and now the nominations could alter things too. "Maybe Gloria—"

Gloria clutched Sloan's arm. "I need you to come with me to a meetin'! Please."

Gloria's brief condolence leave from her job was nearly over, and although Cole was watching Toby today, he too had a full-time job. The clock was ticking on Bo's threat to take Toby, and Sloan feared that Bo could swoop in at anytime. "Please . . . beg her to meet with us as soon as possible. A child's at risk."

———

The Department of Child Services building looked industrial and forbidding from the front, but inside appeared less intimidating, merely shabby and tired. Sloan and Gloria went to the front desk and announced that they had an appointment with Marie Foley, one of the department's child advocate attorneys—as it turned out, the only one. Moments later a heavyset black woman emerged from behind a locked door and led them into a space that resembled a wagon wheel, a secretarial desk in the center and office doors off to the sides like spokes. The woman was a secretary, shared by the office personnel. She walked them toward one door and rapped, and when a voice said, "Come in," Sloan and Gloria did so.

The space was small and packed to overflowing with file cabinets, stacks of files and paperwork, and shelves of books.

A tall woman with salt-and-pepper hair brushing her shoulders stepped from behind a messy desk and held out her hand. "I'm Marie Foley. Clear those file boxes off the chairs and take a seat. The mess is really more organized than it looks."

They did as Marie asked. Sloan kept thinking back to when she'd been a kid and terrified of DCS. Now Toby needed its help. Ironic.

"Melody called and gave me a rough outline of your situation," Marie said, getting right to the point. "To clarify, the boy's mother is deceased and her wishes were that one of you should have custody of her child." Her gaze flitted between Sloan and Gloria.

Gloria raised her hand slightly, like a child to a teacher.

"Fill me in. I want to hear the entire story."

Sloan could almost hear Gloria's heart thudding in the room's silence. Realizing that nervousness held Gloria prisoner, Sloan reached over and squeezed her hand. "You know the history. You have to start, because I joined the story much later."

"Lindsey was my best friend." Gloria's words were mumbled at first but grew more confident as she talked. "After high school we got an apartment together. I went to a local college to learn nursin', and she . . . she met Bo Ridley. He was a silver-tongued devil, a snake, but he didn't show that side at first, and she fell hard for him. Everything was fine when they were datin'. He brought her flowers, took her fancy places."

"How did you react to that?" Marie asked.

"Oh, I missed her, but I wanted to see her happy. Her childhood wasn't the best. She was a daddy's girl, but her mama"—Gloria tapped her finger to her forehead—"she was sick in the head. Doctors couldn't fix her, and besides, she didn't wanna get well. Anyway, Bo talked Lindsey into marryin' him. And then everything changed." She straightened in the chair, raised her eyes to meet Marie's. "As you know, a snake has a forked tongue, and Bo's is almost cleaved in half."

Gloria's word picture was so vivid, Sloan thought it would make a good lyric in a country song. "Go on," Sloan encouraged Gloria. "Tell her everything."

"Lindsey started hearin' rumors 'bout him seeing other women. I knew it was true 'cause I seen him myself with some of them, all lovey and cuddly." Gloria shivered with disdain. "Then Lindsey got pregnant, which did not make Bo happy. He said she did it on purpose to trap him. And I'm thinkin', *You* married *her!* Why *if you wanted to keep datin' and didn't want a family?*"

The more Gloria talked, the fierier her voice got. This was a Gloria that Sloan hadn't met, but she welcomed the change, because the fight for Toby might become very difficult, and it would need Gloria's fierce commitment. "And Lindsey had a sweet baby boy." Gloria's voice and expression softened. "That's Toby. Bo strutted around braggin', but deep down I knew it was all for show. I was visitin' one night when Toby had one of those baby colic aches in his little tummy and wouldn't stop cryin'. Bo picked him up and *shook* him! Any fool knows you don't shake a baby 'cause it can damage the brain."

Marie was jotting notes while Gloria talked. "Later Lindsey started confessin' that Bo was hittin' her. She was covering up the bruises with clothes and makeup, but once I knew, I begged her to leave and move in with me. I had my LPN license by then and a job."

"Did she say anything to her father about the abuse?" Marie asked.

"She was too proud, and she knew he was goin' through his own troubles. And then—" Gloria teared up. "Then Lindsey got sick. Bo wouldn't even touch her, 'fraid he'd catch her cancer. The *dumb ass*."

Sloan and Marie both suppressed smiles. "But he got meaner too, didn't he?" Sloan had heard this much from Cole. It had made her angry then, and made her angrier now.

"He did. He liked slappin' her, even when she was sick from chemo. Then one day he hit Toby, left bruises. Boy was only two."

Again silence settled, the only sounds the scratching of Marie's pen on a legal pad, the hum of the AC unit. When Marie looked up, Gloria continued. "So one day while Bo was at work, I come over, helped her pack, and drove her to her daddy's. Bo was spittin' mad and came after her, but Jerry Sloan had a shotgun, and after a screamin' fight between them, Bo crawled off like the snake he was. Lindsey got a divorce and a restraining order against him, but Bo still come around when he was drunk, and Jerry and his gun was always there to persuade Bo to leave."

Marie lifted her head. "But he agreed to the divorce? Signed the divorce papers?"

"He sure did. Lindsey's cancer treatment bills was adding up, and he didn't want to have to pay 'em. Divorce papers said he'd take none of her debts."

Gloria snorted with derision, and Sloan knew more than ever that Bo Ridley was unfit to raise his son.

"Did he pay child support?"

"Not a dime."

"You have a copy of the restraining order?"

Gloria held up a file folder that had been tucked into her oversized purse. "I have it, along with Lindsey's will deeding the house to me, and a notarized power of attorney to make decisions for Toby after she was gone." Gloria's voice cracked. "She thought of everything she could to keep Toby safe."

"So how did you end up in Windemere?"

Gloria gave Sloan a sidelong glance, and Sloan encouraged her with a nod. "After Lindsey's parents died, she sold their house and . . . and she took off. And I come with her. She picked this town 'cause it was kind of out of the way. Bo had no way of knowin' where we were."

"The courts don't look kindly on parental abductions," Marie said. "What about visitation rights? Did his father have any?"

"It's not in her divorce papers. Bo never cared 'bout Toby. He was glad to be rid of Lindsey and Toby both. Not sure why he's actin' like he cares now. He don't."

"That's conjecture. I have to deal with facts." Marie said the words kindly, and Sloan could see that the attorney was sympathetic. Sloan was glad for that.

"Lindsey didn't feel like she had a choice about leavin' Memphis," Gloria said, defending Lindsey's actions. "Especially without her daddy there to protect her and Toby."

"The law—"

"Couldn't have helped until Bo hurt her." Gloria finished the sentence on a challenging note.

Marie didn't argue.

"Her cancer started spreadin'. I got a job here in Windemere, and I took care of her and Toby, and when she wasn't gettin' better, she signed all these papers hopin' to keep Bo away if he ever showed up."

"Which he has," Sloan added. "If he takes Toby away, no telling what will happen to the boy. So that's why we're here, Ms. Foley. Gloria wants to follow Lindsey's wishes and raise Toby. We both want to keep him safe. Please, help us."

thirty-three

$\sim$

Sloan couldn't sit still, so she paced the floor of Cole's living room as she told him about the meeting with Marie Foley. "Do you know the woman's the only lawyer handling cases for children in the DCS for this whole county? And she has a ton of cases, so there's a long line of people ahead of us. It's not right, Cole."

He sat on the sofa, his arms spread across the back of the cushions, watching her. Dressed in a bright blue tank top and jeans, she looked incredible. However, he was listening and forming his own opinions about Gloria's chances of keeping Toby—maybe not so good. "We can get a private attorney if need be."

"And I will, but I'm hoping Marie can help us. She knows the system, the judges. That's important."

He heard how she had smoothly switched from *we* to *I* and turned Cole into someone on the sidelines. He didn't take it personally, knowing she was used to fighting her own battles—look how far she'd come from her high school days—

and Cole didn't even know her whole story. It was too bad she was mired in this fight. Because of the music nominations, this should have been a time of celebration for her. Instead her time was filled with sorrow for Lindsey and anger at what might happen to Toby. "You know what I do when life gets out of control and I want to calm down?" he asked.

"Drink?"

He tossed back his head and laughed. "Not a bad guess, and I may end up there, but I start in the kitchen. I cook." He rose, took her hand, and walked her around the half wall into his kitchen domain.

"I can't cook," she grumbled.

"Well, come with me and I'll give you a lesson. We'll start with something simple and delicious that only needs six ingredients."

She didn't want to learn to cook. She wanted to rant.

"We'll start with a basic comfort food that people think is difficult to make, but isn't. We'll go with an Alfredo sauce with linguine this afternoon." He let go of her hand, started taking pots out of oversized drawers, foodstuffs out of his pantry and fridge. "*Real* butter, absolutely essential. Heavy cream, fresh Parmesan cheese, garlic, salt, and pepper." He set the items on the countertop.

She rolled her eyes. "Really, Cole, I'm not in the mood."

"It's my job to get you into the mood."

His dimpled smile kicked up her pulse. She sighed, realizing he wasn't going to back down. "What can I do?"

"Fill up this pot with cold water from that faucet at the back of the stove."

For the first time, she noticed a hinged spigot mounted into the backsplash. "A water faucet over your stove?"

"The right tool for the right job. No carrying a heavy pot

of water over from the sink." Once the pot was filled, he slid it onto a burner, drizzled in a bit of olive oil and a toss of loose salt. "If I'd known we'd be doing this, I'd have made fresh pasta. As it is we'll have to use linguine from the grocery store."

She feigned a swoon. "How shall I survive the compromise?"

He chuckled. "You'd be able to taste the difference, believe me."

For Sloan, eating was a simple necessity. She'd grown up on peanut butter and jelly and anything that could be microwaved. She wasn't sure Cole ever used *his* microwave oven. She watched him expertly mince cloves of garlic. "Now what?"

"Melt that stick of butter in that saucepan." He pointed with his chef knife to a second smaller pot. "Keep the flame low and watch it carefully. Don't let the butter turn brown." She followed his directions, and minutes later he tossed in the garlic and further reduced the flame. He handed her a whisk. "Stir from the bottom, keep it moving." The aromas of butter and garlic smelled delicious. "And I'll pour in the cream." He stepped behind her, encircled her with his arms, and began to slowly add the thick white liquid into the butter mixture. "Keep stirring, because when it comes to a low boil, magic happens."

With him pressed against her back, his arms around hers while she kept a wire whisk moving, and his warm breath in her ear, magic was already happening—to *her.* "Don't let it burn," he whispered. *Too late.* Her body was overheating.

Unable to resist the nape of her neck, he kissed her pale bare skin, touched the tip of his tongue to her earlobe, and whispered, "Perfect. Tastes good too."

Her breath compressed, making her feel light-headed. She released the breath, and it came out in a long low tremble. Her heart thumped, the blood racing, searing through her veins. She closed her eyes, tipped her head to give him full access to her neck. He sent a trail of slow lazy kisses from her ear to her shoulder, savoring the journey.

When the cream cup was empty, he set it on the counter, then ran his hands from the back of her neck, along her shoulders, down her uncovered arms, to her waist, to her hips and across the flat of her abdomen, and just inside the waistband of her jeans. She pressed backward into him, away from the lip of the stove, as desire flared hotter than the blue flame of the burner.

Cole wanted Sloan Gabriel. . . . He wanted the heat of her mouth on his, the feel of her skin pressed to his. He wanted to explore and taste every inch of her. He wanted her body, but also her heart, her thoughts, and her love. He was foolish to love her, but he did. *Game over.*

The stench of burning cream sent them jumping aside. Smoke poured from the pot, its contents turned into a thick brown goo. In one smooth movement he snatched up the ruined saucepan and shoved it into the kitchen sink, where it smoked and sizzled. He turned off the gas flame. Their eyes met. Then they dissolved into laughter, bending-over, unable-to-catch-your-breath laughter. "I failed my first cooking lesson!" she wailed when she could finally get words out.

"*I'm* the failure! I'm your teacher!" he countered, wiping laugh tears from his face. Their laughter slowed, faded into chuckles and giggles. "You distracted me."

"*You* distracted *me*! Do chefs usually kiss their cooking students?"

His gaze traveled the length of her before settling again on her face. "Every chance he gets."

She sobered, knowing she couldn't let this happen. She wouldn't allow herself to tumble into him emotionally. Sex was one thing, but anything else . . . ? Sloan rocked back on her heels.

Cole watched her pull away, both physically and emotionally, felt himself fall back to earth, and into reality. He turned to the sink. "I think this pot has to be tossed."

She moved closer, peered down, put her hand over her heart, knowing she'd hurt him, but her withdrawal was for the good of both of them. "Poor Mr. Pot. I'm sure it served faithfully."

Cole's eyes meshed with hers again. "Yes . . . faithfully."

And she heard the underlying message in his voice. Cole didn't dole himself out in pieces when he truly cared for someone. He was an all-or-nothing kind of man, while she believed herself as unreliable as a candle in the wind. So much about her he didn't know. Walking away was her only option. "Cole, I—I—"

They were interrupted by their cell phones buzzing simultaneously with texts. His phone was closest, and at this moment, Sloan didn't want to read any texts. He did. "It's Gloria. She says a sheriff's car has come to get Toby and take him away."

───

The two of them bolted out Cole's front door and across the expansive yards between the houses, to where a white-and-green county sheriff's car was sitting in Lindsey's driveway.

The two of them broke into a run. He was much faster, arrived first, and rushed inside the house.

When Sloan entered, breathing hard, she found Gloria huddled with a crying and frightened Toby on the sofa, and Cole standing between them and a sheriff's deputy wearing a holster full of frightening hardware. A woman in a black pantsuit stood beside the deputy, cajoling Toby to come with them. Cole and the deputy must have recognized one another, because Cole asked, "Jack, what's going on?"

"Please don't interfere, Cole. I have a court order here saying the boy has to come with us." He held up a piece of paper. "Signed by a judge."

Heart pounding with fear and exertion, Sloan dropped to the sofa on the other side of Toby, hemming him in between herself and Gloria. Toby cowered.

"You can't just take him," Sloan insisted. "The boy's just lost his *mother*! Stop, please. We had no warning, no phone call about this."

"We don't call, ma'am. We just show up."

"That's just wrong!"

"He's in temporary protective custody," the deputy said.

"With DCS," the woman added. "I'm Lois Byrd, and Toby must come with us now. His father's filed a petition for custody and—"

"His father!" Sloan shot off the sofa. "That man *hurt* him."

Afraid Sloan would get handcuffed and taken to jail, Cole turned the deputy's attention back to himself. "We can protect him."

The deputy shook his head. "I don't have a choice here, and you know it. Toby has to come for now."

"Where will you take him?" Cole asked.

241

"To foster care," Lois said. "It's a wonderful home with a family of six kids. The dad's a minister, and both parents are kind and loving, and this is just temporary until you both go before a judge for a custody ruling."

Sloan felt helpless and sick to her stomach. She'd been thrust into her former nightmare, but the dark hands weren't grasping for her, but for Toby instead. "Cole . . . please!"

"The law's the law. He has to go with them." His jaw was clenched, his muscles as taut as ropes. He dropped to his knees in front of Toby, put his hands on the boy's shoulders. "Look at me, buddy." Toby wiped his cheeks with the back of his hand, looked into Cole's eyes. "Sometimes we have to do things we don't want to do, Toby, and this is one of them." Toby shook his head. "You and I've spent nights camping, so you know how to be brave. You're going to another campsite tonight, maybe even stay for a few days. I know you can do it, because I know you're strong and brave and will mind the deputy and Miss Lois and the people you're visiting with. You weren't afraid of that tornado, were you?"

"No." Toby's voice was barely audible.

"Then there's no need to be afraid now. Plus you'll get to ride in the deputy's car. Who knows, maybe he'll turn on his siren for you." He glanced up at the cop.

"I will," the man said.

Lois looked at Gloria. "Let me help you pack a small bag for him."

Resigned to the situation, Gloria let Lois follow her out of the living room. Sloan felt shell-shocked. And furious. Cole said her name, but she shot him a warning glance and marched out the door to wait in the sunlight. Minutes later the others trooped out of the house, Lois carrying a sports bag and Toby's bed pillow. The deputy opened the back door of the car, where Toby stopped short.

Cole came forward. "You can do this, buddy."

Gloria knelt, hugged Toby. "Don't forget to brush your teeth." Her voice quavered.

Toby climbed into the car, and Lois followed. The deputy got into the driver's seat, said from the open car window, "We'll take good care of him. He'll be safe."

They watched the sheriff's car back out the long driveway, turn onto the road, and head off. Sloan crossed her arms, shivered even in the heat. "Gloria, call Marie." Gloria hurried back inside the house, leaving Sloan and Cole alone. She had nothing to say to him, and he understood she was being crowded by her own demons, so he said nothing to her.

In the quiet of the afternoon heavy with the scent of cut grass, from a distance came the promised wail of a siren.

thirty-four

"So what's your part in all of this?"

Sloan and Terri were sitting in a trendy restaurant when the agent asked her question. Sloan, picking at her salad, had been in LA for two days, but her thoughts were still in Windemere. Just that morning Gloria had called to tell Sloan that Marie had filed a petition with the court and that only a single primary judge for child advocacy was on the bench in the county. *Backwater town!* Sloan had thought. Gloria had sounded upbeat because Marie knew the judge, and he respected her and rarely rejected her petitions. "It'll take ten business days before Marie and me and Bo and his attorney can go in front of the judge. Bo's got a court-appointed lawyer, but thanks to you, Sloan, we got the best! Toby'll be home in no time."

Sloan hoped that was true, and was grateful that Marie had acted quickly on Toby's behalf. Sloan was no miracle worker. Marie would have the honor of that title if she could get Toby home again. "I'm just trying to help," she told Terri now. "Lindsey wanted Toby to remain with Gloria, but Bo is really trying to muck things up."

"He *is* the boy's father."

"Unfit father."

"So it's personal now?"

Sloan sighed. "It is what it is."

Terri picked mushrooms from her salad with her fork and set them on her bread plate. "I distinctly told the waiter 'no 'shrooms,' and yet, here they are." Terri shoved aside her salad plate and sipped her wine. "I understand your involvement. I'm even sympathetic to it, but you have a performance schedule, some venues already sold out, Sloan. You need to be fully engaged and not trekking back and forth to Windemere."

"Once I get in front of an audience, I'll kick right in and give every stage my all. I'm a pro, remember?"

"Tomorrow you face TV cameras, so give that your all too."

Since her return to LA, Sloan had faced an onslaught of interview requests, all the reporters vying to embellish the angle of her CMA nominations versus losing her sister. A tearjerker. The media loved it and wanted a piece of it, and although Terri had done her best to protect Sloan's privacy, she had to meet with the media. ABC Entertainment had won the biggest slice of her time because they were carrying the November awards ceremony on their network, and that interview would be taped tomorrow in an affiliate's LA downtown studio. She wasn't looking forward to it. "I will."

Candles flickered on tabletops, and a low drone of voices surrounded them. A brazier scented the area with smells of sizzling meat. Sloan pushed her almost untouched salad to the side. A waiter appeared, scooped up both salad plates, and refilled Sloan's water glass and Terri's wine goblet. Another appeared and placed their entrées in front of them.

"You listen to the new material CC sent? Do you like it?"

"Some of it. He said he'll send others, though."

"Well, once you begin working on your second album, you'll be near Windemere again, and perhaps happier." When Sloan didn't respond, Terri added, "Won't you?" Terri nibbled on a fire-roasted shrimp from her plate.

"I'm no fan of Windemere, and you know it."

"And yet you keep returning. And you've yet to deal with the DNA aspect—"

"Don't go there, please." Her whole life Sloan had pictured herself singing and basking in success. The success had come, but not the carefree satisfaction she'd expected. Lindsey, Toby, Gloria, and Cole had set up residence inside her life. "Until Toby's father is out of the picture, I can't walk away."

"Maybe you can't walk away from the town, but what about walking away from her gorgeous next-door neighbor? The one you sang to at the concert?" Terri offered a wide-eyed smile.

Sloan whipped her attention from her food and shot Terri a glare. "It was an act. I focus on someone in the audience at every concert. My fans like it when I single someone out."

"No need to get defensive. I was just asking."

Sloan attacked her entrée. A minute later, Terri said, "By the way, the nominations have brought good things your way. Digitals of 'Baby' have increased ten percent since the announcement, and it was already selling big."

Sloan knew Terri wanted to discuss the nominations. At another time the nod from the CMAs would have sent her into the stratosphere. She was pleased about the nominations, but not optimistic. "I'm up against five great songs and five hot new artists. I don't expect to win."

"'Oh, I'm just so honored to be nominated. Golly gee.'" Terri spoke in the breathless voice of pretense used by Hollywood actresses receiving nominations. "That doesn't sound like the Sloan I first met, hell-bent on winning it all."

Sloan wasn't sure where that version of herself was either. She had six weeks of touring ahead of her, and the awards ceremony the first week of November. And then . . . ?

"Did I mention you've been asked to do a concert in March in London?"

"London!" Sloan jolted out of her lethargy.

"As in Great Britain, across the pond, the queen, and her loyal subjects. Yes, *that* London . . . another perk from your nomination. You're going international. We'll know more after the CMAs." Terri rolled another shrimp in a buttery concoction, popped it into her mouth. "I never eat like this, but this is *so* good, too good to deny myself the calories."

Memories spilled like water as Sloan thought of her past and present—images of people she cared about, flooding into images of concerts in front of cheering audiences. She loved touring and working with CC to make amazing music, and now London lay ahead. Two worlds. Two universes colliding.

Terri interrupted the jumble of her thoughts. "I'll take your silence as a yes for London."

"Absolutely, yes."

Terri smiled with satisfaction and glanced down at Sloan's plate. "I brought you here tonight to celebrate, so I'm confused. We're at one of the hottest restaurants in the city, with cuisine from the kitchen of one of California's top chefs, and yet you order something as ordinary as linguine with Alfredo

sauce." Terri shook her head. "Sometimes I just can't figure
you out, Sloan."

~

"Sara Beth is back in the hospital."

Dawson had been driving home from a long workday
when Lani had called. He was tired, but the sound of Lani's
voice lifted his spirits, even though it wasn't just one of her
hello-how-are-you calls. "Aw, babe, I'm really sorry." He knew
how fond she was of the child in her care at St. Jude's, and he
didn't want her to go into a downward spiral over the death of
this child, Sara Beth.

"When she went home in July, I had hoped she'd beaten
the Beast this time."

"Wish I was there to cheer you up."

"Me too."

"I miss you." His heart hurt for Lani. She never meant
to become involved in a patient's life, but she couldn't help
herself.

"Miss you too."

"So now what happens?"

"Probably a bone marrow transplant."

Dawson knew how iffy the procedure could be. A patient
would be stripped of her bone marrow, a large part of a body's
defense system, and infused with someone else's healthy bone
marrow, which would hopefully grow and make the recipient
healthy again. The procedure was harrowing because while
the patient's bone marrow was medically destroyed, the patient would be susceptible to even the most benign germs—
from a cut, a cold. Plus the patient would be kept in isolation
until the donor marrow was infused and took hold.

"She's just a little girl," Lani said. "Doesn't weigh forty pounds. She's so fragile."

"But they wouldn't do it if they didn't have to," Dawson said. "Do they have a match?"

That was the rest of the equation. The donor had to be an excellent genetic match. The best chance was from a sibling, but Sara Beth had none. "I entered myself into the bone marrow registry last week, but I'm not a match for her." Lani sounded sad and a bit guilty, as if she'd somehow missed the mark. "So the bank has to keep looking. Wouldn't it be nice if everybody in the country registered? We have so many patients who die waiting because there aren't enough donors."

Night had fully fallen when Dawson pulled into his apartment complex and parked. "Would you like me to register here in Windemere?" It was a simple blood test for a donor, but if a match was found, someone's life could be saved.

"Oh, honey, no. I wasn't asking you to do that. I was just wishing out loud for more donors."

They continued talking, telling each other the details of their day, as Dawson let himself into his apartment. He didn't turn on lights but walked onto the balcony and into the slight chill of the coming autumn. Finally Lani said, "I have to study. Big exam tomorrow."

"You'll ace it. Good night, my love."

After they disconnected, loneliness swept through him and he missed her more than ever. He looked up into the night sky and saw a single star twinkling in the dark void. "Star light, star bright, first star I see tonight . . ." He spoke the entire childhood rhyme aloud, then made a wish for Sara Beth, and for Lani.

thirty-five

Cole walked into the fast-food restaurant, saw the crowds and long lines, and turned to leave. He changed his mind when he spied Dawson Berke sitting alone, scrolling through his cell phone. Food could wait. Cole sauntered over, determined to engage Dawson in conversation. "Hey there. Room for me? Or are you waiting for someone?"

Dawson glanced up, gave a nod. "No, I'm alone. Have a seat."

Cole took the chair across from Dawson at the table for two. "Thanks, man."

"You going to eat?" Cole held no tray.

"I'll wait until the herd thins." He thumbed at the swamped cashiers. "I think people in this country are programmed to stop whatever they're doing and form a mandatory line at noon every day."

Dawson quirked a smile, offered Cole fries from the carton on his tray. "Help yourself. I bought two. I gotta roll."

"I'm just getting off duty and going home to bed. Where

you headed?" Cole didn't want Dawson running off right away. He wanted to talk.

"New job site." He stuffed his phone into his jeans pocket, started to rise.

"How's Lani? She was a lifesaver the night of the concert, because that woman Kathy had me backed against the buffet table. I felt like a cornered fish and she was a barracuda."

Dawson grinned. "Lani told me about it. Glad you survived."

"I'm a paramedic, remember. I can suture my own wounds."

That made Dawson laugh and settle back in the chair. "As long as we're talking, how's Toby? Did you get rid of that nasty piece of work who calls himself a father?"

The tight, concerned look on Dawson's face revealed more than a casual interest. Cole said, "Gloria had a dogfight about it with child services, but DCS put him into a foster home." Dawson eyes blazed, and Cole quickly added, "But a good attorney filed a petition, and a juvenile judge appointed Gloria temporary custodian, so Toby's back home now and going to school. Unfortunately, Bo was granted visitation rights, two hours a week, twice a month." Cole quickly saw that his words had again upset Dawson.

"Why? He hit Toby. Why would the court allow him to be around the boy?"

"The visits are supervised by a social worker from DCS, so they meet at a neutral location, a place like this"—Cole gestured—"or a park. Man's never left alone with Toby."

Dawson relaxed, and Cole wondered if Dawson had been abused as a kid, because his body language was all about protecting the child. Dawson took a long draw from a straw in his tall soda cup. "And Sloan? What's her role in this? I mean, now that Lindsey's gone."

Cole's senses went on high alert. He wanted every bit of information Dawson was willing to dole out about Sloan, but he knew that discussing Sloan could be land mine territory. "She became very close to Lindsey while she was sick, and Gloria and Toby too. Toby's crazy about Sloan. Brags to everyone that she's his aunt. Sloan found the attorney, a child advocacy lawyer on loan to DCS."

Dawson held his tongue, toyed with the drink straw, stabbing it up and down in the cup, to rattle and move the ice chips. He casually asked, "Does Sloan visit often?"

Cole chose his words carefully. "As much as she can, given her career and concert schedule." Cole took a breath, plunged into deeper water. "Did you and Lani hang with her in high school?"

"No."

Dead end.

Dawson stood, and Cole felt opportunity slipping away. "Sloan's been very good to Toby and Gloria. Her concert paid off all Lindsey's medical bills, set up a trust for Toby. And now she's doing all she can to keep Toby safe from his father. Not sure how things would have worked out for them if Sloan hadn't interceded."

Dawson held his cup, and with his free hand picked up his tray wadded with burger wrappings and fry cartons. "You like her, don't you?"

The register lines had vanished, so Cole had no reason to linger at the table. He also stood. "Yeah, I like her."

Dawson met his gaze. "Be careful."

Cole's heart hammered. "Why? She's nice to me, has never hurt me."

The implication was obvious, as the question *Did she hurt you?* implied.

Dawson's eyes shaded as if blinds had dropped behind them. "Just be aware, my friend. She runs." He turned, dumped the trash, and strode out of the restaurant, while Cole was left to wonder what Dawson's words had meant. *"She runs . . ."* From what? From whom?

Cole's stomach growled, reminding him he hadn't eaten for more than twelve hours. He walked to a register and gave his order to a cashier. When his food came, he walked it to the table and sat again, but this time with more questions swimming in his head than if he'd never spoken to Dawson Berke at all.

"Who wants popcorn?" Cole carried a freshly made batch in a large bowl from his kitchen to the living room.

"Me! Me!" Toby bounced up and down on the center cushion of the sofa.

Gloria chimed in with, "Me too." She sat on one end of the sofa. Cole would take the other end cushion.

Cole set the bowl in the center of his coffee table and passed out smaller bowls, the buttery scent of the warm kernels filling the big room. "Help yourself."

Toby dug in, spilling fluffy white kernels onto the table as he scooped with his bowl from the bigger one.

"When's it coming on? When we gonna see her?" Toby could barely contain his excitement.

"After this commercial."

"I bet she wins!"

"I've listened to the other nominees," Gloria drawled. "Can't hold a candle to her. She's gonna win."

The three of them were gathered to watch the CMA

awards show on Cole's big-screen TV. The event once held at the Ryman Auditorium in Nashville was now held at the larger and newer theater that also housed the Country Music Hall of Fame. Since the awards show was scheduled to begin at seven central time, Toby could watch a good portion of the program before he'd have to go to bed. Cole was recording the show in case Sloan's category wasn't called before bedtime, so that Toby wouldn't miss seeing if she won, or hear her sing her megahit, "Somebody's Baby." Recording the show was for Cole's benefit too. She hadn't visited since Lindsey's funeral, and extra shifts at work had not taken the edge off how much he wanted to be around her.

"There she is! I see her!" Toby pointed to the screen, snapping Cole's attention, and he saw her strolling in the theater lobby on the arm of a man in a tux. "Who's that guy? Why's she with him?"

"Calm down." Gloria patted Toby's shoulder. "He's someone Terri hired to walk her into the theater. Sloan texted me about it. She ain't got anyone special in Nashville, so this guy's been picked to sit with her. She told me that if she could have, she'd have asked *you* to walk her in, Toby."

Toby giggled. "Would I have to wear one of those suits?"

"Yes, you would."

"Forget it." He stuffed a handful of popcorn into his mouth.

Cole ignored the chiseled man with Sloan, concentrated only on her. She wore a full-length strapless flame-red dress sprinkled with sequins. The gown hugged her body, flared at the bottom, where the tip of a stiletto heel covered in rhinestones peeked out as she moved. Glittering diamond earrings, her only jewelry, winked from her ears. Cameras flashed, and a reporter babbled accolades as she passed him. She smiled and waved at the camera, which was on her far too briefly, but her image, the lady in red, blond hair worn in a simple and elegant French twist, her bare skin dusted with a light sparkle, would remain in Cole's mind forever.

"I bet everyone in town's watchin'," Gloria said.

Cole nibbled a few pieces of popcorn. Physically Sloan was fifty or sixty miles away, but it might as well have been a thousand. The feel of her in his arms during the disastrous cooking lesson had only whetted his appetite for more of her.

The show began, and despite numerous musical performances and awards given out, the evening seemed to drag. The Best Song nominees were interspersed with other performances, and by the time the emcee announced Sloan's number, Toby's eyes drooped and he lolled against Cole's side. "Here she is," Cole said, tousling the boy's hair. He sat up, sleepy-eyed. And then Sloan's image filled the TV screen, stunningly beautiful and larger than life. Her body-hugging red dress glimmered. The camera zoomed in on her face slowly as she sang the song that had swept the charts. Every line, every note seemed to pour from someplace deep inside her, trembling on her full lips, filling the room with melancholy words of something lost, gone, never to be touched again. The song was personal, but what drove it?

Tears sparkled in Sloan's eyes, looking like a fine shimmering mist through the camera's all-seeing lens.

"Why's she crying?" Toby asked.

"She's probably just happy," Gloria offered, missing all the cues.

Cole thought differently. The song had been birthed from pain, a deep hurt. What stood behind the curtain of her past, showing so plainly on her beautiful face for millions of viewers to see? He wasn't sure he would ever know.

255

Minutes later Cole carried a sleeping Toby into his guest room, and he and Gloria finished watching the show.

———

Lani was checking Sara Beth's vitals, and Pam was sitting in a nearby chair watching the CMA show, when Sloan's voice began her signature song.

"Oh, Lani, I just love this song! Don't you?" Pam asked.

Lani turned toward the television, pulled the stethoscope from her ears. She watched the camera zoom in on Sloan's exquisite face, saw her misted eyes, heard the passion in Sloan's voice, and for the first time Lani understood that the song wasn't merely about Sloan's loss, but also about regrets over what she'd missed by the choices she'd made years before. Lani's heart softened, and mist swam in her eyes as memories flowed, sweet and tender, and this time untainted by personal sadness. No one could change their past, only regroup and step into the future. For Lani, Dawson's love had begun her healing. Perhaps fame was bringing Sloan hers.

As the last notes of the song faded and the audience erupted into applause, Lani cleared her throat. "It's quite a song."

Pam blotted her eyes with a tissue. "Never fails to grab me."

"Did I tell you I went to high school with her?"

"No way!" Pam's eyes widened, and she leaned forward. "Tell me everything."

"Nothing to tell. . . . We ran in separate circles. I was invisible in high school. She wasn't, but we *all* knew she was going to make it big." Lani smiled. "It's nice to know that we got it right."

thirty-six

Sloan walked into Terri's front office brandishing her hefty CMA trophy in the air. Workers at their desks stood, clapped, and cheered. Kiley ran up to her. "Let me see! Can I hold it?" Sloan handed it over. "You should have won *both* categories, you know."

Terri stuck her head out from her inner door. "Thought I heard some noise. . . . Welcome home, Best New Country Singer of the Year!" She came out and gave Sloan a hug.

Kiley returned the award, called out, "You should have won two!" as Terri closed the door behind herself and Sloan.

"I was glad to win this one," she told Terri, pouring herself a cup of fresh coffee from Terri's silver carafe.

"I'm with Kiley. You should have won for Best Song too. Your performance was stunning."

"Said the agent. . . ." Sloan blew Terri a kiss. "In the end, I realize the song was too sad for a win. People like upbeat songs, and that's the kind that won. But this award"—she gestured to the trophy she'd set on Terri's desk—"is far more valuable to my career, don't you think?"

Late-morning sun flooded through freshly cleaned sparkling windows. Outside, warm November sunlight painted a blue cloudless sky with pure light. From this height over the busy streets and distant freeways, the whole world looked brand-new. "*All* awards are valuable to a singer's career." Terri poured herself a cup of coffee and settled behind her desk. "I'm surprised to see you so soon. I thought you might hang around a few days."

"I took a red-eye as soon as the ceremony was over."

"No parties? The party circuit is huge after these ceremonies."

"Not my thing. I just wanted to get back." The Rick Searle Band had won for Best Record and Best Band, and backstage Tate had made it clear he wanted to pick up where he and Sloan had left off in Atlanta. She didn't, so the late-night flight had been a perfect escape.

"No visit to Windemere?"

"I'm going for Thanksgiving. Gloria's roasting a turkey with all the trimmings and asked me to come." She wanted to see Cole too, kept remembering the way he looked at her, and the way he made her feel. Not just desirable but cherished. *Nice sensation.* "How 'bout you? Where will you spend Turkey Day?"

"Skiing in Colorado."

"Alone?"

Terri gave an impish smile. "My secret."

Sloan matched her grin. "Take notes." She yawned, stood, and stretched. "For now, I'm going to the apartment and getting some sleep." She started toward the door.

"Aren't you taking your award to put on your mantel?"

"I don't have a mantel. I thought maybe you could hold on to it for me until I do."

"I'll put it on my bookshelf for safekeeping. Do you ever think about getting a place of your own? You can afford to live almost anywhere out here. Maybe buy something in Hollywood Hills or build a place in the canyons. You've got a great future and money in the bank."

"Sometimes I do think about buying a house. Know any good Realtors?"

"A flock." Terri glanced at her computer screen. "I'll gather a list of the best ones in LA and shoot you an email." Sloan started for the door. "You know I'm very proud of you, Sloan."

"Lots of your clients win awards. I only have one, but I promise I'll add more."

Sloan's smile made Terri smile too. Then the agent's expression grew thoughtful. "I've seen a lot of talent come through my door, really fine talent. Some of them took a rocket ride to the top. And after they got there, I've seen their rocket crash and burn, sometimes because of booze and drugs, sometimes because the talent gets very rich very quickly and starts believing their own hype."

"Is that what you thought was going to happen to me?"

"I wondered for a time. Then you did what you did for Lindsey and Toby. I was impressed, because I'm fairly certain you will never take that DNA test." Sloan shrugged off Terri's correct assumption. "I'm saying this, Sloan, because I think your rocket ride is for real, because *you're* for real. It's called character, and I admire it."

Sloan's cheeks grew warm. She was surprised and touched

by Terri's assessment. "Stop before my head explodes. I—I thought it was the right thing to do. But now I'll move on and stay on board the rocket as long as I can. I always told you that being a singer is all I've ever wanted."

Terri grinned. "Enjoy the ride, Rocket Girl."

In the car, while the driver fought with snarled traffic, Sloan thought about Terri's words. Kind words Sloan didn't deserve, because of course, Terri didn't know the *real* Sloan. She was Sloan Gabriel now, but as Sloan Quentin she'd made mistakes, and the guilt lingered, gnawing at her heart. She sighed, stared out the window at people on crowded sidewalks, and cars creeping along. She'd once believed she could get lost in LA, but now realized there was no place to hide from herself.

Gloria's Thanksgiving turkey with trimmings contained more food than Sloan had ever seen on a single dining room table. The table might not have looked elegant, with its mismatched crockery and plastic-coated tablecloth, but it felt as homey as a greeting card.

The only blemish at the table was the chair where Lindsey would have sat . . . empty now, as if waiting for the mistress of the manor. Gloria refused to sit there—out of respect, Sloan figured, but the vacancy made the dining room feel as if the space were lacking a balance that might never be regained.

"Think there's enough to eat? I mean, *really*, Gloria?"

Gloria shook her napkin across her lap and giggled. "You're just jokin' with me, aren't you?"

"There *is* a lot of food," Sloan said, "and only three of us."

"I want mashed taters," Toby announced, grabbing a roll.

Sloan passed the heaping bowl swimming in melted butter. She took a few slices of turkey from the wooden plank. "Sorry Cole can't be with us."

Gloria scooped sweet potatoes onto her plate. "Man never makes it for Thanksgiving. Too many people on the road, too many accidents. He says every EMS team in the state gets called in to work. But don't you worry, I'll make him up a big plate of food for when he gets off."

Sloan's deep disappointment over learning that Cole wouldn't be dining with them had surprised her, and because she had to leave early for a scheduled performance at a charity gala in Los Angeles on Sunday, she wouldn't see him at all this trip. She took solace in knowing she would return before Christmas for a longer visit. "I don't think *two* plates for Cole will make much of a dent in all this food."

"Oh, none of it will go to waste. I'll keep some leftovers for me and Toby and take the rest to the community center for the homeless and poor. That's why I cooked so much for today, 'cause there're lots of hungry folks out there, even in our little town."

Gloria's words brought back Sloan's memories of eating at that same center, because as LaDonna had told her, *"It's free, girl. No need to buy and cook food in this crappy trailer if they're giving food away!"* Sloan shook off the past. "That's nice of you, Gloria. It's a kind thing to do."

Later, after they'd cleaned up and packaged the leftovers for transport and Gloria had left with the food, Sloan played video games with Toby, but she quickly realized Toby wasn't his usual peppy self. He was lethargic, spoke to her only if she asked him questions. After a while she put down her game controller. "What's wrong? I know something is, so please tell me."

"I want Mama."

Sloan's heart went out to him. She fumbled around for soothing words, feeling awkward and ill-equipped to say the right things, wise maternal things. "I know you miss her. So do I."

Toby picked at a loose thread on the sofa cushion. "You're my aunt, aren't you?"

She turned guarded. "Isn't that what you've told your friends?"

He nodded. "So I been thinkin' . . . can I come live with you?"

Jolted by his request, Sloan didn't know what to say. She inched closer to him on the sofa, lifted his chin to study his small face. "What about Gloria? Wouldn't she miss you?"

"I like Gloria," Toby said with enthusiasm. "She's nice and talks to me about Mama." He paused, cut his eyes to the side. "But I don't like that man."

Sloan's heartbeat quickened. "You mean Bo? *That* man?" She refused to call him "your father." The boy nodded, his expression forlorn. "Why don't you like him?"

"He's mean." His words were so soft that she hardly heard them.

"How is he mean?"

Toby looked up with a scowl on his face. "He calls my mama mean names, nasty names with bad words. And me too. Says I'm a 'Mama's boy' and he'd like to show me how a real man acts."

Sloan forced herself not to show the fierce anger she felt. Calmly she asked, "Has he ever hurt you? Has he hit you?"

Toby shook his head. "No. The lady is always with us, but she sits at a different table or on a bench if we go to the park."

He was referring to the social worker who picked him up and brought him to the meetings with Bo. "So the lady never hears him say mean things to you?"

Toby shook his head. "He whispers them into my ears and smiles if she looks at us."

As if they were having a fine father-son moment. Gloria had called Bo a snake, but Sloan decided that was an insult to the reptile.

"Why do I have to visit with him? Why do they *make* me? I don't want him for my daddy. My friends have nice daddies, but he's not nice! I don't like him."

Sloan suppressed inner fury. Bo was smart. He knew better than to leave bruises, but words could hurt as bad as thrown stones. Growing up, she'd heard enough belittling remarks from LaDonna to know that bruises on the outside left marks but usually healed. Bruises on the inside couldn't be seen, only absorbed.

Toby turned pleading eyes to Sloan. "If I lived with you, I wouldn't have to see him . . . so can we go to California?"

The pleading expression on Toby's face knifed through her, and yet she had to be truthful. "I can't take you with me, Toby. And you have to visit with Bo for the time being." He looked crestfallen. "Right now we have to follow the law."

"I *hate* the law."

The law was Toby's only protection right now, but he was too young to understand that. "What you can do is always hang close to the lady who brings you. Make it hard for Bo to whisper into your ear. And I *will* figure out a way to change things. It will take a little bit of time, so be patient."

Toby twisted away, stood, and stomped off to his bedroom. She watched him retreat, defiant and angry, reminding her of herself—a girl who had refused to be broken by an uncaring alcoholic mother and the hatefulness of small-town gossips. A survivor.

thirty-seven

Toby slept. The TV was off, and a single lamp burned in the quiet house. Sloan paced the living room, as restless as a lioness in a too-small cage. She could call Marie when she returned to LA, but truthfully, how could Bo's rights be revoked over whispered hatefulness—a child's word against an adult's, and the biological father to boot.

A rap on the front door surprised her, and fear followed, for she would put nothing past Bo Ridley, even showing up drunk on Thanksgiving. "Who's there?"

"It's Cole."

She flew to the door, unlocked and opened it. He looked totally exhausted but managed a dimpled smile. She gave him a heartfelt smile in return. He said, "I had a few minutes and kept thinking about that plate of Thanksgiving turkey." *Who was he kidding?* What he'd wanted was to see Sloan, had stolen a half hour to run by Lindsey's. Sloan started to hug him, but he stopped her. "I haven't had a chance to clean up, and can't stay long."

For the first time she saw the blood flecking his uniform shirt. "Bad day?"

"Drunk driver hit a van of five people. It was a mess. Where's Gloria?"

"She took food to the community center, but texted that they were shorthanded, so she's helping to serve. Toby's in bed."

He raked his hands through his hair. "And you?"

"Just waiting for Gloria." She told him about having to leave sooner than she'd expected. The news was a letdown. She grabbed his hand. "Well, you can't leave without eating some of the leftovers. I can't cook, but I do know how to run a microwave."

Once in the kitchen, he leaned over the sink, washed up, splashed cold water onto his face and dried off with paper towels. He unbuttoned his blood-flecked uniform shirt, draped it on a chair. Beneath he wore a white T-shirt, stained with perspiration from his battle to save a motorist's life. She didn't seem to notice, only dragged out a plastic-wrapped plate and set it into the microwave oven.

While it warmed, she grabbed him a cold soda and sat with him. Cole popped the top, sucked the fizz, winked. "Best part."

"How long you on duty?"

"Another twelve. A ton of shoppers out getting the jump on Black Friday."

The microwave dinged, and she set the plate in front of him, watched him attack the food. Gloria was no gourmet cook, but the meal had been delicious, and sitting at the kitchen table with Cole somehow felt right. She wanted to tell him about Toby and Bo, but held back, fearful of how Cole would react. What if he waylaid Bo and did the man physical harm? Bo could bring charges, and Cole would be in trouble. Sloan decided to hold her tongue.

Cole's beeper buzzed, and he glanced down, shook his head, and stood. "Gotta run."

"Another accident?"

"Domestic violence call. Sometimes holidays bring out the worst in families." He put on his uniform shirt, and she followed him to the front door.

"I'm coming back for Christmas, and I *will* stay a whole lot longer."

His gaze flew to her face, saw the promise in her eyes, and he grinned. "I'll look forward to that."

She watched him dash to his truck and drive up the long driveway. She closed the door, leaned against it. Seeing Cole, even briefly, had buoyed her spirits but hadn't fixed her problem. She'd made a promise to Toby, one she planned to keep. She had to think of a way to get Bo Ridley out of Toby's and Gloria's lives, not just once but for all time. She owed it to them. And to Lindsey.

———

Lani jogged across the employees-only parking lot toward the employee entrance of the hospital, her heart in her throat with every step. Sara Beth was critical, maybe dying, and Pam had called Lani, sobbing, *"Jimmy's not gonna make it. Weather's got him pinned in."*

Lani had been in testing all day, had fought her way home in heavy traffic, and when the call had come, Pam's little girl had quickly become Lani's priority. She'd thrown on scrubs, grabbed her ID, and hurried back to the hospital. LED bulbs in light poles turned the lot and its cars a shade of icy blue-white. December's cold bit through Lani's coat, reminding her of another winter night when she'd run through a hospital's parking lot, not toward but away from the building, hammered by grief and guilt.

She'd taken a few minutes to let Dawson know she'd be returning to work, because they'd scheduled time for a long lovers' chat that evening.

I promised Pam I'd stay until Jimmy gets here, and I will.

Lani swiped her ID, knowing her supervisors wouldn't approve of the way she'd become entangled with Pam and Sara Beth. She didn't care. She would be returning home to Windemere's children's cancer unit in another week, her fellowship program completed. Tonight she was needed by the mother of a dying child.

The halls were quiet on the ICU floor, and the night-shift nurses were busy with charts at their central station draped with a chain of festive tinsel for the Christmas season. A small artificial tree sat atop the counter, adorned with shiny ornaments and miniature candy canes. Lani approached the desk, and Kesha looked up in surprise. "I thought you'd gone home for the day."

"Sara Beth."

"Ah." Kesha bobbed her head. "Child's under sedation, but her mama's in rough shape."

Lani identified with Pam all too well. "Still no word from the army?"

"Not yet."

"I'll dress for isolation and go hold her hand."

The isolation unit for the sickest of the sick was behind double doors, an airlock, and two more double doors. Sara Beth, waiting for a bone marrow transplant, had been through chemo and radiation treatments to destroy her immune system, and now there was a serious glitch. Lani paused for a moment, sucked up courage, and eased into the room. Sara Beth lay inside a clear plastic oxygen tent, IV lines running into her frail body. Pam, sitting in a chair beside the bed, saw Lani and burst into tears. "Thank you for coming! Thank you so much."

Lani stooped beside Pam's chair and took her gloved hand in hers. "I'm staying until Jimmy comes."

Pam nodded, blew her nose. "Don't seem right, you know. Her all ready for the transplant, and her daddy can't get here."

It *was* sad. After a flurry of testing and blood samples sent from half a world away, and pediatric oncology consults at St. Jude's, it appeared that Jimmy, Sara Beth's father, would be the best match for the transplant. He'd been in the rough mountain terrain of Afghanistan when the army had agreed to return him Stateside, and so they'd lost time extracting him, and now storms held hostage his fifteen-hour flight home.

Pam glanced over at her daughter, looking small and ghostly pale beneath the white sheets. "All she's gone through . . . and now . . . now this."

"He'll come. Have faith." Lani's heart broke for the family. After Jimmy arrived, he'd be quickly prepped for the marrow extraction from his pelvic bone, a simple procedure for him, with a quick recovery. Once his marrow was harvested, it would be slowly infused into his daughter. And even then Sara Beth would have a long road of recovery, often strewn with the kind of setbacks and complications that threatened all transplant patients. Sometimes anti-rejection drugs could overcome the problems, sometimes not. But if the transplant worked, Sara Beth could be cancer free.

"Why don't you stretch out in the recliner chair and let me watch over her?" Lani led Pam toward the chair as she asked. The woman was exhausted, and even a few minutes of rest could be helpful. Lani tucked Pam into the chair with a blanket, and Pam fell asleep instantly. Lani returned to the other chair and sat to wait.

Lani must have nodded off, because a rattle at the door startled her upright. She saw a man's face pressed against the door's window. She jumped up, hurried to the door. He was draped in isolation garb, but the look on his face announced that Pam's solider had arrived.

"Hi, ma'am. Jimmy Reader." His gaze swept the room, grew alarmed at seeing his daughter, gentled when falling on Pam in the recliner.

"So happy to see you, sir."

"They said I have to get upstairs but I could visit my family for a few minutes."

"Go on," Lani urged.

He crossed to the bed. Lani followed, and watched his eyes fill with tears while he stared down at Sara Beth. "My poor baby. Daddy's here, honey." He turned then, walked to his wife's side, knelt on one knee.

To Lani he looked like a prince from a fairy tale, bending to kiss his sleeping beauty. Jimmy smoothed her cheek. Pam woke, saw him, and threw her arms around his neck, and they clung to each other. Lani knew it was her cue to exit, and she did, hoping that their story would have a happier ending than the story she'd lived one cold winter night in Windemere.

———

Sloan gave a stellar performance at the Love and Hope Ball for diabetes research, to a ballroom filled with many Hollywood A-listers—stars and superstars, the beautiful people.

The great ballroom sparkled with silver, gold, crystal, and a king's ransom of jewelry. The tables were spread with red linen and holiday decorations, and glowed with candlelight. On one wall hung a large painting of a looped ribbon dotted with a single drop of blood, representing the countless blood tests diabetics did daily to measure glucose levels. Later the work by a well-known artist would be auctioned to the highest bidder.

Yet despite the glitz and glamour of the evening, Sloan's mind remained on the problem she'd pledged to solve. During the ride back to her apartment in the town car, she ignored the driver's attempt at small talk, focusing on the facts surrounding Bo. Why would he want custody of Toby? Gloria had sworn Bo had never wanted a baby in the first place, and while a baby, Toby had been a source of irritation, to the point of physical abuse. Memories of LaDonna milking the welfare system intruded. Sloan tried to swat them aside, like a bothersome fly, but then she straightened in the car as insight shot through her like an arrow. All the pieces fell into place, and the puzzle was instantly solved. Excitement stirred as she began to formulate a plan.

She glanced at the time on her cell phone, realized it was two hours later in Tennessee and that waking Marie up at three in the morning might not be the best idea, but she needed the attorney's help. She didn't call but sent a text message: Call me first thing tomorrow. Urgent. Then Sloan settled back in the luxurious car seat and watched the glowing lights of LA spreading out as far as the eye could see as the car wound its way down from the hills.

thirty-eight

It was a chance encounter. Dawson was filling his gas tank when he glanced across the station's islands of pumps and saw Sloan gassing up a rental car. She had camouflaged herself with a toboggan hat to completely cover her hair, and huge sunglasses that covered half her face. She wore jeans and an unflattering ski jacket to ward off the cold, but Dawson recognized her at once. He had known her body well, and no amount of ugly clothing could hide her from him.

"Hello, Sloan."

She jumped a foot at the sound of his voice, turned to see Dawson standing behind her. "You scared me."

"Sorry." He nodded toward his truck two islands over. "You coming or going?"

"Coming." Sloan had talked to Marie and asked her to set up a meeting at DCS with Bo and his lawyer. Two weeks later she'd flown into Nashville, checked into a motel, and driven to Windemere. She had wanted to come and go undetected, in case her mission failed. "I guess I didn't do a very good job of hiding in plain sight."

Dawson's dark eyes lasered her. "You seem to spend a lot of time in a town you always hated."

"I have a meeting." She fumbled so badly with the gas cap that Dawson slid his hand over hers and took over the task. "Besides, how do *you* know how much time I spend here?"

"I run a construction crew, so whenever there's a 'Sloan sighting,' I hear them talking about it. You're a celebrity." He folded his arms. "And congratulations on the CMA award."

"Thanks." A cold wind whipped across the concrete, making her shiver.

"Looks like you got everything you ever wanted."

It was her turn to give him a hard look. "Not everything, Dawson. No one gets everything. And sometimes a good thing comes along at the wrong time." She pushed a lock of hair that had crept onto her forehead back under the hat. No use snapping at him. "How's Lani?"

His whole expression softened. "She's finished her fellowship and will be home for Christmas. She'll start her new job at Windemere General after the first of the year."

For a moment time ran backward and Sloan saw the tall slim teen boy he'd been when they'd first met in high school, both of them angry at life, both of them on a collision course with fate. A shared past neither wanted to remember, but that neither could forget. "I hope the two of you will be happy."

"We will be. I love her very much."

His words shut the door of the past, and Sloan was once more at a gas station off the interstate on a cold winter day. "Well, can't be late for my meeting."

He stepped aside, and she went to the driver's door, was

about to climb inside, when she turned to him. "If life had a reset button, I'd use it, but even then I don't think anything would be different. And for the record, you and Lani aren't the only people who lost him. *I* lost him too. And it broke my heart."

Bittersweet memories flooded Dawson as he watched her drive toward Windemere. Sloan was correct, the three of them had lost someone they'd loved, and real life had no "do-overs." His and Lani's love had been their saving grace. Sloan had gained her coveted fame, and perhaps that was enough for her. Dawson pushed the "fast-forward" button in his brain, strode to his truck, and drove off in the opposite direction.

⁓

Marie was waiting for Sloan by the front desk inside the DCS building when Sloan swooped in. "Sorry I'm late."

"Bo and his attorney are already in the conference room. And Bo's antsy."

Good, Sloan thought. She wanted him a little nervous, facing the unknown of the meeting's purpose, which had layers. "You have the paperwork?"

Marie held up a file folder. "All drawn up and ready for signatures. Are you sure you know what you're doing? Because I can't imagine Bo signing this paper."

Sloan's heart pounded like a trip-hammer, but she offered a confident smile. "I know what I'm doing."

"Then let's go."

They walked down a hallway, then stopped at a closed door, where Sloan ripped off the toboggan hat to let her blond hair fall free. She dragged her fingers through the tangles, unzipped the coat to show a body-hugging blue turtleneck. "Do you know Bo's lawyer?"

Marie nodded. "This county is a fishbowl, everyone knows everyone else. Don and I've faced off before, but he's a good guy." She opened the door, and the two of them stepped into the overheated room.

Bo's attorney rose politely. Bo remained kicked back in his chair and looking smug. After introductions, Sloan and Marie took swivel chairs on the other side of the conference-room table. Its surface was scarred and scratched, and had no doubt seen many acrimonious battles.

"Thank you for coming," Marie said. Sloan kept her face as neutral as possible.

"What do you want?" Bo barked, glaring at Sloan.

Don reached over and quieted him. "My client is scheduled to meet with his son tomorrow."

"It ain't real convenient for me to drive all the way from Memphis to visit with my own kid. I got a job, you know." Bo seemed unable to control himself, even though Don silenced him again.

"This arrangement is a hardship on my client. As it is, in order to see Toby four hours a month, he has to drive twice a month."

"That ain't convenient, you know. I got a job, and my boss is giving me grief."

Sloan so far had kept her silence, but now she said, "I'm sure you can find work in Windemere to be closer to your son."

"But my *home* is in Memphis. And that's where I want Toby. I ain't moving."

Sloan glanced at Marie, telling her with a look that she

was going to drop her bombshell. "Well, then this is the perfect time to tell you why we're here. Naturally you know I'm Lindsey's half sister."

"So I heard. So what?"

His tone was hateful. Sloan plunged ahead. "That makes me a relative, and that's why I'm prepared to sue you for custody of Toby."

Bo erupted and slapped the table. "I'm his *daddy*. You can't take him from me! Courts are never gonna side with you!"

Don caught Marie's eye, and Marie offered a shrug that communicated, *What can I say? My client has rights too.*

Sloan locked her fingers in front of her on the table, mostly to control their trembling. "You may be correct, Bo, but I'm going to put up one hell of a fight. I can drag it out for years, can't I, Marie?"

"It could indeed take some time. And money."

Beside Bo, Don said, "Very likely."

Bo stood, as puffed up and threatening as a rattlesnake. "You're some rich bitch who thinks she can jerk my kid away? You are wrong. Just 'cause you got money, you can't have him."

Sloan held up a hand, ready to announce part two—the part where she was certain Bo would show his true colors. "And speaking of money, you *do* know that Toby's trust fund— set up with the concert money I raised for his and Lindsey's welfare—can't be touched until he's nineteen if he goes to college. Or, according to the terms of the trust, not until he's thirty. That boundary is in place in case he gets into trouble while growing up. You know how kids are. One minute they're sweet little boys, and then they hang with the wrong crowd and turn to booze and drugs. So if *that* happens . . ." She let the sentence trail. "Anyway, it was Lindsey's idea, and my attorney in LA who set up the trust thought it a good one. Now,

Lindsey honestly believed that Gloria will raise Toby right and he'll stay out of trouble, but my sister wanted to prepare for all contingencies. So you will be raising Toby on your own, with no help from the trust."

The look on Bo's face told everyone in the room that Sloan had hit her mark.

"It . . . it ain't about the money. It's about me being his daddy."

Sloan knew from contract negotiations that whenever someone said, "It isn't about the money," it *was* about the money. She had asked Terri about rules when negotiating, and Terri had told her it depended on the stated intentions of both parties, but it was best if everyone left a negotiation feeling a level of satisfaction. Terri called it "holding out a carrot." Sloan and Bo had reached an impasse—they both wanted custody of Toby, and she was willing to make it a long drawn-out and expensive fight. Bo resettled in his chair.

"My client is within his rights to fight for full custody," Don said.

"So is mine." Marie smiled sweetly, acquiesced once more to Sloan, who flattened sweaty palms on the table, knowing she had arrived at phase three of the negotiation, completely unknown to Marie. "Over Thanksgiving, Gloria and I cleaned out closets and drawers and boxed up some of Lindsey's things for Toby. You know, items he might want when he's grown. And you know what I found smushed in the back of a drawer in her bedside table?" She let the question hang. "I discovered a codicil to her will."

Bo's head came up. "What's that?"

Don said, "An add-on to a person's will, like extra instructions the person makes, additions perhaps for distributing personal items. Codicils are legal."

To her credit, Marie never flinched, kept silent and staring straight at Bo.

"What did it say?" Bo's gaze narrowed perceptively. He was expecting a trick.

"Lindsey was fearful that you might fight her wishes giving Gloria guardianship of Toby. Turns out, she was right."

"Well, cheers for her, 'cause there ain't no way I'm leaving my boy with that woman Gloria. Or you." He sounded venomous but less aggressive.

Marie inserted herself into the conversation, pulled papers from the folder, pushed them toward Don. "Gloria is Toby's primary caregiver and has been for years. The judge will take that into consideration."

"What judge?" Bo asked.

"The one we go before to argue our case for keeping Toby with Gloria. First of all, Gloria was Lindsey's stated guardian. That will count in her favor with the judge. The number one question in custody hearings is 'What is in the best interest of the child?' And that's what I'll be arguing. . . . Toby's life will be less upended if he remains with Gloria, in the house and place he's known as home for years, and with the person his mother wanted him to be with. If you sign this agreement—"

"I ain't signing nothing."

"Then I will sue for custody, and either way, Toby remains living here," Sloan added.

Bo's glare was murderous.

Sloan swallowed down a fist of fear, knowing she'd have to be absolutely convincing when she spoke. *Don't blink.* "Lindsey thought you'd say that." She reached into her purse. "That's why she wrote the codicil. If you sign the paperwork giving up your parental rights, Lindsey authorized me to give you this. We held it out of the trust money just in case something came up to thwart her wishes. And I've taken the liberty of having a local bank issue a cashier's check for that money, made out to you." Sloan slid the check across the table, faceup. She felt as if her skin were on fire, and perspiration had already soaked through the back of her shirt. An overhead fluorescent light buzzed.

Bo looked at the check. His eyes widened.

The carrot. Sloan sat back in her chair, her gaze never leaving Bo's face. He might have been a handsome man at one time, but now he simply looked seedy. He licked his lips.

Don looked at the check and arched an eyebrow. "Can you produce the codicil?"

Marie intervened. "If we must." She gave Don a smile, and a penetrating look. " 'In the best interests of the child' is the way the law reads, and that's the way judges rule. Especially in this county."

Which had only one juvenile judge, Sloan recalled from her and Gloria's first meeting with Marie, and His Honor had set terms for Bo's visitations because of paperwork Marie had already filed. "Your call," Sloan told Bo, braver and bolder than she'd been minutes before.

Marie whipped out her notary seal. "We'll witness your signature today, and I'll notarize the paper you sign right now and take it before a judge. You don't even have to be present at the hearing."

Sloan put her fingertips on the check, still lying on the table. "Sign the papers and take the check. Or leave the check and fight *me* in court for custody of Toby for years to come."

Don said, "Once the papers are signed and executed, there's no going back, Bo. You need to understand that you're relinquishing your parental rights."

Bo's eyes again went to the check, where Sloan's perfectly

manicured nails rested. Except for the buzzing light, the room was silent. Marie magically produced a pen, and in one jerky motion Bo grabbed it, scribbled his name, and shoved away the petition giving Gloria full uncontested guardianship of Toby Ridley. Marie and Sloan witnessed his signature. Bo stood, his expression stony, but he didn't make eye contact. He simply grabbed the check and hurried out the door.

Don pushed back his chair, gathered his briefcase, and looked Marie in the eye. "Well played, counselor."

"In the child's *best* interests," she reiterated. "Your client's greed was quite obvious, and you know it." Once Don was gone, Marie swiveled her chair to face Sloan, who only wanted to leave, yet remained sitting, waiting for a lashing, knowing she'd crossed lines.

Marie drummed the tabletop with long fingers. "Why do I feel as if everything that happened here today wasn't exactly kosher? You never told me about a codicil or the money."

"I—I was afraid you'd ask too many questions."

"So instead you made me complicit in a lie."

Sloan flushed. "Besides, his lawyer sure didn't put up much of a fight about showing him the codicil," Sloan said defensively.

"When Don didn't request it when it was first mentioned, I crossed my fingers that he wouldn't fight over us producing it, but you still took a heck of a gamble."

"I figured out Bo's reason for wanting custody. All I had to do was walk him through the maze to the truth." She tried to sound contrite, but wasn't.

"Your explanation about the trust fund—that wasn't true either, was it?"

"Not exactly. The terms are much more lenient about accessing the money, but Bo will never know that."

"It was a large check, and I'm assuming it wasn't really taken out of the trust either."

Sloan stood. "What good is money if you can't spend it on something you want? And I sure wanted Bo Ridley to show his true colors. But mostly I wanted to keep a promise I made to Toby."

———

Sloan was driving to the Nashville airport to catch her return flight to Los Angeles, heady from her legal triumph. Running into Dawson had been a shock, but in the end they both were all right. Her cell phone chirped. She glanced at the screen, saw that Gloria was calling.

"Hey!" Sloan answered brightly. "What's up?"

"Oh, Sloan . . ." Fear sounded in Gloria's voice. "Toby's done run away!"

thirty-nine

Sloan's tires squealed as she blasted up Lindsey's driveway and braked to a stop. She parked next to Cole's truck, and was in the house before the engine shut down. "Any news?"

Cole was on his cell phone and restlessly walking across the living room. He held up his hand to acknowledge her but stayed on the phone. Gloria jumped from the sofa. "Not yet. I'm so glad you were in Nashville and not Los Angeles. You got here real quick."

After hanging up with Gloria, Sloan had exited the interstate and zipped onto an eastbound ramp. She'd told Gloria that she'd been at a business meeting in Nashville—a small white lie. Time enough later to tell about Bo giving up parental rights. All that mattered at the moment was finding Toby.

"How do you know he ran away?"

"I went into his room to call him for breakfast, and he was gone. And . . . and so was his sports bag and so's his baseball glove. I called all his friends, and no one's seen him. I'm worried sick!"

"But why? What would make him run off?"

"All I can figure is that he was scheduled to meet with his daddy today and he pitched a fit last night 'cause he didn't want to go. Said he didn't like Bo, and I told him neither did I but he *had* to go." Gloria wiped her eyes with a tissue. "It ain't right, makin' that child hang around with the awful man."

Cole punched off his phone and came to Sloan and Gloria. He looked haggard. "Just talked with the highway patrol, and they're issuing an AMBER Alert for Toby."

"An AMBER Alert! Do you think Toby's been abducted?" Sloan said, feeling sick to her stomach. "Do you think Bo could have abducted him?"

Cole said, "I wouldn't put anything past his jerk of a father."

Sloan's legs turned to jelly, and she sank to the sofa. Gloria had said Bo liked winning. Sloan cupped her hand over her mouth, afraid she might throw up. If Bo had taken Toby, *she* had provided the man with enough money to hide with the boy for a long time.

"An AMBER Alert is the best way for the cops to be on the lookout for Bo's truck. They have a description and his license plate. Local cops are looking for Toby in town." Seeing the ashen color of Sloan's face, he took her hands, as cold as ice, in his. "What's wrong?"

Her eyes darted away from Cole's. "This . . . this could be my fault." She told Cole and Gloria about her meeting with DCS, and how she'd secured Gloria's guardianship permanently. Gloria cried with gratitude, but Cole's expression turned grim, understanding the ramifications of Sloan's actions.

"I—I was only trying to help."

Cole brushed her hair away from the side of her face tenderly. "Don't beat yourself up about this. Bo could have taken him with or without the money. For what it's worth, I don't think he took Toby, especially since he was in a meeting with you this morning. I'm guessing Toby slipped out very early while it was still dark."

"Where would he go?" Cole's words calmed her, but her voice quavered when she asked.

"That's the question, isn't it? The local cops are scouring the roads and woods. Toby's not afraid to hide in the woods. I taught him too much about camping and the outdoors. And getting Bo to abandon his parental rights is a good thing. When we find Toby and tell him, he's going to be one happy kid."

Cole's cell buzzed. He answered, listened, thanked the person on the other end, and disconnected. His look of relief gave Sloan hope that Toby had been found. "That was the highway patrol. They stopped Bo's truck west of Nashville on the way to Memphis, and Toby wasn't with him." He offered Sloan a wry grin. "He was mad as hell." To Gloria, Cole said, "Aside from not wanting to see Bo, what else has been going on with Toby? School troubles? Bullies?"

She shook her head, chewed her bottom lip. "No . . . but ever since Thanksgiving he's been missing his mama somethin' fierce. I told him we'd get a Christmas tree to decorate this weekend, and that seemed to cheer him up, but now?" She shook her head.

"So what now?" Sloan asked.

"We wait."

The day passed with no news from the searchers, and the waiting became excruciating. Gloria made sandwiches that no one ate for lunch. Unable to sit still, Sloan paced the house in a meandering circle. Toby's room was strewn with the stuff of small boys, clothes tossed aside, shoes heaped in a corner, baseball cards strewn over a small desk. In Lindsey's room, she discovered a pile of Lego creations on the bedside rug and a stack of comics on the bedside table.

Sloan also saw that the spread was dented and imagined Toby curled up, reading about some comic superhero. Her eyes misted. He felt comfortable here, close to his mother. Sloan's breath caught, and insight flashed. She bolted from the room, yelling, "Cole! Grab your keys! I know where he is."

―――――

"Are you sure, Sloan? It's a heck of a long walk for a seven-year-old."

"Well, he's had hours to make it." Cole drove slowly toward their destination while from the passenger seat she intently searched both sides of the old narrow road. There was very little cover where Toby could duck and hide from a passing patrol car. "It may be a long shot, Cole, but I'm pretty sure of where he's going."

"He's a resourceful kid, and I wouldn't put it past him. We've played T-ball at every field in the town, so Toby knows how to get almost anywhere." Sloan's hunch made sense to him.

"And he's fearless," she added, seeing the entrance to their destination. "Let's walk in," she suggested. "We'll make less noise on foot. If he hears an engine, he might try to hide."

Cole parked. They got out and walked through the cemetery's gates, past the building filled with a location map and documents on its walls commemorating the dead. Some of the graves, in a special area with headstones, dated back to the 1800s. The more modern areas were considered memorial gardens, with only bronze nameplates flat against the ground, each with a vase so that visitors could leave flowers.

The sunlight was gone, replaced with low threatening clouds promising colder temperatures, twenties and thirties predicted by weathermen. Tree branches were stark and bare, and the grass was shorn and brown, asleep with the dead. Sloan longed for spring. Color. Warmth. LA seemed a lifetime away.

Her heartbeat kicked up when she saw a small shape huddled on the ground. "There!" She pointed.

"I see him. Don't run. Let's take our time," Cole replied.

They walked casually hand in hand, as if a twilight stroll in a cemetery were a normal thing for a couple to do. Toby had spread his blanket, and sat with his arms around hunched knees, staring at the ground. Weed flowers that he'd probably picked along the way drooped in the vase. Cole crouched beside the boy. "Hey, buddy. We've been looking for you." The blanket held Toby's treasures, his baseball glove and baseball, a photo of Toby and his mom wearing smiles. "You setting up a campsite here?"

"I ain't going home."

Sloan knelt beside Cole, felt the cold earth through the blanket and her jeans. "We miss you and want you to come home."

He looked at Sloan. "I thought you were gone to California."

"I came back because I made you a promise that I'd figure a way to change things about you having to visit with Bo, and today I kept that promise. He's gone." If she'd thought the news would make Toby jump and shout, Sloan was wrong. Toby simply shrugged and kept his fingers locked around his knees.

Cole shifted, mouthed that he was going to step away and call Gloria and the police to say the boy was found. Sloan stayed in place, unsure what to say, or how to reach inside the boy and soothe his heart. "You miss your mama, don't you?" He nodded. "I miss her too."

"Why'd she have to die?"

A fist of emotion filled her throat. Hadn't she asked herself that same question about another's death? "She was very sick, Toby. You know that." It sounded more like an excuse than comfort.

Toby glared at Sloan, and she saw tracks of tears through dirt on his face. "Mama left me! Everybody *leaves* me!"

"Gloria and Cole are here."

"*You* leave me."

The way he flung the accusation made her cringe. "But haven't I always come back to visit? You know that I travel and give concerts and make music for people to like. It's my job, like Cole and Gloria go to work and you go to school and play baseball."

He fell into a pouty silence, plucked a few blades of dead grass from the side of his mother's brass nameplate. He wore no mittens, and she wanted to gather his small hands in hers, rub them, hold them tightly, yet she remained in place, her knees numb.

Cole had retreated to a nearby standing position, was waiting patiently, allowing Sloan to take her time, and allowing Toby to unload his pain, knowing the boy would face it many more times over years to come.

287

Toby tossed aside the dead grass. "People say they know how I feel. Nobody knows!" His mind had switched to another lament.

His words hammered her heart. "*Nobody knows. . . .*" "I—I think people who lose someone they love *do* know how you feel." She struggled to find the right thing to say, but in the end knew words wouldn't do—she had to show him. It was the only way, not only for Toby but also for herself. "I want to show you something. It's not too far from here. . . . We can walk. Will you come with me? Please?"

Grudgingly he stood, but refused to take her hand. She walked him along a path that intertwined and linked to other sections of the cemetery. Cole followed at a discreet distance. At first Sloan wondered if she could find her way, but soon realized that she'd never forgotten the way. It was as fresh in her mind as the day she'd first walked it. She stopped, looked down the long rows of brass vases marking the embedded brass nameplates, easily saw the one she wanted, because someone had placed red poinsettias in the vase. Tears welled in her eyes. She walked Toby to the vase of Christmas flowers and pointed down. "Can you read the name on the marker, Toby?"

"I know how to read." His indignant tone made her smile, in spite of the ache inside her. He dropped to his knees, phonetically sounded out, "Gabriel Berke." He gave Sloan a satisfied smile. "Hey! *Gabriel. . . .* That's *your* name."

She felt Cole's gaze drill through her, took a deep shuddering breath. "Gabriel was my little boy. He died when he was three."

"Why?"

"He got sick."

"Like Mama?"

"Different illness, but yes, like your mama." Sloan held

herself together while painful memories thrashed her head and heart. "I lost him, so when I tell you 'I know what you're feeling,' I really *do* know."

Toby nodded sagely, rose, and took her hand in his. He looked up, and his face brightened. "Hey! Maybe Mama and him will meet up in heaven!"

Pressure compressed her chest, making it hard to speak. "I—I'd love that." Never mind that she wasn't as sure about heaven as Toby was.

Cole stepped closer, took Toby's free hand. "I think it's time to go home, Little Man. We'll pick up your stuff on the way to my truck."

They walked hand in hand, with Toby between Cole and Sloan, back the way they'd come, through the darkness, while stars winked on in the night sky.

forty

Moving day. The day Dawson had waited for from the day Lani left. He'd been on his way to Memphis to help pack up Lani's things when he'd run into Sloan at the gas station, but once he'd gotten back on the road, all his thoughts had been on Lani coming home. They were working in different parts of the small apartment, he in the living room area, she in the tiny galley kitchen, maybe fifty feet from each other. "You want to keep this?" He held up a table lamp.

Lani eyed the chipped lamp with its dented shade. "I'll replace it. Put it in the giveaway pile."

She continued wrapping plates, cups, and glassware in paper and filling cardboard boxes. She'd already boxed up her closet and bedding, had left Dawson to pack what was left of hers in the semi-furnished unit, but soon noticed he'd gone quiet. "Are you working?" she yelled.

"I'm watching."

She looked up to see him slouching against the doorjamb,

a sexy smile on his face. "We're never going to get out of here this afternoon if you don't get busy."

She'd pulled her long brown hair into a ponytail and wasn't wearing a lick of makeup, and he thought she couldn't be more beautiful. He crouched beside her, took her hand. "Let's take a break."

"*Dawson!*"

Ignoring the exasperation in her voice, he led her to the broken-down sofa. "Catch me up. How's your little Sara Beth doing?"

Lani's demeanor softened. "Better. Not ready to leave ICU yet, but it looks as if the bone marrow is taking. And having her daddy and mom with her has improved her even more."

"Glad she's making it."

Lani tucked one leg under the other and twisted toward him. She had a question for him and thought now was a good time to ask it. "Were you worried about me going off the deep end if she died? Be honest."

He couldn't fool Lani, so why try? "Yes . . . maybe a little."

"I won't pretend that it wasn't difficult watching Sara Beth sink lower. I thought of Gabe many times, and the dark place I lived in after he died. You know how guilty I felt." He started to say something, but she pressed fingertips to his lips. "I forgave everyone but me. And then a counselor told me that self-forgiveness was *always* the hardest. She said it was an arbitration between my psyche and my intelligence, and made me write down the facts of his case and let my professional side make the choice. I did that, but what helped me the most was seeing you emerge from your dark place."

He kissed her fingers, laid her palm on his cheek. "It helped that Dad was a doctor and that I'd watched Mom die.

I couldn't play the blame game card . . . especially with you. Truthfully, though, I may have gotten past what happened, but I'm not sure I'll ever get over losing him. If it hadn't been for you . . ." He let the words trail.

She picked up his thought. "You healed me too . . . all those months after, the way you loved me."

"That was the easy part."

She smiled. "Coming here and working with so many sick kids gave me a perspective I didn't have from my days at Windemere General. At St. Jude's, I was around a lot of sick children, some who died, but also around a whole lot more who lived."

"And now you're going home and doing it all over again." He grinned. "You make me proud." He ducked forward and kissed her.

She gave him an impish look. "And will probably be living in my car because this place isn't packed up yet!"

"You can always move in with Melody."

She made a face. "And have her riding herd on me? I'd rather we get a bigger apartment in your complex."

She started to get up, but he pulled her back. "Dad called. He wants us to come to Chicago for a visit."

Lani hadn't seen Dr. Berke, her mentor, in ages. "I'd love that."

"Or," Dawson said casually, "we can invite Dad and Connie to come visit us."

"That's fine with me too. When?"

He reached into his pocket, withdrew a ring box. "Maybe when they come for our wedding."

Her heart did a stutter step, and her eyes swept to his. She took the box and raised the lid. Inside a single solitaire diamond in a gold setting lay on a tuft of black velvet. The stone caught daylight and shot off an array of sparkles. It was hard to catch her breath.

"It was Mom's. I asked Dad if I could give it to you. I've been carrying it around for days, had planned to give it to you at Christmas, but I can't wait that long. Will you marry me?"

Choked by emotion, all she could do was nod vigorously and hold out her left hand.

He removed the ring from the box and tried it on her finger. The fit was close, but the ring would have to be resized. Lani's finger was larger. "Mom never took it off, even when she got so thin and sick. Dad wound surgical tape around the inside so it wouldn't fall off."

Lani heard huskiness in his voice. She leaned forward. "And I'll never take it off either. Except when the jeweler resizes it, and I'll wait while he does."

"So that's a yes?"

"Yes with all my heart, body, and soul."

They cuddled together, watching shadows lengthen in the room as twilight fell outside. Lani believed she'd fallen in love with Dawson the first time she'd laid eyes on him, and now, despite all the setbacks, the twists and turns of life, and the heartaches they both had faced, they would be married. Dreams sometimes *did* come true. She admired the ring, then sat up straight. "We still have to finish packing."

Dawson looped his hands behind his head, rested his feet on the coffee table, gave her a sly smile. "Give it a rest, lady. I just got engaged!"

Laughing, they tumbled into one another's arms.

forty-one

"Is he asleep?" Cole asked when Sloan entered the great room. He was on his sofa, flipping through TV channels, the sound muted. He'd been waiting for Sloan to come out of the guest room, where earlier Cole had tucked Toby in to spend the night. He had let Gloria know about the sleepover, and they'd both agreed that since Cole had the next day off and Gloria didn't, Toby would spend the following day with Cole and Sloan.

"Yes—finally." She edged onto the sofa, keeping a comfortable distance between her body and Cole's. "He wanted me to lie there with him until he fell asleep." She rubbed her tired eyes. "And he wanted me to talk to him. 'About what?' I asked, and he said 'Anything.' So I did."

"He and Lindsey used to do that. She told me cuddling with him and talking was sometimes the only thing that helped dull her pain. She'd talk awhile, and then listen to him tell her about baseball, superheroes, friends at school, until one of them fell asleep. He's a bright kid and loves to tell stories." Cole turned off the television, put the remote on his coffee table. "What did the two of you talk about?"

"Music. I thought he'd be bored silly, but no . . . he stayed awake. So I talked about my upcoming tour in Europe. London and now Stockholm, and there's talk of Australia next year. He listened, but never shut his eyes."

"Impressive schedule," Cole said, a weight on his heart. Sloan spoke the language of music, a universal language that knew no barriers, and she was a conduit through which it flowed to the whole world.

She waved away his comment. "But back to Toby. Oh, and before I forget, I told him that when he wanted to visit his mother's grave, someone would take him."

"I'll tell Gloria, and one of us will."

Sloan heaved a sigh. "And when I ran out of things to say, I invited him to come with me to California . . . right after Christmas. Just for a few days while he's out of school. But after hearing that, he was too excited to fall asleep!"

Cole gave a throaty laugh. "Did you mean it?"

"Of course! I promised. Hope I can keep him busy. Disneyland, SeaWorld, the Pacific Ocean . . ." She went down the list of places they would go.

"He'll have a ball."

She nibbled her bottom lip. "Kind of scary . . . entertaining a seven-year-old boy for five days." She shifted her eyes sideways toward Cole. "Maybe you can come with us?"

He patted her hands resting in her lap. "Not this time. This is about you and Toby. He's an easy kid. He'll have the time of his life."

Sloan deflated but realized Cole was right. This trip was for Toby.

Cole stood, led her into the kitchen. "How about some

hot chocolate?" A pot simmered on the stove, and the delicious smell of rich dark chocolate drifted in the air. He'd made it with milk, sugar, and real cocoa while she'd been settling Toby.

"With whipped cream?" She leaned in to inhale the fragrance.

"Homemade." He winked and pulled a bowl from the fridge, of heavy cream whipped into fluffy peaks.

"Big mug," she said, using her hands like a fisherman exaggerating the size of a catch.

He grinned, poured hefty portions into heavy ceramic mugs, heaped the cream on top, and handed her a cup. She warmed her hands around it, licked a dollop of the cream off, and raised the mug to him. "Thank you."

He watched as she sipped the brew, biding his time, waiting until she was ready to talk to him.

Standing in the kitchen, Sloan became fidgety, shifted from foot to foot. She knew Cole was patiently waiting for her to explain the things she'd said at the cemetery, a full account of her history. And her mistakes. Where did she begin? "I—um—I guess you heard everything I told Toby."

"You did a stellar job of talking him down, so that we could bring him home. You impressed me." He paused, knowing it would be simpler if he asked questions, as he did in his job as a paramedic to victims in shock or ashamed of certain actions. "And yes, I heard that you and Dawson had a baby and lost him. Were you married?"

"No, we were seniors in high school. I'm surprised you didn't hear about it, because this town loved to talk about me."

"No one said a word. Everyone I've met thinks you're a star who has put Windemere on the map."

"Well, someday the tabloids will get hold of it, and we'll see how everyone acts. The tabloids aren't always kind, you know."

He heard bitterness in her voice but didn't want her to get sidetracked. "And Lani? Where does she fit?"

"She worked at the hospital and was also Gabe's caregiver at Dawson's house for several months, and she and Dawson fell in love."

His brow furrowed. "How did that make you feel, seeing them together?"

Sloan's heart boomed like a kettle drum inside her chest. *Confession time.* "I wasn't . . . around. You see, soon after Gabe was born . . . I left."

Words spoken by Dawson that day in the fast-food joint clicked into place for Cole. *"She runs."*

Sloan took a long gulp of her chocolate drink for courage, because by now Cole didn't have to ask questions. She simply wanted to be rid of the ache inside. "Dawson gets all the credit. He took care of Gabe, raised him, and by the time I saw them both again, Gabe was almost three, Lani was in their lives, and my little boy had no idea who I was."

Cole searched her face, saw deep sadness but no self-pity. He recalled her telling Toby that an illness had claimed Gabe's life, but there was no way Cole could ask about it now. She was barely holding herself together. "Is that why you took his name for the singing contest?"

Her shoulders drooped. "It's a long story, and I'll tell you anything you want to know."

Cole set down his mug, then hers, and drew her into his arms, the glamorous woman and the wounded child locked inside her. He loved them both. "Not tonight you won't."

Sloan crumbled, sobbed into his chest. He held her until

297

the crying lagged. Then he lifted her chin. She turned away, grabbed a tea towel he always kept hanging on a hook near the stove, buried her face, and in a muffled voice moaned, "Why do I always end up *crying* when I'm with you?"

He rested his chin atop her head, swayed gently. "Why do I always want to hold you if you're an arm's length away?"

His comeback brought a slight smile, and she pulled away to see his face. "Always?"

"Every. Time." She snuggled into his embrace, and he realized she was exhausted, wiped out. "There're clean linens on my bed. Get some sleep. I'll take the couch."

"I shouldn't—"

He interrupted. "Toby will be up with the chickens, and I'll fix him breakfast. You get some rest. Like the song says, 'the sun will come out tomorrow.'"

She was too tired to argue, so she leaned forward, kissed him ever so lightly, turned, and started to his bedroom. She had taken only a few steps when Cole asked, "If Gabe was your loss, what is Toby to you?"

She was quiet for a very long minute, searching for a way to tell him what was in her head and heart. She and Gloria were collateral damage from other people's mistakes, yet here they were together at an intersection of time when they could make a difference in another child's life. "I came to love Gabe too late, but with Toby, it's different. He deserves the best Gloria and I can give him. Toby's my redemption. He's not a substitute for Gabe, if that's what you're wondering. I'm not his mother, and I don't want to be. Plus, Lindsey wanted Gloria to raise him in her house."

Sloan turned to face Cole, this man she'd come to know and care for so very much. "You know, people say, 'Never give up! You can have it all!' And when I won the contest, when they announced my name and all that confetti fell on me, I believed I'd gotten it all. But then Lindsey came along, and I realized that 'having it all' is fluid . . . flexible. Because somewhere along the way, my 'all' got bigger."

She spoke in fits and starts, but Cole listened to every word, offering no interruptions, no platitudes. Visible tears swam in her eyes. "Lindsey's gone . . . that's my loss. But she left me something I didn't think I'd ever have. She left me a family. Toby . . . Gloria too. Just the three of us, Cole. DNA doesn't make up every family, you know. We're a crazy little clan for sure, but we belong to each other." She wanted to add *And my sister made it possible for me to know you too* but didn't have the courage.

Cole was shaken as her words imbedded in his heart. He'd never loved her more, never wanted her more than in this moment. Instead he watched her disappear into his bedroom and shut the door. He longed to follow, to hold her and love her for the rest of their lives. He grasped the edge of the granite countertop, hung tightly to the cold hard stone, taking deep breaths to slow the rising tide of desire to go to her. He was smart enough to understand that sometimes the only way to hold on was by letting go.

forty-two

Sloan arrived two days before Christmas, encumbered with extra suitcases filled with gifts. She'd shopped in LA, had bought everything she'd felt like buying for Toby and Gloria and Cole, and had dragged it all to Windemere, where she shut herself in a room and personally wrapped and tagged every present. She knew she had overdone the buying spree, but didn't care. This year was for all the Christmases of growing up when she'd had so little. For her this Christmas was about giving.

The house had smelled of Christmas cookies and pumpkin pies when she'd first walked in the door. The tree was dressed with twinkle lights, paper chains, gingham bows, pinecones, and candy canes—a homespun replica of a *Country Living* magazine cover. And when the sun set, battery-operated candlesticks glowed from every window, as if lighting the way for Santa up the long driveway. Toby moved at warp speed, excited by every box under the tree tagged with his name, while he gushed nonstop about his and Sloan's upcoming trip on the day after Christmas.

"I can't calm him down," Gloria said, throwing up her hands. She told Sloan that when Toby returned to school after the first of the year, she would be working the seven-to-three shift at the nursing home so that she could be home to meet Toby's school bus. "Just like his mama used to. I surely miss her."

"She's watching from heaven," Toby said with a child's confidence.

For Sloan the only bump about Christmas was that Cole was nowhere around. She remembered he had family in Indiana and asked Gloria, "Did he go home for the holidays?"

"Goodness, no. He's working the Christmas shift so the fellas who have families don't have to." She shook her head. "I declare, that man's done nothin' but work since you left two weeks ago. Taken extra shifts and given some of the men extra time off. Nice of Cole, but I sure don't want him to keel over."

After Toby and Gloria had gone to bed Christmas night, Sloan sat listening to soft Christmas music and staring at the tree—the gifts unwrapped and put away, the ham dinner eaten and stored for another meal—and thought about Cole Langston. For months he'd been in her thoughts . . . no matter where she was or what she was doing. The night she'd spent at his house after finding Toby, and baring her soul to him, had been a turning point.

She'd awakened the next morning to the aromas of bacon, maple syrup, and fresh coffee, had pulled herself together, and left his bedroom to see Cole flipping pancakes and Toby scarfing them down.

"Hey, Sloan! You sure sleep late." Toby had had the exuberance of a puppy, as if the turmoil of the day before had never happened.

"How about you, Sloan?" Cole had asked. "Ready for a stack?" His voice had been casual, his look compassionate. He had *not* forgotten the day before. Or the night.

She had felt suddenly shy, as if they'd lain together and made love all night. As if he already knew every inch of her mind and body. Of course they had not been intimate, but the feeling had persisted. She had walked to the table, ruffled Toby's hair, and sat. "Bring it on, Chef. I'm starving."

Now, this Christmas night, as she gazed at the twinkling tree, she asked, "Could what I'm feeling be *love*, Cole Langston?" Her answer came in a nanosecond. She smiled, satisfied that the bursting joyous passionate feeling inside her heart at last had a name.

Cole tried to ignore the insistent ringing of his doorbell, finally gave up, threw on a pair of pants, and padded to the front door. He threw it open, growling, "What!" On his doorstep in blinding sunlight and a blast of cold winter air stood Sloan.

She checked him head to toe, hair disheveled, eyes bleary with interrupted sleep, face dark with stubble, his chest bare, gray sweatpants hanging low on his hips, brushing the tops of bare feet. She flashed him a sunny smile. "And good morning to you too, Mr. Langston. Don't want you to catch a cold." She gave him a gentle push back into the foyer and closed the door behind her. "Can't stay but a minute. Toby's in the car, and we're heading to the airport."

Her smile coupled with the scent of her perfume hammered him, and all his senses went on high alert. "What time is it?"

"Way too early, but he's been up and packed since five a.m., and Gloria's trying to get ready for work. I thought we might as well go to Nashville and let him run around the airport and maybe wear himself out before our flight. We change planes in Dallas, so—" She stopped talking because the bemused smile on Cole's face and his sexy blue eyes stole her concentration.

"So you stopped over to say goodbye?" *Again.*

She cleared her throat, hoping to calm nerve endings that were snapping like downed electrical wires. "Yes, but also to ask you a quick question."

"I'm listening."

She ran the tip of her finger down his chest, from the hollow of his throat to his belly button. Goose bumps burst on his exposed skin, making him shiver. "You know Toby and I will be back in six days. And I'm wondering, do you have any plans for New Year's Eve?"

His dimple sneaked out with a sultry smile. He would wait a lifetime for her, so six days were nothing. "I serve at my lady's pleasure." He fisted his right hand above his heart and gave a slight bow of his head.

Her knight-errant. "The lady wishes to spend the evening with you."

"Does my lady wish anything special for the evening? Food? Champagne?"

"Whatever the chef chooses will be"—she paused—"delicious, the lady believes." She curtsied.

He lifted her hand to his lips and kissed the smooth pale skin. "As you wish, my lady."

Her heart crashed against her rib cage and she could barely breathe. "Until then, stay away from dragons." Sloan spun and rushed out the door.

———

Sloan meandered down the back road, taking her time, reminiscing over the moments in Cole's foyer that had ignited hunger and anticipation for their upcoming New Year's Eve together. Sunlight streamed through the windshield, so warm that she had turned off the car's heater. She glanced in her rearview mirror and saw Toby in the backseat staring out the window. She was mulling over the days ahead with him in California, when a shape flashed past her peripheral vision. She applied the brakes, looked in the side mirror, and saw a large brick entranceway opening onto a widened side road. *What in the world?*

"Are we there already?" Toby asked.

"No, but I see something I'd like to look at. Won't take but a minute." She put the car in reverse, backed up, and stopped in front of two curved low walls of neatly mortared red brick with an entrance road between them. A sign read WINDEMERE ACRES. The road, as wide as any boulevard in Los Angeles, invited people into what was clearly going to be a new subdivision. She turned in, shut off the engine. "Let's explore."

Happy to be out of the car, Toby hopped and jumped on one foot, then raced down the new asphalt road until it abruptly ended in gravel and red dirt. Sloan followed. Small stakes in the ground flagged with strips of red cloth marked off plots of land. To her right was a brightly painted board showing large wedges of lots, some marked SOLD. The sign read:

FUTURE PRESTIGE HOME SITES FOR SALE—1- AND 5-ACRE LOTS, and had phone numbers to call for inquiries.

She turned again to stare in wonder, a cold breeze blowing her hair. Toby ran up. "What is this place?"

"It's where I used to live." He looked around, confused. "It was a trailer park when I lived here."

Clearly uninterested, he held up a foam coffee cup thrown away by some construction worker. "Look what I found. You know what this is?" Inside the stained cup lay a dead butter-fly with orange-and-black markings on its wings. Before she could say a word, he announced, "It's a monarch," and seemed proud to know it.

"Interesting" was all she could say, still stunned by the view of home sites where she'd spent so many unhappy years.

"Didya know that every spring monarchs fly all the way from Mexico to Canada? And then in the fall they fly all the way back to Mexico and hang in trees—lots and lots of trees. And they make more butterflies and sleep all winter. We studied it in school."

She glanced down at his smiling upturned face. "Long trip."

"I know! Crazy. They just know where to go every time, even though no one tells them. They're programmed that way. My teacher says it's like survival of the fittest."

Nature's programming. Instinct. Sloan turned to study the board, saw that several primo five-acre lots backing onto a faraway tree line were still for sale. And in that moment she knew she would never buy or build in Los Angeles. She would build here, a gorgeous house with verandas and columns and rolling green lawns. Whenever she came off the road from weeks or months of touring, whenever she needed to rest and renew her body and mind, this is where she'd come. Gloria would raise Toby in his mother's house, Gloria's house now. They loved and needed each other. Cole was nearby too. Sloan would make sure Gloria and Toby would want for nothing. Tears filmed Sloan's eyes as she remembered that Gabriel was also here, forever.

"You crying?" Toby asked, his forehead puckered.

"Happy tears." She held out her hand. "Come on, Tobias Ridley. Race you to the car." She let him run slightly ahead of her to the vehicle.

"I win!" Toby shouted when he tagged the car.

Me too, she thought. Like the monarch butterfly, sometimes a person had to travel thousands of miles to find the way back home.

ACKNOWLEDGMENTS

My thanks to Marie Farley and her daughter Jessica Farley. Their input concerning child advocacy laws was invaluable.

ABOUT THE AUTHOR

LURLENE McDANIEL began writing inspirational novels about teenagers facing life-altering situations when her son was diagnosed with juvenile diabetes. "I want kids to know that while people don't get to choose what life gives to them, they do get to choose how they respond," she has said.

Lurlene McDaniel's novels are hard-hitting and realistic, but also leave readers with inspiration and hope. Her best-selling books have received acclaim from readers, teachers, parents, and reviewers.

Lurlene McDaniel lives in Chattanooga, Tennessee. Visit her online at LurleneMcDaniel.com and on Facebook, and follow @Lurlene_McD on Twitter.

Forever friendship
and true love from
Lurlene McDaniel

Discover how lives change
in heartbreaking, realistic fiction
that is sure to inspire.

 @Lurlene_McD

/LurleneMcDaniel